OUT OF THE
WOODS

OUT OF THE
WOODS

WILLIAM D. CARL

POST MORTEM PRESS
CINCINNATI

Post Mortem Press, Cincinnati OH
www.postmortem-press.com

ISBN: 978-0692351147

For Don....
through good times and the bad.

Prologue

They say everyone has a story to tell, but over the years I've come to the singular conclusion that this isn't necessarily true. Let me rephrase that. People will always want to talk about their jobs or their latest favorite music or the prosaic problems they're having with their family, but these aren't truly stories; these are merely personal anecdotes, bits of life's flotsam, adrift on a social media sea where nobody can remain quiet for more than five minutes. A story entertains and enlightens, yet few people can find their way around this concept. They should be striving to dually entertain and teach us a lesson when relating what their Aunt Martha did at church last weekend. Good stories warn people about things - why you shouldn't play with matches, why you don't run through traffic, why you choose your friends wisely.

Or, why you never go into the dark woods.

Well, I've got a story - a real humdinger. It's going to open your eyes to the world around you, expose you to its rather seedy underbelly, then brutally toss you back into reality. Like a trout, you're probably happily swimming along in your own stream, oblivious to everything transpiring in that mysterious, uncharted world above the water. Hopefully, my little tale's going to hook you, expose you to that world on the surface, then toss you back so you can swim better, with a bit more knowledge about how the universe really operates. If I've done my job right, you'll retain the memories better than our friend, the trout, who'll probably just get hooked again ten miles farther down the stream. I know I still have the memories from my experiences with the unknown. I still wake up with nightmares, screaming and sweating, tearing through my bedclothes.

It's a story of a far-away time - 1983. The world was a very different place back then. We were still worrying about the godless communists attacking our shores, but we were confident in our president, who turned out to be a better actor than any of us had realized from his movie career. The music to which we listened pounded to a synth beat, and you never worried if your kids would hear it and encounter new or forbidden words from the DJs on the radio. Nudity wasn't allowed on television, unless you subscribed to one of the closed circuit television networks such as Qube, and Halloween was still a wonderful, rather innocent holiday.

Remember when you could wander the night streets of your town without parental supervision, and you rarely worried about what had been inserted into your candy? Remember how people still gave out home-made goodies, popcorn balls and cookies or cellophane-wrapped slices of cake? Remember when the worst trick imaginable was putting dog poop in a paper bag, setting it alight, and hoofing it after ringing the doorbell?

As I mentioned, they were innocent times. We weren't exposed to the internet, where anyone could see a naked lady at any time they desired. We'd have to search every drawer in the house to discover where Dad hid his cache of Playboys. We didn't get offered drugs at the elementary school yard. We imagined what they'd be like and secretly listened to Cheech and Chong records in our basements, giggling into our cupped hands. We didn't have cell phones, so there were actually times when our folks didn't know where we were. And it was all right, because they trusted us enough to let go a bit earlier back then.

I was a psychiatrist in that faraway year, recently graduated from school. This was when psychiatrists were still coming into their own, still the butt of nearly a third of Woody Allen's jokes. If you were lucky, you discovered a Sybil or a Billy Mulligan and made a name for yourself by actually helping to cure someone and getting a book deal out of it. Otherwise, you toiled in relative obscurity, holding sessions with neurotics on couches or vainly attempting to benefit the delusional people stuck away in mental hospitals.

My story starts in such a hospital. I was toiling in the aforementioned obscurity, banging my head against one red-taped wall after another, truly helping no one. And the ramparts of my self-confidence were crumbling faster than the old building in which I spent my long days.

I feel as though I'm rambling.

On with the story... It involves a boy, an old man, horrors from another dimension, death, illusion, life, sex, and the falling of scales from my eyes.

Hooked yet? I hope so. The future of the world may depend upon it. I wouldn't want this to result in a population, a swarm, of trout, blindly swimming along in yet another stream.

Oh, yeah. And my story is mostly about a girl. A wonderful girl. A girl named Deena Bierce. You'll love her as much as I did.

In any case, here's my tale. I hope it's entertaining...scary and suspenseful, maybe even a little bit funny.

Just remember, these words are all true. There aren't a lot of survivors who can vouch for that fact, but I still have a few witnesses up my sleeve. I can bring them forward if need be. Since it's an authentic account, I hope you can take this as a warning. I hope you're enlightened. I hope you don't just shrug this off as some sort of creature feature to be read under the covers with a flashlight on a dark and stormy night.

I hope you believe me.

Please, believe me.

PART ONE
October 30th

"*The whole drift of my education goes to persuade me that the world of our present consciousness is only one out of many worlds of consciousness that exist.*"

William James (1842 - 1910)

Chapter 1

I was on my hands and knees, peering under my desk, when I heard Deena Bierce ask, "What gives? Someone escape?"

"No," I answered, standing and dusting off my hands on my pants legs. "Just making sure nothing gets left behind. Look, two pens and a dried-out magic marker. See what I just saved the county in office supplies?"

She leaned against a file cabinet on the other side of my office, crossing her arms over her impressive breasts. I'd seen that look before - the 'disappointed in me' look. I opened and closed empty drawers, searching in vain for a reason to delay the mandatory lecture I was sure I was about to receive.

"I know, I know," I said. "I've had weeks to pack everything and ship it out, but I waited till the last minute. By now, you should know me well enough to figure I'd procrastinate."

"The hospital closes the day after tomorrow, and all this crap's got to be moved to your new office in town by that evening," she said, a flustered tone creeping into her voice.

"It'll get done," I said, and I stepped over to her, wrapping my arms around her trim waist. "I promise. You worry too much."

"You knew that when you asked me to marry you."

"I think your superb sense of efficiency complements my own lack of productivity."

"Kiss me before I tell you how full of shit you are," she said. I obliged. "Now, get back to work."

"Yes, ma'am," I said with a grin.

Deena was a fellow psychiatrist at the soon-to-be-closed Saint Michael's Hospital for Mental Illness. I'd been practicing here for almost three years, but I still felt green when I was around her. It wasn't just the fact that she was three years older than I was. She was infinitely more productive. I'd watch her with patients, admiring the skills she used to pry their secrets from their subconscious minds. Even the manner in which she chose her words bespoke multitudes about her professionalism. Every phrase was thoughtful, every sentence sculpted to attain the most information from any patient. I learned a lot from her.

One day, six or seven months after I'd started at Saint Mike's, as it was known by those familiar with its crumbling halls, I had been observing her from across the room while she questioned a woman with suspected multiple personality disorder. I was smiling, proud to be a part of her team, but also admiring the way her ash brown hair fell over her eyes and the unreflective way she brushed the stray locks behind her ears. Looking up at me, she caught my attention, and I must have blushed. As though she could read my mind, she grinned at me, momentarily forgetting the woman speaking with two different regional accents across the desk from her. She focused all her consideration upon me, and I felt something, a little electrical something I hadn't felt since high school when Mary Anne Huenamann had let me proceed to second base in the back seat of my father's Dodge Colt. When she'd completed her interview, she'd approached me, and I still felt the burning redness in my cheeks.

"You want to go get a cup of coffee?" she'd asked me, her eyes promising so much more than the momentary lift of caffeine. "I mean, if you want to get out of here for a while. We could talk or something."

Her clumsy phrases, so out of character for her, had belied Deena's nervousness around me. As a result, I became emboldened.

"Yeah," I'd answered. "I'd like that a lot."

Coffee had led to conversation, mostly concerning the eerie and rumored to -be haunted place we worked. Everyone who worked there had mentioned the ghostly patients seen on late nights, but neither of us believed them. This had been followed by a lot of laughter, which was succeeded by unabashed kissing in front of her apartment. Before the night was over, we'd explored every part of each other's bodies, noticing funny lines and moles, discovering what happened when she touched me there or there or especially there. Afterwards, we had lain next to each other and talked all through the night in hushed, urgent voices, as though we were afraid of breaking whatever spell had overtaken us. Then, we had made a date for the next evening, and the next, and the many more which ensued.

We'd known it was frowned upon, what we were doing, two doctors working in the same institution screwing like horny little bunnies, but we couldn't help ourselves. The more I got to know her, the more I wanted to know about her. It had evolved into a complex relationship, hidden from our boss, Dr. Steven Carmody, although, I had my suspicions he knew exactly what was going on. In any case, he'd turned a blind eye to the whole matter.

Six weeks ago, when the anticipated announcement had fallen from the upper echelon of the Montanya County Mental Health Board, I'd discovered I was being displaced, that the damp halls of Saint Michael's Hospital for Mental Illness were being demolished because no amount of paint and plaster would make the necessary repairs worth the tax-payers' money. I was being sent to a hospital twenty miles to the north, near Pittsburgh, and Deena had been placed farther east, close to Altoona. As we would no longer be working in the same building, it seemed an opportune time to pop the proverbial question. To my relief, she'd said yes, and we set about informing everyone at the hospital. They were polite enough to feign surprise, but I could see the delight hidden beneath their 'my goodnesses' and 'congratulations'. Only crusty old Dr. Carmody said what everyone felt, "Well, it's about damn time."

We had set a date a year in the future, started all the elaborate machinations that go into setting up a wedding. We'd informed our parents, hired out a hall, and finally moved in together. It had seemed a bit odd at first, living with someone else, even though I loved the woman to bits. There'd been tiffs about leaving the toothpaste out or the toilet seat in the raised position, but these never resulted in much more than a discussion, an apology, and furious make-up sex. Eventually, everything seemed to run smoother, and my apartment had never been so clean and tidy. I'd also started gaining weight due to Deena's expertise in the kitchen.

We'd written to our supervisors, and they'd been surprisingly accommodating with our requests. As a result, Deena would be practicing in a hospital only an hour's drive from where I'd been placed. There would be no ridiculously long commutes for one of us to work, and we'd be able to find a good apartment in the vicinity of either institution.

Now, making the final preparations for the move to our new hospitals, we'd been seeing a bit less of each other. There was so much to do - files to check, patients to discharge, and everything had to be packed and properly shipped. The hospital was only scheduled to be open another two days. Then, the remaining patients, the most disturbed still in our care, would leave their cells empty. The electricity would be turned off, the phones disconnected. The place would be vacant, haunted only by the ghosts of psychotics past, an old ruins eventually integrated into the encroaching woods.

And I was running behind schedule. Not a big surprise or anything.

After Deena left, I glanced around the room at the towers of boxes, the files neatly stacked within each cardboard prison. The pictures had been removed from the walls yesterday, leaving ghostly, pale imprints on the pea-soup green plaster. The water stains were easier to discern on both the ceiling and the walls after being bared.

It was definitely time to lay Saint Michael's Hospital for Mental Illness to rest. The old building had done its job for more than fifty years, and the asylum looked exhausted. The electricity had been fading in and out with little recourse to reason for the past several months, lights often flickering crazily or going out altogether. The plaster walls were cracking beneath the pressure of time, leaving mysterious little piles of dust in inexplicable places throughout the hallways. Doors and windows had warped to a point where many of them refused to open or close any longer, letting in even more rain, along with the damp forest air. Roots from the woods that surrounded the old hospital were poking their way through the weakening concrete floors, and the staff often found themselves tripping over tendrils while leading a patient to their cell. It all gave the 'ghost patient' rumors substance, and I caught myself peeking back over my shoulder more than once.

Saint Michael's had been built more than fifty years ago in the center of a deep forest in rural Pennsylvania. Surrounded by ghostly, white-barked birch trees, it had been a grand three-story building, once as high as the woods encompassing it. It had been thought it would be a safe place to put the most dangerous of the lunatics, distanced from civilization in case any of them escaped. Over the years, the breakouts had been few and far between, but none of them had ever made it to one of the suburbs about twenty miles distant. The trees always seemed to confuse the fugitives, and they were either picked up by local police or they returned, shame-faced and befuddled, to St. Mike's.

In some ways, I was sorry to be leaving the old hospital. This had been where I'd interned five years ago, and I had remained in place afterwards. I ran a hand along the familiar cool plaster of one of my office walls, bringing it back damp. It smelled of rust and rotten wood.

The dampness had been worse lately, creeping in from so many locations it had become impossible to locate them all to put a stop to its perpetual encroachment. The water seeped into the very walls, poked its way from roots into the mortar between the sodden bricks. Most of the moisture was probably coming from the trespassing woods around the building. The birch tree line had grown ever closer to St. Mike's. What had always protected the institution was now destroying it from the inside out.

The roof was also leaking in many places, dotting ceilings with Rorschach water-spots that sometimes frightened the more mistrustful of our patients. It seems they resembled judgmental eyes to the paranoid, ever watchful of their frantic, darting movements. There was one spot on the third floor where so much water damage had occurred, a hole had formed in the floor after the roof nearly collapsed. It was being held up by some hastily constructed scaffolding. Michael, the last remaining janitor on duty, had told me the whole ceiling could come down on that wing, and he wasn't certain the other two floors would hold up to the strain for much longer. In other words, the place was a house of cards just waiting for a good, strong wind to blow it down, and the few of us remaining in the structure were whistling in the dark until the day we left.

About forty-eight hours from now.

Glancing out the window, my worst fears were confirmed. The day was more than overcast. It was downright gloomy. Ash-colored, cumulonimbus clouds could barely contain the lightning and thunder stirring within them. At any moment, they could burst, soaking the institution, doing who knows how much more damage to the old place. I just prayed it would remain standing for the next two days. Then, it could collapse into rubble for all I cared. Oh, who was I kidding? I'd grown somewhat fond of the monstrous place with its creaking doors and shadow-filled hallways. I'd even miss those alleged ghosts.

As I watched the woods from my window, I marveled at the various changing colors of the leaves. Autumn in mountainous Pennsylvania could be brilliant, with as many variations of shades of trees as was possible. I hoped the approaching storm wouldn't blow the last of them down. Then again, it was almost Halloween; October 30th, to be precise.

Somebody had a real sense of humor in the upper management offices, closing the mental hospital on Halloween. They'd obviously been watching the recent John Carpenter flick when they'd struck upon that brilliant plan.

With a sigh, I started unpacking my file cabinet. Careful to maintain their order, I loaded the cardboard file trays. I realized it wouldn't take very long to finish the whole chore, so I started humming to myself - the theme to *Halloween*.

I was closing up the last of the cartons, taping down the top, when I heard a screaming ambulance outside. Peering through my window, I watched as it pulled up to the front gates. *Curious*, I thought. *There weren't supposed to be any new deliveries while we were shutting the place down. Where the hell will we put them? Gotta be a mistake.*

Two men emerged from the ambulance, zipping up their jackets against the rising wind. Leaves fluttered around them like moths, and I knew the lovely autumn shades were probably gone for good. The storm would end up sweeping them all away, leaving the mountainside in a palette of brown and darker brown with only the white birch bark to show any bloom of color. In the distance, I heard the first ominous clap of thunder.

The ambulance driver and his buddy opened the back of the truck and pulled a gurney from its innards. Strapped to the contraption was a thin figure, struggling against its bonds. From my window, I couldn't make out any features, but the person was really straining against his or her restraints. There was almost an animalistic quality to its attempt to free itself, and I wouldn't have been surprised had the patient tried to chew through his/her bonds, growling all the time.

What the hell are they doing bringing someone here? I mused. *We only have a few days left, and we'll just have to transport him...her...it again.*

There was a rapping at my door, and Deena popped her head into the shambles that had once been called my office.

"You see this?" I asked her, motioning to the window. Thunder rumbled in the distance, as if in answer to my question.

"Why are they bringing him here?" she asked, looking past my shoulder and out the window.

"That's what I want to know."

"Well, there's only one way to find out," she said, heading for the hallway.

I was right on her heels.

As I closed my office door, I hesitated, feeling a vibration in the doorknob underneath my fingers. I raised my hand in front of my face, checking it for the shakes. With a sigh of relief, I saw I wasn't trembling. A crash of thunder fairly close by announced the real cause of the motion of the brass knob.

The storm was getting very near, but at least I was still in control.

And I had to stay that way.

Although, I suddenly felt very thirsty, and I wished the day was over so I could return to my little apartment and pour myself three fingers of good Scotch. This was all I could do any more - wish for a drink, imagine the harsh taste of it scalding my throat. I couldn't trust myself to imbibe anymore, not after what had happened the last time. But, sometimes, wishing was enough. Sometimes.

"Are you coming or not?" Deena called from around the corner.

"Be right there," I said, double checking my hand.

Steady as a rock.

Chapter 2

Saint Michael's Hospital for Mental Illness was three stories high with a half-basement, played out in an inverted 'U' shape. As I mentioned before, the top floor had been sealed off for some time, the victim of a leaky, precariously rickety roof and too much water damage to even attempt to salvage it. Until two weeks ago, the second floor had contained the low security wards, where patients could visit with each other or meet in the game room or cafeteria for a hand of cards or lunch with the ladies. The first floor contained our offices inside the left arm of the 'U'. The middle of the building accommodated the guard stations, the entrance (quite grand for an old school mental institution), and the admittance area. The twenty two cells in the right wing of the 'U' shape held the worst cases, the high security alerts. Behind Plexiglas windows set in steel doors, under the constant gaze of numerous cameras, we watched over some of the most hopeless, most violent patients. I hated this ward, but it was where all the interesting stuff happened.

We had sheltered one Mr. Jim Stephens, who'd stabbed his wife thirty seven times before slicing off her flesh and boiling it to serve at his company picnic as Bar-B-Q. There'd been Miss Jane Dahlee, who had left her children to die in a closet in one hundred degree heat, then pretended they were still alive, playing with them at all hours of the night. Mr. Alan Weisenthal had such terrible agoraphobia that he'd locked himself in his house, starving nearly to death, because he didn't dare leave the security of his home. Mrs. Louise Fallow had been my favorite patient, an elderly spinster with at least six certified personalities, all of them bitter and angry at the world. She was one of the very few documented true cases of multiple personality disorder on record, and I had watched her be interviewed.

Of course, she'd already been transferred to another institution, far away in another state. I'd mailed my notes to her new doctor, who would probably write a paper on her which would end up in Psychology Today and win him the Nobel Prize. Lucky bastard.

To be blunt, this was the ward where we stuck the people who were going to either go for your throat and try to kill you, or they were certain to inflict serious harm upon themselves. The worst of the worst, the hopeless, and the damned; the cries and gibbering from the locked cells drove away at least one guard a month. They'd rather face unemployment than listen to the hellish bedlam of inhuman articulations from the west wing. Only the stoutest souls continued to work there; or the sadists. Although I hate admitting it, many of the long-term employees of the high security area were hard, cold people. Sometimes, even cruel people. We watched over them as much as possible, making sure nobody was ever injured or beaten, but you didn't catch the doctors or nurses eating lunch with the high security guards. One of them, an ex-wrestler named Rollo, stood six and a half feet tall and had to weigh at least three hundred pounds. Solid muscle, too. His head was shaved, and his mouth was continuously set in a grimace. If you looked at him long enough, you knew there was no soul behind that steely glare. It's what made him such a good guard, his lack of humanity, his assertion that the high risk patients never required coddling.

With the callous, unemotional guards standing sentry over the isolated prisoners and the general frightening atmosphere of the west wing, even doctors weren't fond of traveling there. I certainly wasn't. Of course, I had to attend patients there, but I always felt somewhat slimy and dirty after spending any time around the severely affected lunatics. I know, as a doctor, I shouldn't be bothered by something as vague as an atmosphere, but the gloom hung in the air in a dense poisonous fog, and it was almost hard to breathe through that smog of human suffering. When you left there, you were stained by the overwhelming dementia.

Most of the medical staff didn't even call it the west wing any longer. We just referred to it as 'Siberia.'

And Siberia was where Deena was heading, with my sorry ass right on her heels. If they were bringing in somebody to admit at this late date, when we wouldn't even be open except for another day and night, something big was going on. When it's something big, somebody's being exiled to Siberia. Somebody's done something truly whacked, or they'd truly whacked someone. Either way, my curiosity was piqued.

I caught up to Deena, walking swiftly, matching her usual brisk pace. She looked over at me and grinned. I knew that grin. Intimately.

Deena loved being a psychiatrist in the way that most people love their mothers. She was one of the brave, foolish few who still believed that what they were doing was useful to somebody, that they were helping in some way. Cynicism had yet to take root in her pretty little head, even though it had infested mine several years ago.

Deena never saw a new patient. No, she saw an opportunity. She never made a diagnosis. She worked with somebody, coached them through their weaknesses and their various crises. And she was damned good at it, too. I have to admit, her success rate was staggering.

"You think this is something juicy?" she asked, as we approached the admittance desk.

"Don't you?"

"Hell, yeah," she answered. "No other reason why they'd bring someone in at this date."

The nurse behind the desk was a veteran of twenty odd years at St. Mike's. Vicki Hellings was a tall, blocky woman with long red hair that fell around her shoulders and tended to make her look permanently exhausted and frazzled. A cigarette dangled from her large bottom lip as she typed. Dr. Carmody had once attempted to curb Vicki's smoking habit, but was vocally thrashed for at least fifteen minutes before he declared the smoking area of the hospital was now to be located at the admittance desk. Then, he ran in fear. Vicki had that effect on a lot of doctors. I had never seen her take a sick day, had never even seen her with a cold. I presumed germs were afraid of her.

"Hey, Vicki," I said, leaning against her desk. "What's the story with the patient getting admitted?"

She looked down at where I was leaning on her desk then raised her eyes to mine in mock derision. Her thick eyebrows elevated. Stepping back, I felt the daggers from her reptilian gaze pricking the skin of my arms.

"Figured you two'd hightail it down here," she said, the cigarette wobbling with each syllable. The ash on the end clung to the paper for all it was worth. "Couldn't keep yourselves away, could you?"

"It's good, isn't it?" Deena asked.

"I don't know. Looks like just another nutjob to me."

"We don't use words like nutjob, Vicki," I said. "Call them what they really are - whackos."

"Well, it appears you've got one for the books," she said. "There's a hell of a wreck on I-90, ten cars involved, so they need all the ambulances they can get. This guy was on his way to Pittsburgh, so they dropped him here for the night. They'll pick him up tomorrow when everything's back to normal."

"Pittsburgh, huh?" I asked. I glanced at Deena. "Our new home away from home."

"Oh yeah, you've been transferred there, haven't you?" she asked. The ash on her cigarette was becoming dangerously long. "Carmody will probably want you to examine him. Do the preliminaries."

"Awesome," I said, smiling at Deena. She looked as though she just won honorable mention in a contest with only two contestants.

Vicki shrugged towards me, but she looked at my fiancée. "You really marrying this bum?"

"Don't tell anyone," Deena said. "I wouldn't want word getting out. They might lock me up for loving him."

"Ha. Ha. Ha," I said. Sarcasm's one of my best social skills, and I utilize it every chance I get. "If you two ladies have finished dragging my good name through the mud, I'd like to hear about the patient. Spill it, Vicki. What kind of a bird do we have on our hands?"

"Looked pretty quiet when they toted him in," she answered. The two-inches of ash finally gave up the ghost and dropped onto her keyboard. "Probably all Thorazined up. His name is...let me see here...Gary McCoy. Not much on the chart yet, but the EMTs who brought him in are right over there."

She pointed towards two muscular guys in blue and white uniforms who rushed past us, wheeling an empty gurney in between them. As one of them held the door for the other, I ran behind them.

"Hey, fellas, who's the patient you brought in?"

"Ask your boss," the one with the blonde hair said as he got behind the ambulance's wheel. "We got at least twenty injured people in a wreck, buddy, and we don't have time to stop and chat. Maybe I'll come back and have tea with you."

"Wise ass," I muttered.

With sirens wailing and lights twirling, they zoomed out of the parking lot. Over the clamor of their departure, I heard the loud rumble of the encroaching storm. I looked up and got an eye full of cold rain. Swearing, I wiped it from my face and did a hoppy dance back into the admitting room, as though my elaborate, jerking motions would ease my body between the raindrops and keep me nice and dry. Instead, they just made me resemble a jackass with severe hemorrhoids.

When I entered the room, Vicki was lighting a cigarette with the still burning end of the one she was finishing. She grinned, mischievously, shaking the match out and leaving it in an ashtray towering with lipstick-smeared butts.

"Well, Pocahontas, it appears as if your little rain dance worked."

Lightning flashed through the windows, a bright, momentary flare as though someone had taken a picture. The thunder followed almost immediately.

"Looks like it's going to be a big one," Deena said as she tried to wipe the dampness from my hair. Her hands felt good on my skin, and I had to remind myself I was on duty. No nookie till we were home in bed. "I hate storms."

I heard familiar, tapping footsteps echoing from the high security wing, and I knew someone was hiking back from Siberia. The shoes definitely belonged to my boss, the head of the institution, Dr. Steven Carmody; I'd know those clicking heels anywhere. It often sounded as though he was wearing tap shoes. When he turned the corner, I flagged him over to our little group. He adjusted his thick glasses, smoothed down his graying goatee, and ran a hand back along his balding hairline. I couldn't help but notice the brown folder clutched in his hands.

"Ah, good," he said, walking over to me. "Bob, I want you to have a look at our newest - and probably final - patient, please. He'll be transferred tomorrow night to the hospital in Pittsburgh where you'll be stationed. I spoke briefly with Sara, your new boss, and she agrees that you can continue monitoring him once you both make the switch. I'd do it myself, but there's so much to see to, and there's so little time. I don't know where to begin. You *will* look in on him, won't you? Give him a regular preliminary analysis? I hope I haven't stepped on your toes."

"Of course not. I'd be glad to see Mister...what was his name again?"

Carmody rechecked the chart before handing it over to me. I felt a zap of static electricity from the file, and yelped at the shock. Shaking my hand, I answered everyone's puzzled looks.

"Shocked me," I explained.

"His name is Gary McCoy. I haven't had much of a look at his file, but the EMTs doped him up to the gills before they left. They said he was violent."

Flipping the file open, I glanced through what the two burly men had written. The handwriting was so bad, it took me a while to decode it, but what I saw made me salivate for more. I knew I had to interview Gary McCoy right away. There'd be no delaying this one.

This could be the case that would make my name.

"Is it good?" Deena asked as Carmody hurried away to his office.

Nodding, I said, "Oh, yeah."

Chapter 3

I dashed back to my office to grab a few pens and a yellow notepad. I usually write my notes in personally developed shorthand then transfer them onto the word processor on my brand new computer at a later time. I always took more than one pen in case I ran out of ink. You couldn't stop a raving lunatic from raving once he got started.

And from what I witnessed from my office window, this boy sure looked like a raver. Or, at the least, a good thrasher.

The file stated Gary McCoy had been picked up on a country road near a gas station, where he'd caused quite a disturbance. He'd entered the place and started screaming about monsters swimming through the air, that creatures were going to eat everyone alive. He'd grabbed an eight year old girl and shook her so hard he dislodged one of her shoulders, screaming into her face that she was going to die, that everyone was going to die, and the world was going to end.

Apparently, the world wasn't going to end so suddenly that Gary couldn't use a beer, so he had swiped a six pack of Old Milwaukee (the choice of beer a valid case for incarceration, in itself). The clerk at the gas station let him walk out with it. Probably figured it'd be easier and safer just to lose the beer than to confront this impassioned maniac ranting about the end of the world. Still, he had called the local police, and they discovered Mr. McCoy waltzing by himself down the road, four beers into the six pack. Seems he put up quite a fight, but they got him in the back of their patrol car until the EMTs showed up so he could be checked into the psych ward of the local loony saloon. Then, the monstrous accident happened, and poor Gary McCoy was dumped, almost literally, on St. Mike's doorstep.

Deena mentioned something about seeing me later then she was off to do some mysterious thing dealing with the move. I'm not sure what she was accomplishing, because my attention was already focused on this new patient.

You'd think we would get a lot of apocalypse watchers, but we really don't. Every once in a while, somebody gets a little too religious for their neighbors and winds up locked in St. Mike's, but it was rare to get someone actually stomping up and down and declaring that the end was nigh. That was something for the movies.

Until today.

I'd just had a primo case of paranoia land in my lap. Who knew what else was wrong with the poor guy? All I could be certain of was if Gary McCoy lived up to his file, I'd soon be published in all the journals. My name would be made. I might even be able to go into private practice and get away from the harsh realities of Siberia and all the other Siberias in all the other hospitals. If nothing else, it was a nice dream.

I gave security a quick buzz to let them know I was on my way and to secure a room for the preliminary interview. Rollo was working, and he grunted assent, which was pretty much all you ever got from Rollo. Hanging up, I whistled as I made my way to the west wing.

Passing Vicki, I gave her a jaunty little salute, and she coughed up a phlegm ball into a handkerchief in answer.

"Good luck," she said, lighting up another Virginia Slim.

"You've come a long way, baby," I said.

"Yeah and there's a helluva long way to go," she hacked.

As I approached the corner of the first floor, I gave a cursory wave to Rollo where he was standing on the opposite side of the Plexiglas. He buzzed me in, and I pulled the door too early in my rush of anticipation. It caught, and he had to buzz me again. As I stepped into the security corridor, he glared at me, chewing at a toothpick in the corner of his mouth. I shrugged.

"Sorry," I said. "Just a little anxious to see the new guest."

He grunted, pulled the keys from his pocket, and opened the door at the other end of the little hallway where the head security guards on duty maintained their desk. I couldn't help but notice a Penthouse magazine on the surface, turned over so the centerfold kissed the Formica. I should have told him the magazine wasn't allowed on hospital premises, that it wasn't a very bright idea to leave sexually explicit material where the crazies could get to it, but this was Rollo. He'd snap my neck like a string bean if I so much as told him his fly was open.

Following me through the second door, he locked it behind me. A red metal folding chair rested against the wall of the hallway, very distinct in the glare of the bright lights and the pea-soup green paint. Motioning me into the examination room, Rollo plopped down on the chair and proceeded to pick at something deep within the coils of his ear. As he examined his fingers, I entered the room, closed the door behind me, and listened as Rollo stretched and contorted his body then turned the key that sealed me into the chamber. He'd remain seated next to the door, outside of hearing range, until I gave him the signal to let me out.

Gary McCoy sat in a twin of Rollo's chair, his hands folded together on top of a long table as if in prayer. His face was down, and his long brown hair fell forward so I couldn't discern any of his features. His legs were strapped to the ends of the table, and handcuffs secured his arms. He was breathing very heavily, and I detected a bit of a wheeze. Asthma, perhaps?

"Hello, Gary," I said, sitting across from him in a blue aluminum fold-up chair. We were separated by six feet of table, so he couldn't reach me even if he tried. He didn't. Placing a blank tape into the recorder, I started the machine and let it quietly unspool for a full thirty seconds before I addressed him again.

"I said, hello Gary."

He remained perfectly still, placidly gazing down at the table as though it was holding a secret conversation with him.

"Can you hear me?" I asked. "My name's Doctor Robert Gaskell, but you can call me Bob if you prefer. Or Doctor Gaskell. Or Robert. Rob. Whatever you prefer." I tried to sound friendly, jocular.

Still no answer - only the labored breathing with that hint of rattling mucous behind it. The more I heard him, the more I suspected he had a minor case of walking pneumonia. There was definitely some liquid action in those overworked lungs.

I flipped through the folder again, looking for any sign that he might be deaf. Nothing indicated such an infirmity, although it also didn't refute it.

Sometimes, getting to know a new patient is a matter of waiting for them to become comfortable, coaxing them along until they could easily talk to you. There wasn't enough time to mess around with McCoy, though. I had to get a primary analysis completed before he was shipped off to the new mental hospital. Otherwise, they might assign him to someone else once he arrived. I couldn't lose this guy, not when he was so promising. I tried another approach.

"Gary?" I asked. "What are you seeing? What's on the table?"

He muttered something too low for me to hear. His voice seemed imbued with the same fluid affecting his lungs. While he spoke, he didn't move. He remained in the same face-down position he'd assumed before I had arrived in the room.

"I can't hear you, Gary. Tell me about the things you see."

More muttering, but it was getting louder, almost perceptible.

"Gary, tell me about the monsters."

He slowly raised his head. Even though his long, stringy, unwashed hair covered most of his face, I could see his eyes between the strands. I could also see the madness behind his mismatched eyes. One of them was blue, and the other was dark brown. Both of them were rimmed in red and bloodshot. When he opened his mouth, I could see his rotting, mossy teeth.

"They's ever'where," he whispered, then breathed in that phlegmatic manner. "I sees 'em in the table. In the room. They's ever'where."

Finally, a contact had been made. So, he didn't really want to be here talking to me, but he was willing to converse about his hallucinations. I decided to run with it.

"Okay, Gary, what are they? Tell me about them."

"They's all different. Some of 'em swim through the air, like big eels or snakes, mouth all lined with teeth. Some of 'em look almost kin ta you or me, only they's got three feet and six arms, or they's got eyes that look like a bug's."

"Multi-faceted?"

He shrugged. "I dunno'. Big, like a bug's. Some of 'em are all tentacles...million legged octopuses crawling along, just big balls of arms. They's all different kinds. They's all around us, only most can't see 'em."

"Why not?"

"'Cause they ain't got the gift of the sight. That's what Pa calls it. The sight. Most of the village folk can see 'em."

"Which village are you talking about, Gary?"

"My home. It ain't got no real name. It's always just been the village to me. To us what lives there."

"Where is it?"

"Up in the mountains. Only about fifty of us left now. Pa says the babyies ain't turnin' out right no more. They's so twisted, they can't live in this world, so they go to the world of the monsters."

"This Pa, he's your father?"

"Near as I can reckon. He brung me up, along with five brothers, though two of 'em ain't right in the head."

"What about your mother? Is she still alive?"

"No," he said, shaking his head. "She passed on givin' birth to my youngest brother, Abe. I think Abe was too much for her. He's a big sucker. Even as a babe, he was big."

"Did you love your mother?"

"You askin' if I laid down with her? Well, sure. The drawin's in the hills show us what to do. They say the mother should take care of her babes. In ever' way. We got to follow what the drawin's say, else the monsters might get us."

"You had sexual relations with your mother?" I was scribbling frantically in shorthand. *Incestuous relationship with his mother?* This guy was better than I'd ever hoped.

Gary McCoy actually blushed. "You make it sound dirty. She taught us the way. Showed us where to stick our peters, how to make a woman feel good. Pa showed us with the men, and we all did it to make more babies. That's what the drawin's said to do. We got to do what the drawin's say."

"Where are these drawings?"

"In a cave by the village. You got to go pretty deep to see 'em, but Pa said villagers been followin' the lessons of the drawin's ever since he can recollect. Pa's pretty old, so it must be a real long time."

So, the people in this village were incestuous and bisexual, to boot. If what Gary was saying was correct, they were living their lives by the scrriptures of some ancient cave drawings. Suddenly, I was out of the realm of scientific journals and into National Geographic territory.

"Is there marriage in your village? Are there strict families - father, mother, sons, daughters?"

"Only real family is the village. We all family there. Ever'one's related to ever'one. Been that way since Pa was a babe. Only now, the family's gettin' smaller and smaller. Too many babes dying. Too many babes twisted up so's they can't breathe the air of this world. That's why they go to the other world, the one only some of us can see."

"The world of the monsters?"

"Yeah. I ain't supposed to call 'em monsters, though. They's just like us, only not made for this world. Pa says, they's formed that way 'cause they're supposed to go to the next world. The one behind the curtains."

"What curtains?"

"The curtains that stop people like you from seein' what's all around us. See, accordin' to the drawin's, there's a lot of worlds, all of 'em one step away from another. That step's hard to get through, same as big heavy curtains. Only, we been followin' the gospel of the drawin's, and we can see it. We can even touch it sometimes. Ain't so solid."

"Can you cross over into it?" I wondered how far his delusions could carry him. To other worlds, possibly?

He shook his head, cast his eyes downward again. "No. I don't think we been breedin' right. The monsters, I ain't supposed to call 'em monsters, but they are - the monsters can sometimes swim into this world. I seen 'em. We all have sometimes."

"Because you've all had sex with each other?" I asked, hoping to follow his jagged trail of logic. "Because you've bred only with the others in the village, you can all see the monsters."

"Most of us can. Not all. Some ain't so blessed as I am."

"You can see them all the time?"

He nodded. "Yeah. All the time. All around me. Swimmin' like eels in a lake, only there ain't no lake. Only air."

"Why have *you* been blessed?" I asked, latching onto the word.

"I'm the final brood. The one who was sexed just right. My Ma and Pa must have had the right juice inside 'em to make someone like me."

"Someone like you?"

"A preacher. That's what they call me in the village - Preacher. I can see the things all the time, so I can tell 'em what the things want."

"The monsters actually talk to you?"

"Not talk, really. But, I know what they want...in my mind, sorta. In my head. They whisper whisper whisper to me."

"What do they ask for?"

"Different things. Mostly sacrifice to the Old One."

"Old One?"

"The god of the monsters. He's from some other world, but he got lured into the world behind the heavy curtains. The one right next to ours. Sometimes, the monsters tell me to ready a sacrifice to him. When they ask, we got to do it, or they take one of our own people in the village."

"They can kill you if they want?"

He nodded. "It happens ever' once in a while. We'd

find someone all chewed up, parts of their bodies all over the place. Then, when we'd eat 'em..."

"Wait a minute," I said, gazing at the man in wonder. "You eat each other?"

"Only when someone dies. Or when the Old One wants a sacrifice. The things they know pass into us. Pa calls it something...a big word...trans...trans somethin' or other."

"Transubstantiation?"

"That's it. That's what Pa calls it. We get all the knowledge from inside the brains of them that we eat. Oh, don't worry. We cook 'em first. We ain't animals."

Jesus Christ, I thought. *Ritual cannibalism, incest, pagan religions... What the hell have I stumbled onto?*

"So, Gary," I said, trying to get myself back on track again. "What made you leave the village? When the police picked you up, you were on the highway, trying to tell other people about the monsters. Why'd you leave the hills?"

"Because they whisper whisper whispered to me."

"The monsters did?"

He nodded.

"Go on, Gary."

"They said the Old One needed a big sacrifice. A really big one. They said he was hungry, that he needed souls brought to him. A lot of souls."

"Why is the Old One hungry? Did the monsters say?"

"They said he was preparin'."

"For what?" I asked, though I thought I knew the answer before he spoke.

"'Cause he's gettin' ready to go through another curtain. He wants back into our world. He's gonna try and get through the curtain, but he ain't strong enough yet. He needs a lot of souls to get strong. More souls than are in the village."

"So, the voices wanted you to kill people?"

"Yes. But, there's only about fifty left in the village. It ain't near enough, even if we all die, to get him through the curtains. It won't matter. He needs more."

"So, you were going to kill the people in that gas station?"

"No, Mister," he said, and his eyes grew very wide. The two different iris colors drew my focus.

"Then, what were you doing so far from your village?"

"I was tryin' to warn them people. If the Old One gets into this world, he's gonna kill ever' last person on Earth. He can't always kill the monsters. They're too tough, too fast for that. They're real slippery. But, people...the people on Earth. We ain't no match for the Old One. We ain't no match for a god like that. He'd kill us all."

"Does your Pa know you're down here?"

"He does by now, I 'spect. He's gonna be pissed as hell, too."

"He wants the Old One to get into our world?"

"It's what the drawin's say will happen. There's one of this black cloud, and there are tentacles and such comin' outta it. They's snatchin' up people on the ground, and it's rainin' blood outta that black cloud. It's rainin' blood."

"Is the black cloud this Old One?"

"I 'spect it is. Pa says it is. He says we can't stop a prophecy. No ways. No hows."

He began thrashing in his chair, jerking the table back and forth with his violent trembling. It looked to me as though the meds were wearing off.

"But I don't wanna see that black cloud with them monster tentacles. I don't wanna get killed. I don't wanna see it rain all that blood down. We got to warn people, Mister. We got to warn 'em he's comin' through that curtain. He's comin', and we all gonna die. We all gonna die! We all gonna..."

He collapsed, fainting. His head hit the table with a loud clang, and I rushed over to him.

"Gary? Gary?" I asked, checking his pulse. "Are you all right? Gary? Preacher?"

"We all gonna die," he mumbled, his eyes closed.

The words were soft, almost translucent, but they brought goose bumps to my arms.

"We all gonna die."

I knew I needed to get him back into that room, out of his poisoned head, away from any of the terrible thoughts he was having.

"Gary, snap out of it," I said, and I pounded hard on the top of the table. It was louder than I'd expected, and the man across from me stopped shaking for a moment and regarded me with those strange, clashing eyes. He pushed his hair back, revealing all of his face for the first time.

"Oh God," I stammered. "What did they do to you? What the hell did they do to you?"

Scars criss-crossed his face in circular, tribal patterns. These weren't little, neat scars, either. These were big, pink, swollen keloids. They hadn't healed well, and it was obvious these were not surgically precise operations.

Someone had been hacking into Gary McCoy's face, probably years ago. The one on his left cheek was a spiral, flowing in a clockwise direction. The other one was a succession of circles within circles, probably representative of the worlds within worlds philosophy that dominated the village's religion.

I cleared my throat then asked, "Did your father do this to you? The scars on your face?"

"I don't rightly know," he said, and he traced the keloids with trembling fingertips. "They been there long as I can remember. Since I was a little, bitty baby. They's marks of distinction."

"Because you're special? Because you're the Preacher?"

"Yeah, I reckon that's right. 'Cause I can see the monsters and I can hear them whisper whisper whisper about the Old One and his plans."

Holy shit! Ritual mutilation.

"Are you tired, Gary?"

He blinked a few times, then he answered, "Yeah, I 'spose so."

"Tell you what," I said, pushing a paper torn from my notebook and one of the pens over to him. The pen was a felt-tip, so he couldn't harm himself. "I will tell you what, Gary. You draw me a map from the highway to the village, make a spot for the cave with the drawings in it, and I'll get you a nice, soft bed prepared. Can you do that? Can you draw me a map to the village?"

"I reckon I can. I'll show ya where the cave is, but do not go to the village. No matter what, you gotta promise me. You'll piss off Pa, and he'd come here and we all

would just die faster. And the monsters. The monsters...
Just to the cave. Promise me that. You gotta promise me."

"Okay Gary," I said. "Just to the cave."

As if I would miss any opportunity to see the hellhole
he'd described. But, hey, he didn't need to know my
intentions.

As he picked up the pen and started sketching an
elaborate cartogram, I had to admire his artistic abilities.
The man could really draw. If he'd been raised in a city,
he'd probably be attending art school somewhere,
preparing for a job in the advertising industry instead of
frightening small children with end of the world stories.

"That's good, Gary. You just keep on drawing, and I'll
tell Rollo to get your room ready. How many pillows do
you want?"

He didn't answer. He merely concentrated on the
paper, on his developing map into the mountainous forest
surrounding route 90.

Chapter 4

Newly drawn map in hand, I practically skipped to Deena's office at the other end of St. Mike's. It was all I could do to restrain myself from bursting into a Broadway musical number right there in the hallway. When I finally waltzed into Deena's office, I found her resting at an empty desk, boxes stacked neatly around it, each one labeled as to its contents. Her total preparedness took some of the wind out of my sails, especially when I thought about the haphazard way I'd packed, but it couldn't entirely stifle my glee.

"I love this new patient," I said. "At first, I was envisioning scholarly articles for psychological journals, but now I'm seeing book deals, mass market paperbacks, New York Times bestsellers."

"He's that good, huh?"

"Deena," I said, sitting on the edge of her unnervingly clean desk. "The man's a gold mine. Hears voices, raised in a society of abuse, ritual scarring, possesses all the symptoms of a typical paranoid schizophrenic. Get this; he was raised by people who believe he's somehow holy, because of his incestuous family line."

"Holy shit!"

"And have I mentioned the cannibalism or imaginary religions based upon metaphysics this dude couldn't even begin to comprehend, let alone have read about in some book left lying around."

"You're serious. This really is big," she said.

"Yeah," I said, suddenly solemn. "The kid's as fucked up as anyone I've ever seen, and you know some of the basket cases we get in here. I look into his eyes, and I see...Hell, I don't know what's there. He looks dead, but there's something lurking behind that lack of emotion. Something simmering, about to boil over at any minute. I wouldn't admit it to anyone else, but it kind of scares me."

She reached out and took my hand in hers. Smiling, I clutched it tightly in mine. She knew me so well, could almost read my thoughts. Sometimes, she finished my sentences for me. But, on that day, she let me speak, let everything pour out of me - my doubts regarding my abilities to handle Gary McCoy's case, my lack of expertise in the field of schizophrenia, my fears that I would end up making the boy worse.

I told her the whole ugly tale, everything McCoy'd had divulged during his interview with me. I told her about the village in the woods, the hysteria of the villagers, the sexual abuse, the encouragement of incest, the death rites, the cannibalism, the voices murmuring within Gary's head, and finally, I told her about the Old One.

"Have you ever heard of such a thing?" I asked her. "I mean, I've heard of schizophrenics hearing the voice of God before, but all this garbage he's spouting about the whisperings of the Old One, of the monsters in the air - it seems pretty far-fetched. The guy's invented a god to tell him what to do, to give him instructions. An aural manual to the Apocalypse."

Deena shook her head. "No," she answered. "I haven't heard much like that, except in old H.P. Lovecraft stories."

It took me a moment to place the name. Then I remembered.

"The New England writer who invented Cthulhu? Wrote all those freaky stories I read when I was fifteen?"

She nodded. "A lot of modern doctors think he might have been mildly schizophrenic. He certainly tapped into another world."

"He's a science fiction writer. He's supposed to invent other worlds, isn't he?"

"Well, maybe he did it a little too well. He was an isolationist, rarely seeing people, shunned by the public and most magazines. The only ones that would print his crazy stories were the pulps. Certainly, some editors found him to be too involved in this alternate universe he created, as though he truly believed it existed. He called his ancient race of gods the Old Ones. Plural."

"You think McCoy read H.P. Lovecraft and just extrapolated upon his original mythology?"

"Sounds like it," she agreed. "Or maybe, one of the elders in the village...Christ, it's as if we're talking about a lost tribe in New Guinea or something, not a village in Pennsylvania. These people, if they truly exist, are living just a few miles into the woods, up on a mountain somewhere."

"I think it's Pa," I said.

"What?"

"I think the person who has adopted the Lovecraft mythos is Gary's Pa. The boy treats him as if he's some kind of clan chieftain. You should have heard him. 'Pa said this,' and 'Pa said that.' Everything came directly from his father's mouth. I'd bet money that the source of the religion is Pa McCoy."

"From the fathers to the sons."

"And his mother died in childbirth. Reverse Oedipal tendencies."

"Jesus, Bob," Deena said. "I think you're on to something. This could be as big as *The Three Faces of Eve*."

"I need to visit the village, try to see for myself if any of his babblings are factual. Hell, the guy could just be making up everything, stringing me along with his line of bullshit."

"But, you think it's all true? A village hidden away in the mountains, where a whole community has reverted back to a savage state?"

"I don't know," I said with a Cheshire grin. "But, I had him draw me a map just in case."

I placed the sheet of paper on the empty desk in front of her, and Deena leaned over, carelessly pushing a stray lock of hair behind her ear. The map was quite detailed, especially when considering McCoy'd completed it in just a few minutes. He'd drawn arrows entering the woods from a spot off Highway 90, just north of West Gershon, close to the gas station where he'd been arrested. If what he'd drawn was accurate, a pathway would lead me through about two miles of woodland before ending at several cliffs. The caves where the drawings were located were cached in the walls of these bluffs, and the village was another half mile further into the forest.

"This map is beautiful, Bob," Deena said, running her finger down the side of the drawing. "Your new patient is quite the artist."

"Makes you wonder, doesn't it?"

"Hmm?"

"If he was all right in the head, if he hadn't been influenced by his father. What could he achieve? What kind of life would he be living if he was born to a wealthy family in the suburbs instead of in a hovel in the hills? Pretty sad, really."

"If you cure him of his delusions, he could still achieve a lot," she said, always the optimist. "This is exquisitely rendered."

Only, Deena hadn't seen Gary McCoy when he was raving about the end of the world and the monsters swimming in the air like giant lamprey eels. Just as it's easy to admire the beauty of a Van Gogh without considering the fact that the man lopped off his own ear in order to impress a woman. Honestly, what kind of woman would that impress?

And what was running through McCoy's labyrinth of a mind when he spouted such nonsense?

"I'm going to check this out tonight," I said, refolding the map and tucking it into the back pocket of my jeans. "I need to know how much of his story's true, what they're really doing in this village of his. I need to know if the place even exists at all before I get into my diagnosis."

"Tonight, Bob?" she whined.

"Yes, right away."

"We were going to carve pumpkins and watch horror movies tonight. It's Halloween tomorrow. Besides, you aren't even done cleaning out your office. We need to be ready to evacuate St. Mike's tomorrow evening."

"It's one office," I said. "If I'm not finished, I'll just sweep it all into crates to sort out later."

"You always procrastinate."

"Not this time, sweetheart," I said, kneeling in front of her. "I need to ascertain the truth before McCoy's shipped off to another hospital. I need to make the initial prognosis so I can follow up on it later. This has fallen into my lap, at the worst time, I'll admit, but I'm not going to look a gift nut-job in the mouth. I can taste this, Deena. I know this is the big one that'll establish my name."

She sighed. "You want me to go with you?" she asked.

"No, that's not necessary."

"Come on, Bob. It could be dangerous. Who knows what these villagers are like? Plus, I know you," she said, wagging a finger at me. "We've been camping before. You'll be lost for weeks in the woods, surviving by eating berries or possibly poisoning yourself on toxic mushrooms."

"You know me all too well," I said.

"Thus, the ring on my finger," she said "I suppose we'd better drive home and change. I'm not traipsing around the woods in high heels and a skirt."

"Okay, come on. I'll cite you in the articles."

"Oh, maybe I'll just take it out in trade. But first, give me a kiss." she said.

I was happy to oblige.

Chapter 5

We drove back to the apartment through a fine, misty rain. The storm seemed to have subdued itself, as though it consciously realized we would be taking a nature hike soon. Still, when Deena pulled beside me in the parking lot, I could feel the sogginess of the ground beneath my shoes. It felt as though the heavens had opened up and dropped an inch of water on the Earth, too much for the soil to absorb in such a short time.

Shutting her door, Deena said, "I can't wait until we don't have to drive separately to work. This 'putting on an act' crap is really starting to get to me. Besides, we'd save so much in gas."

"Well, it won't be long now," I said. "Just a few more months until we're hitched. You realize, of course, everyone knows about us already at St. Mike's. It's not a very well-kept secret. Hell, we made an announcement to anyone who matters."

"Oh, I know, but it still seems wrong to be engaged to the person in the next office. Kind of like in-breeding."

"Of which we'll probably get more than our fill of tonight," I said.

Opening the door to our apartment, we shook off the dampness and started preparing for our little sojourn into the woods. I changed into loose jeans and a sweatshirt, and I watched as Deena replaced her more formal work clothes, too. She was wearing a black bra and matching panties, and I debated committing a little afternoon delight before she caught my gaze.

"Don't even think about it," she said, throwing on an outfit eerily similar to my own. "We want to get in there and get out before nightfall. I, for one, don't relish going out there in the first place. In the rain and in the dark, and you, my love, will be all on your own."

"Then, you shouldn't wear such attractive underthings."

"I'm not saying anything about *after* our hike. There's always the night. Anyway, you were the one who bought these for my birthday. More of a present for you than for me."

"Ready?" I asked, as she handed me a yellow raincoat. I looked down at it distastefully. "Well, at least I won't be shot by any deer hunters."

Deena struggled into a dark green rain poncho. "No, but I want you sticking close to me. This damn thing may as well be camouflage."

"We could switch," I suggested.

"I think it's time we hit the road. It's almost one-thirty now. Who knows how long this is going to take."

I unlatched the door and held it open as she walked back outside. It seemed ridiculous at the time, but I felt a surge of love for this woman as she walked past me in what amounted to a green garbage bag that completely swallowed her form. The hood even covered most of her face. Still, my heart wanted to pound its way out of my chest with the emotions she exhumed when she was near to me.

I knew she didn't have to take the rest of the day to help me in my search for Gary McCoy's village. After all, it could just be another delusion, and we would be wasting our time when she could be helping others in Saint Michael's pack up their belongings. She had already prepared everything in her own office. She could even be taking the rest of the day off, sitting in our warm apartment, carving pumpkins, and watching scary movies on TV. A local horror host was presenting a double feature starting at eight. Instead, she'd opted to accompany me on my journey, to aid me in finalizing a diagnosis on the McCoy boy. It told me more about Deena than any glimpse of her half-naked body, and it revealed a lot about my own feelings for her, as well.

She had been there when I needed her most, when I'd lived with a bottle of whiskey no farther than ten feet distant from me at any time. I'd stashed bottles in my office, at home, even in the car. After completing my work, I'd high tail it to a bar or the nearest hidden reserve, eager to put the day's madness behind me. Nights were spent in a drunken stupor and days went by in the haze of a hangover. I knew it had affected my work, but, at that point, I didn't care.

Then, she'd looked over that clipboard at me and flashed that smile. It acted as a substitute, or perhaps I finally had something worth staying sober for. In any case, I'd joined AA that very week. Now, I rarely went to the meetings, able to hold my urges in check. Every once in a while, I felt the need for a drink, but I pushed such desires aside, concentrating on Deena and the life we were building together. It was enough. Nearly always.

I still probably had forgotten hidden collections of whiskey all over St. Mike's. I know I would've been better off without the temptation lurking so close at hand, and I wouldn't have suffered the enticement at home, but what was the point of overcoming a handicap if there was nothing left to tempt you? It felt good to step past those bottles without giving them more than a courtesy remembrance.

I drove my car, a beat up, five year old Honda Civic that sputtered and choked when it rained. I kept it in the hopes of saving money for a cash down payment on the next car, something with a little more style, but the money never seemed to go as far as I'd prefer. Even with Deena splitting the bills in half, we were having trouble building a nest egg. A lot of money went towards the rent and utilities, but a lot of it was blown on frivolous things - movies, better groceries, the gas to my A.A. meetings whenever I was compelled to attend one.

I told myself that's why Gary McCoy was so important. A good write-up in the professional journals would definitely demand an increase in my salary at the new hospital. A book deal would set us up for the next several years, get my name out there as someone who had actually helped a patient. My record at St. Mike's was rather superficial. I'd helped plenty of people with issues they had brought in with them, but nothing ever stood out from the rest of the cases every psychiatrist sees every day. I needed to set at least one subject apart from the others.

Gary McCoy was different, even if the entire village scenario turned out to be a figment of some fantasy playing itself out in his skull. I'd never heard so many problems coming from a single patient. I believed the issues were linked somehow - his delusions, the religious overtones, the prophecies about the end of the world. If I could link them, connect all the dots, I could get a job in a really good hospital - a better one than where I was being sent. Maybe even become Deena's boss.

I turned on to Highway 90. Traffic was heavy, due to the rain and the slick roads, but I managed to restrain myself from speeding past the other cars. I didn't want to go hydroplaning into the bushes.

Soon, both sides of the highway were lined with dense thickets and trees. The woods seemed to sprout up out of nowhere, magical apparitions of the end of urban sprawl. The trees were old, huge elms and oaks, birches and walnut. They'd maintained sentry over this wild part of the state for a long time, towering over the landscape. When the highway began to rise and lower over small hillocks, I turned to Deena, who was holding the map, playing navigator.

"What did he draw to indicate the pathway? Some kind of split tree?"

We passed the gas station where he'd verbally assaulted the little girl and the cashier. Its neon lights formed mini-rainbows in the mist. I knew we had to be close.

"Yeah, he drew two trees growing in a 'V' formation," Deena said. "He also drew the gas station, so it should be...right over there. Holy crap! Look, Bob, there it is."

As I pulled the car over onto the berm of the road, I saw what she was pointing towards. Two white birch trees seemed to have sprouted from the same trunk, each one rearing upwards at approximately forty five degree angles away from each other. I could see a path cut from the underbrush at the left of the tree. It would have been well hidden if you didn't know exactly where to look.

"There's the way in," I said. "So far, so good."

"It's starting to rain harder," Deena said, eyeing the windshield and the water spattering against it.

"At least there's no thunder or lightning," I said, looking at the dark, overcast sky. I wasn't going to hold my breath that we wouldn't get caught in a storm. Those clouds looked downright pissed off.

I locked the car after me, and then I held out my hand to my fiancée. She took it, and I shrugged the backpack onto my shoulders. Inside, I had packed several pens and blank notebooks, along with the notes I'd taken while interviewing McCoy earlier that day, two flashlights, extra batteries, and some bags of chips. Just in case we got hungry.

We were only twenty feet into the forest, following the narrowing path, when I had to let go of Deena's hand. We could no longer walk next to each other, and I gave her the option of walking in front or in back.

"Well, since most monster movies show the person in back getting killed first," she replied, "I'll lead. You can follow, but I want the flashlight. It's already getting hard to see, and these thorns are becoming downright hazardous."

Handing her one flashlight, I gripped the other and zipped up the backpack. Returning it to its position on my shoulders, I trudged after her, trying to avoid the afore-mentioned thorn bushes, which were scratching the hell out of my hands. I didn't know what they were, but I was quickly learning to despise them.

The ground was muddy from the previous rainstorm, and the path was dotted with puddles that often tried to suck off one of our shoes. Roots emerged from the dirt trail, tripping us up, and I fell more than once. Somehow, Deena managed to keep her balance, although she sometimes performed elaborate ballet moves, arms wind-milling, feet tapping all over the place, that kept her retaining her upright position.

The farther we traveled, the denser the woods became around us. The girths of the trees grew wider, and the branches, half devoid of leaves in the cool October air, seemed to reach out for us. The meager sunlight was all but obscured by the tall trees and the canopy they provided. Luckily, this covering managed to deflect a lot of the rain, which, alarmingly, seemed to be increasing in volume. I could hear it pounding away at the overgrowth. I was thankful I'd packed the flashlights, because without them, we would have had to stop our progress and return home. Either that or light a torch using my shirt, and I actually liked the sweatshirt I was wearing. It featured the words 'Penn State', and I'd had it since attending school there.

Thinking of college always brought back the nights spent drinking with my comrades in the Psychology department. Beer is always cheap in college towns. A thirst for the stuff seemed to tickle me in the back of my throat. I looked ahead of me, at Deena's flapping, green poncho, and I smiled.

Although, I'll admit, in that rain, in those dark woods, a beer would've been more than welcomed.

"How far do you think we've come?" I asked, surprised by the whiny tone of my voice.

"Probably about a mile. What time is it?"

I checked my watch. "Two-thirty or so."

"Maybe a little more than a mile, then."

"Sheesh, Mom, are we there yet?" I asked, trying to lighten the mood. The darkness of the forest surrounding us was starting to creep me out. It was almost Halloween, so I decided those chills traversing my spine were merely by-products of the season.

"You want to talk about the wedding?" I asked, latching onto a subject Deena found inexplicably thrilling.

"Not really," she answered. "This place seems to call out for quiet. For peace. It makes you humble."

"It makes me wet and cranky," I said, slapping at my bare neck as some buzzing insect bit me.

"Keep up with me, and we'll be there soon. If we maintain this pace…"

"…we'll cross the state line by six-o-clock." I finished for her.

We continued in silence. I tried to admire the beauty of the forest, but it just seemed creepier to me all the time. The trees were nearly bare, and their branches stuck out, clawed fingers splayed wide. Leaves crinkled under my footsteps. My legs had become encased in mud, which was starting to dry and crust on my jeans. It became more and more difficult to maintain a steady, quick pace, as we kept getting stuck. The muddy trail turned swampier, and the insect population was definitely increasing, as testament by the swelling pocks on my neck and arms.

"You aren't getting bit," I said, slapping at another of the little black bugs that swarmed around my face.

"They must not like the taste of me."

"Well, if it's any consolation, I like the way you taste."

"You're a pervert."

"And damn proud of it."

"Hey, I think those are the cliffs from the map," she said, pointing ahead.

I couldn't see anything at first, but as we stepped closer, the whole panorama came into view. I gasped, stopping at Deena's side where the path widened.

The trail ended suddenly, dropping off a short cliff of about fifty feet or so. A creek ran through the valley, wide and swollen with the recent rain, the muddy water filling the bottom of the crevice. Scraggly trees lined each side of the cliffs, green vines dangling from them, and stairs had been created in the side of the bluff by carving out the earth and placing rotting two by fours across each 'step.'

"Do you see the cave?" I asked, leaning over the cliff and peering down into the dark gorge.

Deena moved her flashlight from side to side. "No," she said. "Wait a second. What's that? Looks like a hole near the bottom by the water."

My gaze followed her flashlight's beam and I saw a darkened patch. It could have just been a discoloration in the mud, some strata of clay, but I didn't think so. It resembled a cave.

"Come on," I ordered.

"Be careful," Deena warned. "The wood is rotted right through."

She was referring to the hand-made steps that inched down the side of the bluffs. Indeed, they didn't look very sturdy, but I didn't have any choice. Confirmation of at least part of Gary McCoy's tale awaited discovery just fifty feet below me. I needed that corroboration if I was to get anywhere with the boy's case.

"I'll be careful," I said, and I started down the steps.

The wood was pulpy, wet through and through, and it seemed to squish beneath my sneakers as though it was a sodden sponge. I grimaced at the sensation.

The rain was having an easier time falling on us without so many trees blocking it. It made the wood even more slippery, and I grasped hold of several roots that were sticking out of the earth. Once, I even held tightly to a scrubby bush. Deena clutched tightly to my yellow slicker, the rubber material tight in her fingers. I had a sudden vision of her falling and taking me with her, never letting go of that yellow coat, the two of us plummeting into the brown water.

By the time we reached the cave, my hands were covered in mud and clay from grasping at anything to keep my balance. We stepped into the small cavern, thankful from the relief from the onslaught of rain. I shook my hair and hands, and water flew in every direction. Deena laughed at me.

"You look like a dog," she said, covering her mouth. "A mongrel."

"Better than a drowned rat, I guess. Man, look at this place."

The cave wasn't very large, perhaps twenty feet deep, narrowing as it went, and about ten feet wide. Stalactites and stalagmites grew together in strange, amorphous shapes, and the walls were smooth limestone. We waved our flashlights around, searching for the drawings Gary had described, but there didn't seem to be any unusual markings on the cavern walls.

"Well," I said. "I guess he's just another delusional schizophrenic, hearing voices and-"

"Wait a minute," Deena said, moving to the back of the cave where the stalactites appeared lumpy instead of flat. I could hear water trickling somewhere, but the acoustics of the cavern created an echo, so I couldn't decide where the noise came from.

"There's more to this place," she said, stepping behind one of the limestone growths that resembled an abstract female form. "The cave goes farther back."

I followed her and found a much larger cavern hidden behind the stalactites. This one resembled a cathedral, with huge, dripping ceilings, spiked with dagger-sharp calcium deposits. It was so large, I couldn't determine how far back it went or how high. The flashlight beams dissipated and were lost in the darkness. You could have at least fit a football field within the subterranean place. The floor was relatively smooth, and there was a circle of stones in the center, filled with the ashes of long dead fires. Placing my hand over the stones, I realized that the fires weren't so dead, after all.

"There's still some heat here," I said. "Someone's been here recently. Maybe yesterday."

"Think it might have been McCoy?"

"I don't know," I answered, moving towards the walls. "Holy shit."

Deena moved to my side, and we looked at the primitive art that covered the limestone. There were dozens of elaborate drawings, done in a style reminiscent of the grade school pictures of children you'd spot taped to the windows of elementary academies. The people were little more than stick figures with either balloonish breasts or incredibly long phalluses to determine their sex. The animals were blobs, with four legs and horns, obviously primitive attempts at sketching cattle.

"There's a lot more," Deena said, signaling with her flashlight.

As we looked, we saw the walls had about a dozen pictures drawn upon them, and they appeared to tell a story, a sort of antediluvian stations of the cross. Figuring that they read from left to right, we started at the far left corner of the cave, with the sketch of the men and women tending to their bulbous cattle. There were also several small houses drawn in the background of the picture.

The second picture displayed what appeared to be a family tree, starting with one man and one woman at the top with three lines drawn from them to two men and one woman beneath their stick feet. Lines were then drawn between these two men and one woman, probably brothers and sisters of the first two people, to several other men and women beneath their feet. And so on and so on.

"This must be what McCoy was talking about when he said the drawings said that brothers and sisters should mate," I said, following the diagram with my fingers. "See how the brothers and sisters are connected with the lines, then to their children?"

"As though someone was trying to say have sex only with your own family. I don't know how anyone so primitive could comprehend genetics, but, perhaps, someone wanted to preserve some specific gene, or create it through incest."

"As in creating the Preacher? Could be. An elaborate breeding chart that could result in a specific person with a specific ability - the aptitude for seeing into other dimensions."

"We're only postulating here, but I think that's got to be it."

"Gregor Mendel would be so proud."

Deena moved to the next picture and illuminated it with her flashlight. This one showed a single man with a triangle emerging from his face, point-first at his nose and growing as it moved further away from him. The end of the triangle was obscured by smudges or smoke. A single line connected the man's feet with the previous drawing.

"See," Deena said, getting excited. "This line must mean he's the product of all that in-breeding. The Preacher."

"And the triangle is what he's seeing. Why is it all smushed and smeared?"

"Let's look at the next one."

The fourth pictogram was much more elaborate than the infantile drawings before it. Long creatures that looked like lamprey eels, their mouths ringed in rows of teeth, swam through the air. Three legged, bearish beasts walked on the ground. Clawed, bat-like creatures flew next to the eels, their paths crossing with the primitive looking people on the ground going about their daily business.

"This is what McCoy says he's seeing," I said. "The monsters coexisting with the people, only the people are oblivious to them. Only the Preacher can see them or hear them whispering to him."

Deena shivered, and I hugged her, wanting to tell her I was feeling the same eerie apprehension. The cavern was creepy, and the pictures only added to the uneasy mood, combined with the quiet plop-plopping of water dropping from the stalactites to an underground lake somewhere.

"Notice anything about this picture?" I asked.

"Well, the monsters look much more elaborate than the people, as though they were..."

"...drawn by someone else. The artwork looks terribly familiar, don't you think? Like the map?"

"You're right," she whispered. "It's definitely the same artist. Your patient's been a busy boy."

We got closer and noticed the elaborately sketched monsters, with all their minute details, had been drawn over a much simpler picture. In the earlier drawing, the monsters had exhibited much of the childish primitivism of the stick people, all angles and crude lines.

"Gary McCoy has drawn over the old picture," I said. "He's drawn the monsters he's seeing, instead of the original artist's rendition. He's clarifying how the creatures actually appear."

"This is what he's seeing? These eel things?"

I nodded. "So he says. What's the next one?"

There followed an elaborate series of circles connecting to other circles, an extended Olympics symbol. In the first was a picture of waves on an ocean. The next interconnecting circle was filled with the same stick people from the first drawing. The third contained the same three species of monstrosities, drawn in Gary McCoy's hand over what appeared to be a bunch of wavy lines and creatures made from blobs and sticks, very similar to the cattle of the first picture. The fourth was filled in with inky blackness. Black, writhing tentacles snaked out of the fourth disk, feeling their way into the circle of the monsters and into the fifth circle, which only showed wavy lines, like the ocean on its side.

"The different dimensions McCoy talked about," I explained, "the way they cross each other, overlap, that must be where he gets this 'heavy drapes' idea. The drapes separate the different dimensions, but only where they overlap. And this bad boy," I said, pointing to the black shape with the tentacles. "This must be the Old One, the god who wants into our world."

"It gives me the heebie-jeebies."

The next picture was very similar to the last with its rings, but a man stood in between each of them where they overlapped. The Old One's tentacles were reaching much further now, entering most of the way through the monster's realm, and the beasts were all facing it, as though worshiping, kneeling to that blackness. The next one showed the circles all breaking apart. The sideways ocean flooded the people's land, the monsters were devouring the stick figures, and the huge black thing had grown large enough to fully inhabit all three dimensions. It had two humans wrapped in its black tentacles.

"You notice," I said. "McCoy's gone through and drawn over all the creatures, as though determined to show them the way they really are."

"Why didn't he elaborate upon the people? They're still just stick figures."

"I don't know," I admitted. "Probably part of his psychosis."

"Or maybe he drew them all, getting his hallucinations out of his head, as it were, and the people aren't as important to him as the monsters are."

"Honestly, I don't know. But that sounds pretty good. He *is* focused on the creatures he's describing to me. Only, the stick figures, the early pictures, all seem pretty old. I'll have to get someone in here to date them."

"I have a friend at Penn State who could do it. She's doing her doctorate thesis on primitive American cultures, especially their artwork. Native American art as opposed to South American or European. She'd be fascinated by all this."

"Call her when we get back," I said.

The final drawing in the series depicted the Old One hovering over the earth, a huge black cloud in outer space. It was surrounded by stars. Tentacles dropped from its amoebae-like body, grabbing at people and pulling them into its smoky, amorphous mass. Just as Gary had mentioned, red blood, the only color used other than black on any of the pictures, fell like rain from the creature.

Deena asked, "Have you seen enough?"

"Yeah," I said. "Let's get out of here and come back with a lot more people. I'm getting, well, kind of..."

"...freaked out?"

"Yeah."

As we turned back towards the smaller cavern, something moved in the darkness behind us. It wasn't the sound of water splashing against water, but something big moving through liquid. Then, a thin laugh emerged from the darkness.

"Hee hee hee..."

Deena grabbed me, and whispered, "Bob, someone's back there."

"They've been there all along," I said, unable to suppress a tremble. "Waiting in the dark. Waiting for us to get to the end of the story."

We waved our lights into the cavern, and something pale and thin rushed towards us, laughing crazily with every step.

Chapter 6

Deena screamed, but she ceased when the beam of her flashlight illuminated the white figure. It was an old man, long gray hair flowing over his naked shoulders. He wore a pair of filthy jeans, cinched around his puny waist with a rope, and his chest and feet were bare. He was so emaciated, he looked as though he hadn't eaten a proper meal for several months; his ribs jutted out, his belly was slightly swollen, and his shoulder blades threatened to burst through his paper-thin skin at any moment. His skin was not really white, as I'd first assumed, but a sallow, sickly yellow. His mouth was open in a howl of rage, exposing diseased gums and a single tooth lodged halfway back to his throat. His white pupils exposed the fact that he was blind, and he held his arthritic hands in front of him, feeling his way as he hurried towards us, cackling with manic laughter all the way.

He stopped a few feet away from us, moving his outstretched hands back and forth in front of himself, trying to feel out our position. His head swerved, unsteady on his thin shoulders. He licked his gums a few times.

Looking at Deena, I put a finger to my lips in the international symbol for 'shush.' I wasn't sure yet if it was safe to expose our position. She nodded at me, and we looked back at the man who'd emerged from the cave.

Fingers splayed, he continued feeling his way closer to us. Finally, he asked, "Who's there? I heard ya. Can't see worth a blue bitch, but I can hear ya. Ain't dead yet, ya know."

I looked back at Deena, shook my head so she'd understand we shouldn't say anything yet.

"Aw, come on," the old man continued, his arms slapping back against his sides. "You just come here ta look at the dyin'? Well, I ain't dead yet. Ain't dead yet, even though you all put me here. Left me ta die. Well, fuck y'all, I ain't dead yet."

Deena's face was starting to display that compassionate look she had for homeless people and lost pets. I knew there wouldn't be much time before she rushed to the old man, put her arms around his bony waist, and tried to comfort him. It was her way, and there wasn't anything I could do to change her. I didn't want to change her.

"Watchin' the old man die...it's sick, I tell ya. Sick! You bastards just get along now and let me starve ta death. Just let an old man starve..."

He started to turn, and Deena took a step forward. I shook my head, but she ignored me.

"Hey, sir?" she said, placing a reassuring hand on the old guy's shoulder. "We can help you."

In a flash, faster than I would've thought possible, the old man whipped his skeletal hand upwards and grasped Deena by the wrist. She squirmed and moaned. His grip must have been tight, because her expression told me she was in pain.

"Come to see the dyin' old man, eh, girlie? Come to see me fall over in weakness? Well, I ain't so weak, am I?"

"Ow! You're hurting me," she squealed.

"Let her go," I shouted, and I was surprised at the loud, authoritative nature of my voice. I'm not a big man, but I sure impersonated one in the confines of that cave. The bellow echoed off the limestone walls.

The old man moved his head, searching for my location. Taking advantage of his momentary confusion, I ran towards him and knocked him down with a tackle-block I'd learned in high school. He fell to the floor of the cave, letting loose of Deena. My fiancée hurried towards me, and I wrapped an arm around her. For a moment, just a brief moment, she pressed her face into my chest. Then, realizing how she probably looked, she turned her gaze to the old man.

"Now what'd'ja have ta do that fer?" the old guy gasped, clutching at his side where I'd struck him. "Ain't nice ta' hurt the old and dyin'. I was just funnin' with ya."

"Who are you?" I asked, trying unsuccessfully to emulate my previous strong, he-man voice. "Why are you lurking in this cave and attacking people?"

He started to giggle again, and the laughter turned into genuine guffaws. The old man slapped at the floor of the cave, but he didn't try to stand. I thought he might be too weak for that.

"You two ain't from these parts, are ya?" he asked. "You talk like rich folk...city fuckers."

"You're right," I said.

"What in tarnation you doin' out here in the woods? This ain't a good place for people like you. You ain't gonna understand it. None of it."

"What won't we understand?" Deena asked, and I saw that tender, piteous look falling over her face again. "Why you're in this cave? Did someone leave you to die?"

"Always leave the old ta die, lady," he answered. "Ain't doin' nothin' but gettin' in the way. I got so sick and blind and all, my sons couldn't take care a' me no longer. Dropped me off in here ta starve. Then I hear ya makin' noise out here, and I thinks that mebbe one of the boys has come back fer me. Mebbe, one of 'em cares enough."

"We can get you to a hospital. They'll nurse you back to health."

"A hospital?" he screeched, spitting out the word. "You ain't got no idea, lady. It's my time. The boys know it. I know it, even though I ain't gonna admit it to no one. I ain't of no use to no one in the village no more, so I get left here ta die. Just wish it weren't takin' so damn long."

"You're from the village?" I asked. "The one in the woods?"

"Where the fuck else am I gonna be from?"

"You know where it is?"

"'Course I do. I'm blind. Not stupid."

"Do you know the Preacher?" I asked.

His face turned towards me, and I could see his befuddled expression. He licked his lips, thinking for a moment then he asked, "How you know about the Preacher?"

"Gary McCoy? He's a friend of mine," I said. "I just talked to him earlier today. He told me all about the village, but he didn't mention any old man in a cave."

"Preacher is the special one. He's gonna bring about the new world," the old man said, and he resembled someone caught up in the holy spirit in a Pentecostal church. "He told ya about the cave and the things a'swimmin' in the air?"

"Yes, he did."

"He tell ya about the Old One?"

"Just this afternoon."

"The time is near," the old guy said, and he stood, wiping the dust off of himself. "I don't know a lot. I'm just a old man who ain't got many days ta live, but I know me one thing. I'm glad I ain't gonna be around when those curtains open and we can all see what the Preacher sees. They say it's gonna rain blood down on the earth and a lotta people gonna die. They say that Old One's hungry...even hungrier than me, I s'pose. He been starvin' for so long, millions a' years."

"How can we stop it?" I asked, getting caught up in the mythology the people out in these woods had created.

"Oh, ya can't. Ain't no stoppin' a god, sonny. It's too big, too ornery, bein' caged up like that fer so long. No, sir. Ain't no stoppin' a god."

"Bob," Deena said. "We need to get to the village before it's too late. I don't relish being in the woods after dark."

"You're right."

"Hey," the old man snapped. "You say you was talkin' to the Preacher this afternoon? Today?"

"Yeah, at the mental hospital where I work," I said.

"He's in a hospital? In the city? He ain't out in the woods where he's supposed ta be?"

"He's locked up, safe and sound."

"We wouldn't hurt him," Deena said. "Don't worry."

The old man laughed again. "You city folk think you know it all, don't'cha? You think you're so damn smart. You took the preacher into the city? You don't know what kinda hell you brought down on yourselves. Hoo! When the Old One gets loose, he's gonna make tracks right for that preacher like he was a magnet. And your city, it is gonna be right in that Old One's path."

With that, the blind man sprinted into the darkness at the other end of the cave. I could hear him laughing, hooting and braying in the back of the little grotto.

I ran after him, "Hey, what do you mean?"

Deena, left behind, cried after me, "Bob! Bob don't go after him!"

I ignored her, moving towards the back of the cavern, wishing my flashlight beam were brighter. It illuminated a small swath in the darkness, taking the shape of a cone of light. I could see an underground lake appearing to my left. That must have been where the water dripping noises I'd heard were coming from.

"Oh Bob, don't leave me here alone," I heard Deena say. Then I discerned her footfalls approaching me from behind. She was running to catch up, splashing through puddles.

I could still hear the laughing blind man in the depths of the place, which seemed to stretch back farther and farther into the side of the hill. The lake was almost to my left when I saw the first white bit of bone sticking out of the shallows. Deena caught up to me, and her flashlight beam merged with mine to double the brightness.

"What is it, Bob?" she asked. Then, she looked towards the lake. "Oh my Lord."

The lake was filled with human bones, which spread across the shallow water and onto the shore. Human and some animal skulls lined the shore, and others had been placed on top of stalagmites, their empty eye sockets glaring down upon us. Other bodies, some still decomposing, were laid carefully along the side of the cavern as though they were awaiting the Apocalypse they'd been promised. The scene was like that of a newly discovered, exhumed graveyard, and the maniacal laughter of the blind man who hid in the shadows didn't do anything to dispel the disturbing aspects of the area.

"How many are here?" she asked. "How many people have just been left to die?"

"Come on," I said, taking Deena under my arm and turning her around from the sickening gleam of bones. "Let's get out of here."

"Sounds good to me," she answered.

We heard the blind guy laughing behind us all the way to the entrance of the cave. Occasionally, he'd shout out words, but the echo distorted them to an extent where I couldn't understand anything.

Chapter 7

We rested for a bit outside the cave, leaning against a huge tree that managed to block most of the rainfall. The storm seemed to be brewing heavily in the west, and we sometimes heard a distant growl of thunder from that direction. At the moment, however, it was still merely raining, and the pitter-patter of the drops hitting the trees was loud enough to block the crazy old man's incessant giggling from within the cave.

"I have to tell you," Deena said, "I'm not liking this a bit, Bob. Why don't we go home, celebrate Halloween by watching a horror movie and not living one? I think I hear the pumpkins calling our names."

"Sweetie, you can head back if you want to," I said, rubbing her knee. "I won't mind."

"And leave you alone out here? With crazy people who dump their elderly in caves to die? Jesus, this is America, not some far away third world nation. What kind of people do that?"

"Well, that's just the sort of thing I need to find out. If Gary came from someplace prehistoric, then I'll know better how to treat him. I didn't even think this village was really out here, but I'm starting to believe Gary's psychosis isn't, well, so psychotic. Maybe, all of this stuff is true to him."

"Oh come on, Bob. Old gods crossing through dimensions to attack our world? It's a myth based on a bunch of cave drawings."

"Yeah, but how'd it develop? Myths come from someplace, and if our boy back at St. Mike's was raised in a belief system that believes in Cthulhu or some derivation of Lovecraft, then I need to know that."

"I really, really don't like this," she said. "We have creepy people lurking in caves, monsters in the air, and a storm approaching. All we need is some Bernard Herrmann music, and we got ourselves a very special Halloween episode of The Outer Limits."

"Why don't you go back to the car?" I asked. "Wait for me there."

"No way am I going any place in this spooky forest alone. Let's just find the village and get the hell out of here."

"Okay, where's the map say we should go?"

We perused McCoy's drawing for a while longer, figuring which direction to take. Soon, we discovered a pathway, and we started walking towards the bottom of the little canyon. The ground was getting muddier and muddier, and our feet made squishing noises as the earth sucked at them. We seemed to wade through two inches of fallen leaves, yellow and brown, attached to twigs which crunched beneath our feet. It made the going slow. At least the bugs had stopped swarming me, preferring to hide from the rainfall.

Before long, the path opened up, broadening until we could once again walk next to each other. Deena took my hand in hers, and the little bit of contact, skin on skin, brought reality crashing down upon me.

What was I doing hauling my future wife out here in the rain and hunting for some group of people who may or may not actually exist? I didn't know if the village's inhabitants would be dangerous, friendly, or crazy as a bunch of loons. At the very least, she was probably going to catch a cold from all the damp weather. I chastised myself. I was being a bad fiancée.

And then, the path spread wider, became more navigable, exposing a glen with several pitiful structures huddled within it, as though they were cowering from the poisonous influences of the outside world. The shacks were built of anything that people could get their hands upon - pieces of wood, fallen trees, limbs tied together with brown twine, sheet metal, and long pieces of rotten carpeting. They were arranged in a circle, and a bonfire smoked in the center of them, as though daring the rain to extinguish it.

"The village," Deena said. "My God, it's real."

Chapter 8

Calling the little group of hovels a village was an absurd exaggeration and a misnomer. I counted twenty one of the buildings, if you could refer to these heartbreaking shelters as buildings. If what McCoy had said was correct, and so far the guy had been batting a thousand, then fifty people lived within the glen, but I couldn't see any inhabitants. They must have all been inside, shielded from the rain, which pinged loudly on the tin roofs and sheet metal coverings.

"Where is everyone?" Deena asked, once again displaying her uncanny ability to read my mind.

"I don't know."

I wanted to take a few steps towards the epicenter of the huts, but the silence of the place stopped me. Other than the ping of the rain, the wind through the branches, and the crackling fire, I couldn't detect any noise. If there were people in those hovels, wouldn't they make some sort of sound? Wouldn't they be preparing dinner or talking or snoring or something?

The thought came to me with a chill.

Not if they're waiting for us.

"Stay here," I said, moving away from Deena.

"Oh no. You are *not* leaving me here in the dark all alone with God knows what kind of incestuous, monstrous *Deliverance* extras hidden in the bushes. Are you crazy?"

"I need to see what's in this place. I need to talk to the people."

"It's twilight. It'll be night soon. Let's return in the daytime. When it's sunny and not so freaking creepy."

"I think this place will always be freaking creepy. Even at high noon."

"I should have stayed in the car, huh?"

"Yeah, you probably should have," I said. "But I'm glad you didn't. I'm glad you're here with me. This seems so important somehow, as though it's going to change my life...our lives. I wouldn't want to be doing it alone. It's good having you by my side."

"Oh, I bet you say that to all the girls."

I nodded towards the quiet ring of homes. "You ready to check these people out?"

"Yeah, but we aren't staying all night. We just solicit a few interviews to learn about McCoy's background. No thorough research yet."

"Trust me," I said. "I don't want to be out here when it gets really dark. With those clouds, there's not even going to be any moonlight tonight."

We stepped forward, taking our time, watching the doors of the hovels in case someone rushed out of one of them. As we walked through the village, we began to hear hushed conversations from within the shacks. Once, I thought I heard mumbled chanting. All this dialogue was being executed in soft whispers, so I couldn't actually hear what the citizens were saying. I could just discern the velvety sibilance of hissed, sibilant tones, and it created the effect of some sort of gathering of snakes.

I was thankful when we arrived at the fire, unharmed, unmolested. The blaze wasn't very large, just five or six logs, but the heat it generated was a welcome relief from the cool October air. The wood spat and popped as it burned, and the rain sizzled upon contact with it.

Deena put her hands out to the fire and grinned at me. "Feels good."

"Who in hell are you two?" asked a thin voice from behind us, tinged with a backwoods accent.

I turned and saw an old man, more ancient than the blind guy in the cavern. Lines were etched into his face as if carved with a knife, and his legs and arms were twisted with severe arthritis. Hobbling from one of the huts, he limped towards us on feet cruelly turned inwards, so he almost had to walk on his heels.

At the sound of his voice, others began emerging from their shacks. They moved cautiously, as though wary of Deena and me, and many of them suffered from similar arthritic conditions. Their movements in the twilight gloom were jerky, spasmodic. As they gathered closer to the fire, clustering behind the first man who had approached us, I could see why they moved so strangely.

The inhabitants of the village were supposedly the result of generations of incestuous couplings, and, looking at them in that glen, I didn't doubt it for a second. Their eyes were set very close together, and more than a few of them possessed the same brown eye / blue eye combination of pupils as Gary McCoy. Sometimes, their eyes were set one higher than the other. Mouths gaped open, and saliva drooled from the corners. Any exposed teeth were either rotten or in serious need of an orthodontist. I could see several people with shriveled, useless arms or legs twisted nearly backwards, making the act of walking almost impossible. More than a few had malformed spines, curving their backs so that they hunched over.

"Bob," Deena whispered, pointing to a particularly twisted specimen. "That man has thirteen fingers."

The birth defects kept mounting as I looked over the gathering denizen of the village. I saw one woman whose naked back exposed a spinal column located outside of her skin. One man had legs half the length they should have been and a torso far too long. There were several enlarged craniums, and, as I looked around the pitiable group, I witnessed a few faces displaying signs of Down's syndrome and / or severe mental retardation. Many of them tried to speak, but could only make sounds, similar to a seven month old baby. I winced when I saw a child dragging its body along by two elongated arms, its fingers enclosed in flipper-like pouches of skin, its boneless legs dragging behind it.

"Oh God," Deena said. "These poor people."

"Who are ya?" asked the old man again. "I asked twice now. I ain't gonna do it again."

"We're friends of the Preacher," I said.

All around us, the people began whispering. Gary's nickname excited them, stirred them into motion, and they started to rush to us. Deena cried out.

"Wait," the old man said, holding up a withered claw.

Upon his order, the group stopped in their tracks. They seemed humbled, ashamed of their sudden movements. I realized this old man was their chief or leader. He obviously held sway over these deformed people.

"How you know the Preacher?"

"He's come to us," I answered. "He's staying at a hospital where I work, and we're trying to help him."

There was some laughter around us. Glancing around, I saw the twisted smiles, the empty, rotting mouths forming 'O's of delight.

"Are you..." I said, looking at the old guy. "Are you his Pa? He talked about you."

"Aye. I am the boy's papa. I sired the preacher."

Deena was clutching on to me so tightly it felt as if she was squeezing the air out of me. I tried to unlatch her from my side, but she wasn't about to let go. I would have bruises in the morning.

"Can we talk somewhere?" I asked. "Out of this rain? Maybe in your house? I'd love to see it."

The old man nodded, raised his arm, and swept it around the circle. The gathered people immediately turned and headed back to their own homes, as if they were dismissed from the warmth of the fire. They obeyed the silent command without a complaint, without any sound whatsoever.

"This is my house," the old man said, limping towards a ten by fifteen foot shack made up of haphazard pieces of plywood and a portion of sheet metal on top for a roof. "Come on in. Tell me what ya know 'bout my boy."

Entering the one room place, I was struck by the disgusting reek of the quarters, a mixture of body odor, stale sweat, and sex. There was little in the way of furniture - a bed, a small oil heater, a single chair. The old man sat in the chair and motioned towards the floor. Looking down, I saw black beetles scuttling across the dirt, their carapaces so shiny I could see my reflection. With some distaste, we dropped down and sat Indian style. Deena removed the notebook and started writing in it. I heard a sound behind us.

A woman lay on a bed across the place, younger than Pa, but she was more deformed than any of the people we had seen outside. Her body was so malformed and disfigured that she appeared to have no legs or arms at all, but upon closer inspection, I saw she had flippers. She rocked on her twisted back, flapping at the man, muttering nonsense and drooling on the filthy bedclothes. A child played under the bed. I could hear it, but, thankfully, I could only make out its dystrophic shape.

"So, ya got yer hands on the preacher, did ya?" the old man huffed. "The little bastard go to you or did ya come to him?"

"I don't understand."

"Why'd ya steal away my boy?" the old man hissed, leaning forward. "He's our preacher, and he's our deliverer, and he sees the visions for us all."

"You can't see the monsters?" I asked. I heard Deena scribbling as fast as she could, and I realized she was noting the old man's facial expressions and tics as well as his words. We both knew how valuable these notations could be in later sessions with Gary.

"Sometimes I think I see one of 'em, but only outta the corners of my eyes...same as them little floatie things. Preacher, he the one who sees 'em. He the one who gonna deliver us to the Old One."

"When's the Old One supposed to come into this world?"

"Soon. That's all I know. It's gonna be soon. Ask the Preacher, if you're so dang friendly with 'im. He can tell ya better'n me."

"I wouldn't say we were friends," I said.

"Then why you meddlin' in our business, you sorry-assed little bug fucker?" His tone had become laced with rage. I could see him shaking, trying to control the fury that threatened to boil over at any moment. "He's my spawn. I raised him right. Had him right with his older sister over there on the bed. You shoulda heard her squawking when he come outta her. Heard it all through the woods."

"I didn't take him," I explained. "He came to us. He wanted to warn someone about the Old One, about the prophecies. We have him safe and snug at Saint Michael's Mental Hospital. He won't be harmed, I can assure you."

"Oh, I ain't worried about the boy," the old guy said with a terrible leer. "I think I'd be worried 'bout whether that there hospital will still be there in the mornin'."

"You think your Old One's going to destroy everything?"

"Well, now, we ain't gonna know for sure till he arrives, are we? And since he's supposed to arrive through the Preacher, I reckon your pretty little hospital ain't gonna be much more'n dust come Arrival Day."

"Through the Preacher? Your son is the gateway?"

Deena added, "What's Gary have to do to let him into our world?"

The old man smiled, but the effect wasn't one of pleasure or happiness. There was a kind of smug knowledge there. I'd seen the same 'cat that ate the canary' look on certain evangelical ministers who damned everyone to hell then committed the same sins they were deprecating.

"We don't have all yer answers, missy," he said. "We only know what the drawings tell us, and I reckon you've already done seen the drawings since you come from that direction. They told us how to breed with each other, who to screw so we end up with our precious preacher-boy. They tell us some of what the preacher can see, but they don't say a lot about what happens to the preacher when the Old One comes. It sure don't look good for people, though."

"Yeah, we know, it'll rain blood from the skies."

"See, you been there and learned what we know."

"Did your son draw over the cave pictures?" I asked. "The monsters looked different, as though a different artist rendered them."

"He's been doin' that fer years. See, that's how we can be so sure he's our preacher. No one else can see the beasts in the air, but some of us catch 'em outta the corner of our eyes, like. We can almost see 'em, enough to know they're there. But, my boy, ever since he was a little baby, would look around, watching the air, and he could see somethin' no one else was seein'. It weren't till he was a bit older, maybe seven or eight, when he started in on the drawin's. Then, he started makin the graven images."

"The what?"

The old man asked, "You didn't see 'em on yer way into the village? Well, I s'pose they're on the other side and you didn't get no clear view of 'em. You wanna have a look-see? 'Course, ya do! Ya come all this way for a look at the crazy people and the monsters they believe in, didn't ya?"

"We wanted to help your son," I said, although he was closer to the truth than I would have wanted to admit. "We needed more information to help cure him of his delusions."

"Well, how 'bout we go take us a good gander at those delusions," he said, standing with a loud snapping of bones. He moaned, rubbed his back, and said, "I'm gettin' old. Real old, so's I can feel it. Ain't gonna be long till the Old One comes, and I'll welcome him. I'll welcome the darkness and the end he'll bring to all these aches and pains of mine. Come on. This way."

He led us from the hut, pushing aside a piece of plywood that serviced as a door. I looked back at the woman on the bed, flapping her feeble arms in the air, and I saw a movement from under the bed. As I closed the door behind me, the baby crawled out from beneath the mattress, and I only saw it for a moment. Its face was a snarling mass of hair and teeth, and its hands were shaped into claws. Plate-like scales covered its body, and red skin gleamed between the cracks. I lowered the plywood of the improvised door, trying to control my revulsion.

We followed Pa McCoy through the huts, listening to the whispers coming from between them. The wind had picked up, and Deena's hair flapped around her face. The air smelled as though a storm was brewing, a heavy electrical one, and lightning crackled from the sky, God's fingers trying to touch the Earth He'd created, attempting to erase His mistakes. The thunder rumbled a bit, low as a dog bristling at some new person it didn't trust.

Deena said, "It's dark, Bob."

"I can see that, sweetheart. Hard not to notice it."

"I wanted to be back home by dark."

"Yeah, well, things happen. You wouldn't miss all this, would you?" I asked. "Try to think about the papers I'll write. The book deals. The film rights. It'll make my reputation. We could be set for life."

"If we make it back to civilization," she whispered. "I can't believe these people live just a few miles from the city, so isolated from everything."

"It's the way we want it," Pa said. "Don't wanna be no part of no city. People such as yerselves, you think they know it all, but you don't know nothin' about the Old One and what he wants. You don't know nothin' about raising yourselves a preacher. I've heard priests rail against the breeding, calling it incest and evil and a sin. Ain't no sin when it pleases a god. And we all wants ta please our gods, don't we?"

"Do you ever go into town?" I asked as we headed for the back of the encampment.

"Sometimes, but don't like it none. Ain't got much use for the places nor the people, and they don't give no rat's ass for us. We keeps to ourselves, hide when need be. It's important ta stay where your damn laws ain't got no effect. Still, there's things we need sometimes, things we ain't able to make. City does have its purposes...for now at least."

The shacks seemed more pitiful as we walked towards the edges, as though Pa's home was the best constructed place in the village at the epicenter. The farther you got from his shack, the more dilapidated the other homes became, the less relevant and important the citizenry.

I wondered about the people within these hovels that lived without even a door or window, but little more than a sheet of tin on some two by fours tied together with vines. How badly were they deformed? How closely did they even resemble humans?

As we rounded the last pathetic cluster of huts, lightning illuminated the glen, and I saw what Pa McCoy'd been talking about - the graven images.

"Oh my God," Deena said. "Your son made these?"

"Yes, ma'am. Copied 'em from the things he's seen that the rest of us can only catch a glimpse of. These are the real monsters."

Tree limbs and sticks had been bundled together with vines and other found objects to construct three astonishing sculptures. The first was almost benign, with three legs emerging from a barrel-shaped body, ending in four spindled toes per foot. Two arms stretched out from the sides of the body, each ending in three claws, the tips of which had been sharpened to knife-sharp points. The head atop the barrel was foxy, with pointed ears and a triangular face that ended in what looked like a pointed beak.

The second sculpture was perched atop a thick pole driven into the ground. It displayed a monster with a bat-like face, complete with fangs made from some thorn bushes, four long wings that sprouted from its back, similar to those of a dragonfly. Only, these wings were heavy, again, almost identical to those of a bat. The thing's body was serpentine, curling down around the perch it clutched with hawkish talons sprouting from its long tail.

These two sculptures represented fanciful beasties, almost comical in their melding of bits and pieces from known animal species of this world. The last work of art was something else altogether - something hideous, simplistic, and horrifying. I felt Deena draw nearer to me.

It was displayed upon three poles that held its writhing body in the air, emulating a squirming, swimming motion. In form, it looked like a gigantic lamprey eel, only its entire head consisted of nothing more than a few bumps surrounded by a gaping maw. Within the open mouth, Gary McCoy had arranged rows and rows of large thorns - a shark-like succession of teeth. There were no eyes, ears, or any other sensory organs. The manner in which he'd tied the sticks together, emulating the twisting, serpentine motion, was uncanny, chilling. He was a true artist, even if nobody had ever seen his work except for the fifty or so feeble-minded zealots inhabiting his village.

"This here's what he sees," Pa said with that same bit of smugness trailing back into his voice. I was once again reminded of Jerry Falwell and other self-righteous evangelicals. "They're all 'round us all the time. Watchin' and waitin'. Every once in a while, one of 'em breaks through for a second, and someone spots it or gets bitten."

"Bitten?" I said. "People have been wounded by these delusions?"

"You call 'em what you wanna. But a few suffered from bites. Not many."

"Are there any here? Any we can see?"

"Oh yes," he said, and he unbuttoned the front of his dirt-encrusted flannel shirt. "I believe I can show ya a lil' somethin'."

Pulling the material away from his flesh, he exposed a terrible scar on his shoulder and collarbone. It looked as though four or five rings of teeth had punctured the skin, clamped down upon the shoulder. The scar was old, and probably not well tended to, so the wounds shone in the beam of my flashlight, raised and angry.

"Was one of them eel things," he said. "I saw it for just a second, then it latched onto me. Hurt like holy hell, but it was gone when I reached for it to try and pull it off of me. But it left its bloody rings on me. They healed up, but they stung a lot for weeks. Must be some kinda poison in its spit makes it burn like that."

I wondered how the old man had done that to himself, for the wound had to have been self-inflicted. With a knife, perhaps? Or the thorns Gary'd utilized for teeth in the sculpture? Puncturing himself hundreds of times in a row in special, circular designs?

Or had he really been bitten by some eel monster? Could all this bullshit really be true?

I shook the thought away as Pa McCoy buttoned his shirt back up. I couldn't go down that path, couldn't follow that kind of logic. That's the kind of thinking that starts witch hunts and executions at the stake. There wasn't anything supernatural going on in the woods twenty miles from civilization. There was a logical explanation for it all. As a scientist and doctor, I needed to discover that rational explanation.

Gary McCoy had been raised in a world where people had assembled their religious belief system upon a group of drawings found in a cave. They could have possibly even drawn them themselves, based upon phantasms wrought from damaged minds. The whole degradation of Gary's mind would've been aided by his father, no finalist for stable person of the year himself. He'd told his son repeatedly that he was their preacher, their savior, their gateway, and the boy had finally begun to believe it himself. He saw the monsters his Pa described, and he used his considerable artistic abilities to bring them to life, albeit through sticks-and-stone effigies. Now, he'd finally had enough, and he'd sought help by running to the outside world, a world he didn't understand, that he was afraid of. He'd wanted to warn everybody, perhaps save some of the damned from the bogeyman implanted in his young head by a village full of inbred rednecks. It all made sense. Nothing supernatural about it.

But, in these darkened woods, with a storm on the horizon, it was easy to see how Gary had swallowed the whole fairy tale.

"You see these things," Pa McCoy said, motioning towards the statues. "My boy sees 'em. He's the first to actually get a good look at the monsters. They follow him everywhere, so they's probably all over your nice hospital. I wouldn't be too surprised if they was breaking through already. When they do, it's gonna start the comin' of the Old One, and it ain't gonna be pretty if'n he ain't here in his village where he belongs."

"He has to be here for the Old One to come through the curtains?" I asked.

"I dunno'," the old man said with a predatory grin. "But that's how it looks in the picture in the cave. Probably needs to be near all of us, so we'd all really appreciate it if you was to bring him back to his folks."

"He's been admitted to the mental hospital," I said. "It's not so easy to just let him go. Besides, I think I can help him, and if it takes holding him against his and your combined wills, then that's what I'm going to do."

"You're so brave," Pa said. "So fuckin' brave and so fuckin' stupid. He needs to be here."

"That's probably the last thing that boy needs."

"Oh, he'll be here tomorrow night. When the Old One wants to come through, when the different worlds are separated by somethin' so thin as paper, the beasts will claw their way into our world. Ain't nothin' gonna stop 'em. Not me, not you, not some fancy-ass hospital."

"Is that a threat?" I asked. I tried to sound brave, but the attempt was feeble at best. At least my voice didn't crack.

"Maybe," the old man said, looking at me. "You bring the preacher back here afore tomorrow night when the sun sets. He needs ta be here."

"And if I don't do it?"

He rubbed his shoulder where the scar was located under his pauper's shirt.

"Then I reckon we'll just have ta come and get him ourselves."

I took him in, the grubby clothes, the grimy, sallow skin, the weak eyes and weaker expression. He blinked, and his eyes seemed to glow with some elegant expression - longing, jealousy, or maybe assured hillbilly confidence. I couldn't decide which I saw, but he looked terribly calm considering the end of the world was happening tomorrow and his son was in my custody in a state run mental institution.

He rubbed his chin, and I heard his whiskers bristling against the calluses on his big hands. He squinted, and I backed up a step, defensive.

"What the hell do you mean by that?" I asked.

"I mean, Mr. Fancy Pants, I aim ta have my boy here with me when the Old One parts the curtains and comes through. If you ain't gonna let him go, I 'spect I'll have to go and get him."

"They aren't going to let you just up and take him," I explained, as though to a child.

He didn't look anything like a child when he answered, "I done told you, I'll have ta go and get him myself. And with some help. You think the Old One's gonna get this far and not finish enterin' our world? You think he'd let a little thing such as a hospital or guards or even you stand in his way? He's a god, you got ta understand. He's a god, and ain't nothin' comin' between him and my boy tomorrow night."

"That's a threat?"

"That's whatever you wanna make of it. Anyways, you'd best be skiddadlin' home. I think your little hospital," he practically spat the word, "is about to have some unwelcome guests."

Chapter 9

I grabbed Deena by the hand and started back through pathways of the village. Behind us, Pa McCoy started to laugh, deep from within his chest, an audible lava overflowing from the open crater of his mouth. It had all the bite of molten rock, too, bilious and frenzied. If I hadn't sensed it before (and I certainly had), I knew at that moment the man was hopelessly, incurably mad.

Glancing behind us, I saw the unaffected statues in the small clearing. The three legged fox thing, the bat monster, and the horrible, slithering eel were briefly illuminated by a blast of lightning that lit up the scene like the Universal Studios backlot, the effigies exposing twigs and limbs tied together to resemble muscle in the chiaroscuro luminosity. I thought I saw the statues' eyes glowing red in the electricity, and then the whole area erupted in what looked like fireworks. Fingers of lightning struck the earth all around the horrible landmarks, always hitting the ground, never touching the wooden monsters or the crazy old man who stood between them, raising his hands to the heavens as if welcoming the assault of the storm. He began jabbering, some monotonous chanting I couldn't hear over the rising wind and the inevitable crack of thunder a half second later.

He was looking directly at me and Deena, his gaze focused. He lowered his hands and pointed towards us. I almost expected lightning bolts to zap from his fingertips - Zeus atop Mount Olympus playing with the poor mortals who would never understand his godly ways.

"Come on," Deena begged, pulling on my arm.

I began moving with her, dodging through the huts as the inhabitants peeked timidly from the interiors. Their narrowly set, mean eyes glaring at me, their malformed hands reaching out towards me - too many fingers, no opposable thumbs, fingers melded together with taut, pallid skin. They emerged from their homes, flopping into the mud and paddling on flipper limbs.

And they started moving towards Pa McCoy. They crept towards him slowly, reverently.

"Goddamnit, come on, Bob!" Deena shouted.

The rain broke from a cooling mist to a throbbing downpour, the water bouncing off the earth, instantly soaking every exposed bit of us. It partially obscured Pa in its torrents, turning him into a shadow of himself, a silhouette with arms raised and fingers pointed at us.

"Follow them," I heard him bellow to his acolytes, his voice loud and distinct. "Follow them and bring the Preacher back home."

They turned towards us, more than thirty malformed faces, jaws too wide with too many teeth crammed into them, tongues lolling, empty, unstable visages. As Pa McCoy began laughing again, they lurched towards us.

"Bob!"

Deena slapped me out of my thoughts, and I held her hand and started running through the muddy, narrow paths that acted as streets in the village. People continued to emerge from the shacks, reaching for us, groping at the air, almost corralling us where they wanted us to go. Eventually, we found the way back into the woods towards the cliffs and the cave where Gary McCoy had expressed himself so artistically, covering primitive representations with his own delusions of monstrous beasts that inhabited his dark, soiled mind.

I could hear the slapping of bare feet in the mud puddles behind us. Turning briefly, I saw the denizen of the hidden town fumbling their way in pursuit. Most of them were impeded by some imperfection or other, but some of them skittered along like rats, coming upon us fast.

Deena shrieked, and I pulled her with me, running as swiftly as I ever had in my high school football days. I hadn't known I could still travel so quickly, and I was shocked that Deena was keeping up so well. Adrenaline pumped through my body; I could hear my heartbeat in my ears, pounding louder and louder. I'm certain Deena felt this same rush, as well.

Branches got in the way, but I let them whip against me as I hurried along the narrowing path. Soon, I pushed Deena in front of myself, as we could no longer run side by side. I wanted to place myself between her back and the horrors that chased us. She did me proud, taking off with a burst of speed that would've put Steve Prefontaine to shame.

We kicked up dirty water and slick mud, and it caked our legs up to our knees. I felt a switch hit me across the face, and I knew it had drawn a welt. I could feel it swelling as I ran.

Every now and then I glanced over my shoulder to see if any of the villagers were following us. Every time, I saw a part of one of them, a leg or a head or a withered section of an arm, retreat behind a shrub. Once, I thought I witnessed one of them climbing a tree, pulling its legless body up the trunk, arm over simian arm. They were in the forest, surrounding us. They knew this land better than anybody, definitely knew it better than we did. They roamed the woods regularly. Now and again, one of them would hoot in good humor, caught up in the thrill of the chase.

The rain pounded down on us, smarting whenever it hit bare skin. The temperature was dipping down into the forties, and the wind was picking up even more. It rattled the branches above us, brittle bones knocking on each other.

When we reached the little cliff, we saw the old, blind guy waiting for us at the mouth of the cave. His white eyes, suffused with cataracts, gazed out upon the drama unfolding before his vacant stare. It was almost as if he could see what was happening.

"You think we should shelter in the cave for a while?" Deena asked as we started up the wooden steps to the apex of the cliff. "At least it's dry."

I shook my head and answered, "No, we need to get as far away from here as we can. It's just a little rain."

As if to repudiate my words, a bolt of lightning streaked down from the heavens, through the heavy raindrops, and split an ancient oak tree in half about a hundred feet behind us. Something screamed in the woods beyond the lightning strike, something animalistic, primeval. I could smell the electricity in the air, and I noticed Deena's long, brown locks were standing away from her head. The scent of burning wood filled my nostrils.

Giving a little 'eeep' sound, Deena began rushing up the side of the bluff, trying to get away from what could end up being a forest fire. I grappled my way up the stairs, which were slick with water and oozing mud. I held on to Deena's rain poncho with one hand and groped through roots and brush with the other, trying to maintain a precarious balance. If we fell, we probably wouldn't die - not with the creek running beneath us and the earth soft with moisture. But, we'd certainly break a leg or worse, and I didn't relish the thought of being incapacitated with fifty redneck, inbred religious fanatics running around through the forest. Especially since they seemed to have an agenda to meet, the advent of the Old One, and I was their biggest obstacle in bringing their god through the veil.

For a moment, during our chancy scale past the cavern, I thought of Gary McCoy back in St. Mike's Hospital. I thought of how he'd been raised by these freaks, how he'd been brainwashed into believing he was some sort of natural prophet. It was a wonder he wasn't raving and tearing at the walls, a miracle he'd had the clear conceit to come to town and warn people about his beliefs. Foolish as they were.

My foot slipped, and I almost went tumbling down the muddy side of the cliff. Deena grabbed hold of the hood of my yellow rain slicker, allowing me just enough time to regain my footing, although my heart was threatening to beat its way through my ribcage.

"You all right?" she asked before continuing her climb.

"Yeah. Fine."

My mind turned immediately back to the mission at hand, escaping from the villagers.

We'd reached the summit, although now our hands were cut and bleeding from grasping hold of shrubs, some rife with thorns. The mud on them probably saved us from getting scratched any worse than we were. We looked down the side of the cliff to witness the malformed people fashioning a semi-circle around the base of the bluffs. They looked up at us, eyes mismatching, one higher than the other, too close together. The rain was really hard now, and it must have been pummeling their faces. They gathered silently, and then Pa McCoy walked through them - Moses parting the red sea - to take his place at the front of the group of twenty or so inbreeds. When he raised his countenance to look at us, I could see the gleam of his evil smile from the apex where I stood.

"Come on, Bob," Deena said, tugging at my arm.

"What are they doing?"

"Who gives a shit? They're nuts. We've got a pretty good lead now, let's take advantage of it."

She was right, and I followed her. We struggled along the trail, Deena in the lead with me pulling up the rear. We'd slowed since our sprint below the cave, but we were still walking at a brisk pace.

The air was getting cooler, and I could see my breath emerging as little puffs of cloud from my mouth. I wished I had brought a heavier coat. The night was getting downright frigid, and I thought it would probably frost for the first time tonight. Autumn was quickly evolving into winter.

As we hurried through the woods, I would occasionally hear a twig snap, and I spun around, looking for one of the villagers to be on our heels. I didn't see anyone, but that didn't prevent me from looking every time I heard a sound. It didn't stop my heart from leaping into my throat whenever the wind rustled a patch of leaves.

Sometimes, I swear, I could see someone or something moving just out of the corner of my eye. There was never anything actually there when I looked, but it happened several times. I was reminded of what Pa McCoy had said about the monsters, how he could sometimes see them for half a second, then they were gone. Shivering, I continued until we emerged from the forest to the highway where our car was parked.

And where Pa McCoy and his minions were waiting for us.

They surrounded the car, some of them sitting on the hood in awkward positions. McCoy leaned against the driver's door, his arms crossed nonchalantly in front of himself. None of them were even breathing heavily.

"How...?" I gasped. "How did you...?"

"I lived in these here woods my whole life, Doctor," he said, and I could almost taste the bile in his throat when he spoke the word 'doctor.' "I know ever'thing about them. Where to hunt, where to get the best berries, all the goddamn short cuts."

"You let us past," I said, hoping I sounded more authoritative than I felt. I pushed Deena behind me, just in case.

Pa McCoy laughed. The others around him chittered, too, but the laughter seemed to belong to wild animals rather than humans.

"I ain't stoppin' you," he said. With a sweeping gesture, he moved aside and brushed his arm backwards in an inviting way. "Please, get in your automobile. Go back to yer pretty hospital. And return my son ta me. Tonight."

"I don't think I can-"

"Did I ask for excuses? I ain't askin' for nothing. I am tellin' you the preacher needs to be brung back tonight. If not, well, I reckon I'll be seein' you again."

With that, he cricked his neck, made a 'let's roll' circular gesture in the air with his finger, and the denizen of the village spilled off the car and started moving awkwardly back into the forest on their malformed limbs. He threw us a final look, and then he followed them wordlessly into the tree line. In a few moments, there was no sound at all, except for the storm raging around us.

We ran to the car, hopped in, locked the doors, and made a U-turn. Somehow, speeding on the wet roads didn't impress me as such a dangerous crime, so I buckled in, kept my hands at two and ten-o-clock, and I did eighty miles per hour all the way back to the city.

Chapter 10

"**R**emind me never to accompany you anywhere ever again," Deena said as she closed the door of our apartment behind her. "We could have been killed. Several times."

"I know," I said, heading for the bathroom. I handed her a towel and began drying my own hair. "I'm so sorry, but, can you believe it? It's all real - the village, the in-breeding, the cave drawings inspiring a whole religion. What are the odds that someone like this Gary McCoy will ever land in my lap again?"

"I'd pray for never."

Moving into the bathroom, she began to strip off her stained, soaked clothes. She looked at the hamper for a moment then she dropped them into the garbage can beside the sink.

"I don't see me ever wearing these jeans again," she explained. I heard her open the shower door and turn on the water. "I'm going to take the longest, hottest shower of my life," she said. "Maybe it'll get the stink of that place off of me."

I removed my clothes, feeling the uncomfortable stick as they tried to remain glued to my body. In my boxers, I put my own jeans and sweat shirt in a plastic garbage bag. I loved those jeans, and they deserved a second chance. I'd wash them in the morning. Meanwhile, Deena stepped into the shower.

"Oh my God, that feels so good."

I stuck my head into the bathroom. Steam was pouring out of it, and the mirrors were already fogged up to an extent I couldn't see my reflection. I looked down at my hands, at the cuts that criss-crossed the palms and the gouges on my arms.

"I think I'm going to need some iodine," I said.

"I just need to stay in here for hours and hours," Deena moaned from the shower stall. "Everything else doesn't matter."

I could see her form through the frosted glass, and I admired her, leaning against the sink. She had a beautiful body, trim, but rounded at the hips and breasts. Nothing was too big or too small for my tastes, and she kept lean by jogging four times a week. Her legs were long and sculpted, probably her best physical feature. I felt myself getting aroused at her silhouette, and I opened the door of the shower, intending to step inside for a little 'I'll wash you if you'll wash me' action.

She held her hand in front of her and stopped me. "Don't you dare come in here now that I've gotten clean. You're covered in mud from head to foot. You just wait until I'm done."

"But, honey, I thought we could..."

"Oh, I know what's on your mind, but I'm not about to get filthy again just to have to take another shower. You let me finish, then you take a shower, then I'll meet you in our nice clean bed on its nice clean sheets, and we'll have some nice dirty sex."

And she slammed the glass door, leaving me cooling my heels for the next ten minutes while she washed her hair. Twice.

When I finally got my turn under the scalding stream of water, my muscles relaxed. The steam and the heat soothed my aching shoulders and back. I heard Deena moving around in the bedroom, making the little noises that occur in any shared household - drawers opening and shutting, footfalls. They were as comforting as the persistent barrage from the massaging showerhead.

In my loosened state, I felt myself craving a whiskey and Coke. The taste of alcohol after so long would scald my tongue, but the feeling of it warming me from the inside of my throat and stomach would put me in an even better state of mind. I could almost feel the way the glow would emanate from within me, coursing through my muscles, flushing my skin.

It was a craving that never left me for very long, and when it returned, as it did in the shower, it came home with a vengeance. The veteran alcoholics I remembered from my A.A. meetings had mentioned the sensation, the desire - how it would strike without warning and you'd abruptly need a drink more than oxygen. This was how I felt that night.

I needed to feel that security that only Knob Creek could provide. I required it just to get the energy to turn off the shower and dry myself. It was no longer something I craved. It was a necessity to get me through the next hour before sleep overtook me.

But, I'd cleared the temptation from my home, tossed out all the bottles, even if they were full back when I'd started dating Deena. There was nothing within reach. I wouldn't be imbibing any time soon without a trip to the store. Or to a hidey hole at work.

And I was far too tired for such an excursion. Getting chased around the woods by a crazy man and his even more whacked-out followers will do that to a body.

Nothing in the house.

I knew I could try to drive to a store, make a quick purchase.

Too exhausted. And Deena was in the bedroom right now...

Deena...

The thought of her brought me to my senses, nearly expunging my urge to drink. Nearly...

She was in the next room, probably naked under a sheet, waiting for me. She would brace me for the long night, and I found myself turning off the hot water tap and sticking my head under a stream of coolness. It woke me up a bit, enough to find my way out of the shower.

I dried off, wrapped a towel around my waist, and marched into the bedroom. Deena had lit some candles while I was in the shower, and she lay back on the bed wearing nothing but a smile and her earrings, no sheet covering her body. Dropping my towel to the floor, I moved towards her then leapt across the room onto the bed. Giggling, we made love, slowly, passionately, carefully avoiding the cuts and scrapes that covered our bodies alongside the darkening bruises.

When we were finished and we lay gasping next to each other, admiring the ceiling, she exhaled long and slow.

"Wow. Near death experiences sure bring out the animal in you."

"It was all that talk of breeding. Got me hot to trot. Hey, you want to carve those jack-o-lanterns now?" Sex nearly always brought me to a more awakened state.

"I'm too tired," she said. "Anyway, tomorrow's Halloween. We can do it then."

"All right," I said. "Hey, you think Halloween has some significance to the villagers? That's when they say the Old One's coming back - tomorrow night. It must mean something. I'll have to ask Pa about it."

"Seriously, Bob. I don't want you going back into those woods again. It was actually dangerous. We could've been killed by the villagers or that crazy, old man. Looking back on it now, I'm surprised we weren't."

"I don't think they wanted us murdered," I said. "I'm supposed to let the preacher out of our dreaded, psychological clutches, and how could I do that if I'm dead and rotting in a cave someplace?"

She shivered and drew the blanket over her naked body. Putting an arm around my middle, she said, "How many people do you suppose were killed in that place? It looked like hundreds of skeletons. Maybe thousands."

"Over the years, who knows? But, I do intend to ask Gary McCoy about it tomorrow morning."

"So, you aren't letting him go back to the village?"

"Are you kidding?" I asked, letting her spoon against me. It felt nice, comfortable, how you'd imagine an older couple would feel after having been together for fifty years.

"What if his father retaliates, somehow?" she asked. "What if he shows up at St. Mike's demanding his kid be turned over to him?"

"Gary's at least twenty years old. His father has no hold over him any longer. It's not as though he's being claimed on a tax form somewhere."

"All those people, living like that out in the woods," she said, and I recognized her sleepy voice. She'd be snoring lightly in a few more moments.

"Yeah," I said, holding her hand.

"It's really hard to believe they're so close to the modern world, yet still so primitive. How'd they live so long..." Her speech was interrupted by a yawn. "...without anybody knowing they're out there?"

"I guess people aren't looking for them," I said. "It's easy to stay hidden if you're so superfluous to civilization. I guess, if they don't mess around with us, we'll just leave them alone. They aren't hurting anybody."

"Says you."

"Yeah, well, they aren't hurting anyone important. Nobody from the cities."

She was breathing hard against my neck, and I could tell she was asleep. I was glad she could retreat to slumber, and I hoped her dreams were pleasant. I wasn't having any such luck.

My mind kept busy, mulling over everything that had happened that day - the admittance of Gary McCoy, the interview, the hike, the cavern, the blind man, Pa McCoy, the statues of the monsters and the cave drawings. So much to process in a single day.

Somewhere, in the back of my mind, that little alcoholic demon kept needling me, telling me how much a drink would help me to sleep. I tried my best to ignore it, but the bastard kept niggling at me.

Eventually, lulled by Deena's soft snoring in my ear, I submitted to the sandman. Falling asleep, I thought about Gary, locked in his cell, alone, probably terrified, but safer than being around the people in the village. Had I finally saved someone? Could I do anything else for him? Or was merely getting him away from the village and their belief system enough?

After a while, Deena mumbled in her sleep and turned to the other side, facing the window. I rolled over and spooned against her back. Opening my eyes, I saw the storm was still raging outside the second floor of the apartment. Rain pelted the windows, sounding like hail.

And a dark form was pressed against the glass, peering into the room, a black, human shape outlined by a burst of lightning.

I leapt back, instantly awake. "Deena, wake up, someone's at the..."

Second floor window? There's no ledge...nowhere to stand...

Lightning once again illuminated the scene, and I could see Pa McCoy's leering face pressed against the glass. His eyes glowed red, and his saliva smeared the window where his tongue darted in and out of his mouth.

"Tonight," he hissed.

"Deena, wake the fuck up!"

She rolled over, exposing mismatched eyes, set far too close together. Her hairline was receded, and her face looked pinched at the nose. Grabbing me with two appendages that mimicked flippers, I saw her fingers had all fused together, and her arms weren't jointed correctly. I struggled to get out of her grip, but she shoved her face against mine, kissing me, forcing her tongue down my throat. I could feel it writhing in my mouth, and it didn't feel right. Probing it with my own tongue, I discovered it was forked, split in two parts at the end.

"I told ya, tonight..." Pa McCoy said.

And I fell from the bed to the floor, screaming, entangled in the sheets. Awakening, I looked around and saw Deena watching me with a mixture of concern and amusement dueling on her face.

"Bed hog," she said. "Jesus, what were you dreaming about?"

As I sat on the edge of the mattress, I saw my hands shaking violently. I ran them through my hair as I checked out Deena's arms. They looked normal, beautiful, long, and lithe as usual, and I lay back on the bed.

The telephone's ringing startled both of us. I was the first to reach it, and I mumbled, "Yeah, hello?"

"Doctor Gaskell? It's Stan, the guard at St. Mike's?"

I remembered him, vaguely - big guy, red hair, beard, a real lumberjack character.

"Yeah, Stan, what is it?"

"It's that new patient of yours," he said. "I know you only have him another day or so, but I think you'd better get in here."

"What time is it?"

"Four a.m.. Little after, maybe."

"What's the problem again?" I asked, trying to shake the sleep and, by proxy, that horrible dream from my head.

"He's bouncing around the room like a rubber ball's the problem," Stan explained. "He's screaming loud as hell in there, and...well, something else. I don't know if you'll believe me or not."

I was alert, wide awake now.

"What?"

"Well, something took a bite out of Rollo's arm. A big chunk's just gone. He says your boy McCoy did it, but I don't see any blood on the kid's face, and with a bite like that, there would be blood all over him."

I heard Rollo bitching up a black cloud in the background. "I tell you there wasn't anyone else in the goddamn cage with me. Had to be the little bastard. Had to be him."

"Anyways," Stan continued, "I really think you should come in."

"I'll be there in half an hour," I said, hopping out of bed and hanging up on the guard.

"What is it?" Deena asked, wiping her eyes.

"The Preacher seems to be caught up in the spirit," I said. "Really having some sort of anxiety attack or something. I'm going to check it out."

"You mind terribly if I stay here in bed? It feels so good."

"You rest up," I said, dressing. "I wouldn't have it any other way."

"Thank you so much," she murmured, laying back down and cuddling a pillow from my side of the bed. "I'm all worn out."

I kissed her on the forehead and raced to the car, wondering what was happening to McCoy and if it had anything to do with his father's demands.

And just who or *what* had bitten Rollo?

PART TWO
October 31st

"Deep into that darkness peering, long I stood there, wondering, fearing, doubting, dreaming dreams no mortal ever dared to dream before."

Edgar Allan Poe

Chapter 11

My mind was racing faster than my car when I pulled into St. Mike's parking area. I had to flash my badge at the guard at the gate surrounding the place, even though he'd seen me dozens of times. I suppose it was a good thing, in that nobody had ever escaped. Almost every security measure was still being executed, even though only a few of the worst of the worst patients remained in the cells.

A word about the security at the hospital is probably overdue here. Saint Michael's is surrounded by a fifteen foot fence, curved inwards, with loops of razor wire curled around the top. Once upon a time, there'd been whispers about electrifying the fence, but when the money didn't appear, it was forgotten. A guard patrolled the exterior grounds at all times, and another guard was stationed at a post at the only gateway in and out of the place. The grounds were illuminated with plenty of bright lights, including two searchlights waiting for use at the uppermost east and north corners of the building. Thick woods surrounded the whole area, almost impenetrable, overgrown with thickets and thorn bushes and briars.

To get into the building, you had to be buzzed in by the doorman then buzzed into the lobby by the head nurse on duty, where we'd spoken to Vicki Hellings earlier that afternoon (it seemed so long ago). She would then check credentials and unlock the door inside, which was secured with three locks, the kind that utilized old-fashioned keys instead of electrical devices, a caution against power outages happening at just the wrong time. The halls were patrolled by two to four guards at all times, and the high security area, where I'd visited Gary McCoy, was separated from the rest of the hospital by two more steel doors with multiple locks.

It was a very safe environment, really. Our escape rate was a perfect zero.

Now, only the gatekeeper and the nurse at the front desk remained along with two patrol guards. It still offered plenty of collateral against escape attempts.

"Bit of a brouhaha in there tonight, Doctor," the guard at the gates said with a jaunty little salute. I wished he wouldn't do that.

"So I heard," I answered before driving into the nearly empty parking lot. I hurried up the front steps and was buzzed into the building by the night nurse, a tired looking woman whose hair was mussed and make-up smeared. There were a few drops of crimson on her uniform.

Looking at me with a haggard, lined face, she rasped, "They took him to the operating room."

"Who? McCoy?" I asked, momentarily confused.

"No, that fat guard. Whatshisname?"

I turned towards the left. The operating room, as she put it, is only there for emergencies, so it's not usually very well stocked at the best of times. The day before the whole hospital is shut down, they would probably be lucky to find a Band-Aid and antiseptic.

I knew I should be checking on my patient, especially if he's freaking out in the way Stan described to me on the phone. But, something made me go left to look at Rollo's wound. Maybe that little piece of me left over from childhood that still believed in monsters.

I burst into the room. Rollo sat on the operating table with his shirt off, tossed across a chair in the corner. He had the body of a full-back gone to seed, bulging muscles covered with a layer of fat. Dr. Carmody was tending to it, and I was surprised by his presence at this late / early hour, although I shouldn't have been. He was one of only four doctors left on staff to care for the few remaining patients, and he *was* the head psychiatrist on staff. He'd probably been called during the emergency right before I was.

Rollo grunted while Carmody poured antiseptic on the terrible-looking wound. "Goddamnit, man! That fucking hurts."

"Bite down and bear it. You're a big boy."

The clear liquid bubbled and fizzed as it hit the guard's arm, and Rollo gritted his teeth against the sting. Moving closer, I got my first good look at the bite, and I was surprised Rollo was holding it together as well as he was.

Five concentric rings of cuts and slices, each about a half-inch wide, oozed blood and clear pus. The whole bite measured approximately a foot across and three quarters of a foot wide, and in the center, a good two inches of flesh had been scooped out from the guard's bicep, as though something had hacked away the fatty part of his arm.

"Holy shit, did McCoy do this?" I asked as Dr. Carmody started stitching up the wound.

"Does this look like that little bastard bit me? Been thinking about it, and the bite doesn't match up. The kid's mouth ain't even that wide. It couldn't have been McCoy."

"Was there anyone else in the room with you?" Carmody asked.

"Nope, just that little fucker. He was running around and screeching - sounded as if he was speaking in tongues in one of those snake handling churches. You know the kind...ow, damn it, Doc!"

"I'm just suturing it closed. You'll still need to go to a hospital, but this will stop the bleeding."

"Aw man, I don't wanna go to a hospital. My insurance has a two hundred dollar deductible, and I don't have that kind of cash lying around. You fix it, Doc. I trust you."

"Could you make out *any* of the words McCoy was shouting while he was excited?" I asked, distracting him while Carmody did his work. My boss looked over at me, grateful for my intrusion.

"He was just shouting. I wasn't paying a lot of attention. Something about a village and the curtains opening or something. Any of that make sense to you?"

"Yeah, it does. Think hard, Rollo. Try to remember anything that boy said."

"All I remember is talk about curtains opening and something about a village. About someone going to the village. That really seemed to drive him batshit."

"The fact that someone went to his village?"

"Yeah. He seemed really pissed about it. I go into the room to try and calm him down. You know, Doc, to give him a shot, get him to sleep the next twenty four hours so's I can be rid of him. Soon as that door shut behind me, I see that boy across the room. He's all hunkered down in the corner on the floor, hiding his eyes like a little baby. I start over to him, hypodermic in my hand, and damned if something to my left took a hunk outta my arm. Just bit me. I could hear the crunch, and the blood started pouring out, so I got the hell outta there quick as snot."

"And McCoy was all the way across the room, in the corner?"

"Yep, so you see it couldn't have been him that bit me. I thought an animal was loose or something, but I couldn't see anything else in the room. Just that kid, and he really starts in to wailing after I've been bitten. He's running around the place, flapping his arms, and I swear he's gonna take off flying like a bird. He's screaming about that village. He says someone went there. Someone shouldn't have gone to that village, but someone did. Hey, see I remembered after all."

"Did you ever get him calmed down?"

"Nope," Rollo said. "Last I seen him, they were taking me away to get me fixed up in here. He was still running around that room, clawing at the walls. Still screaming at the top of his lungs. Crazy fucker."

"There," Carmody said, snipping off the catgut. "All stitched up. Twenty-two stitches. Whatever nipped you got you pretty good, Rollo."

"Well, it hurts a lot."

"And it will for a while. How about I prescribe you some pain-killers, and you take tomorrow off."

"That's the last day we're here," he said, and he almost looked morose about it. "I been a guard here for almost twenty years, Doc. I want to see it through. Hate to leave you in the lurch like that."

"Well, then, if you feel up to it, go home and rest until tomorrow night. We'll need you then, I hate to admit. The more hands the better on the first to transport those last twenty - oh, twenty one now - people. It's certainly not going to be a pleasant job."

Carmody tore off a page from his prescription pad and scribbled on it in his achingly bad handwriting. Rollo took the paper and left quietly. At the door, he turned and said, "You guys go in that room, you be careful. Something's in there. I don't know what, but *something* took a chunk outta me."

Carmody began cleaning up, and I helped, wiping up the spilled blood. There was more of it than I was actually comfortable with, and I wondered briefly if Rollo should drive home.

"You know what's going on here, Bob?" he asked.

"No, Steven, although I'm piecing it together bit by bit."

"An unfortunate choice of words," he said, and his mustache twitched in mirth. "I suppose you'd want me to accompany you to visit your patient?"

"I'd be delighted," I said. "This is a complicated case, Steven. More so than I first realized."

"I'm beginning to suspect that. Well, it's almost five a.m. I have a lot to do today, so I'll go with you. Then, I'll start on finishing up the move."

"Let me tell you about what happened tonight," I said as we walked from the office room into the hallway.

As we made our way to Siberia, I explained the occurrences of the day to him, leaving out nothing except some of my inner thoughts. I didn't want to reveal that my main reason for aiding this kid was sheer, unadulterated ambition run rampant. I also down-played the danger we experienced, making the villagers seem more comical in their zealotry than frightening, although I sensed he picked up on the fact I was scared shitless. He was a very observant man, after all.

"It appears as though you placed yourself and Dr. Bierce in danger," he said when we approached the outer locked door to the high security area. "Probably not a good idea when you intend to marry her."

"I know, and I hate that I did that, but I didn't realize-"

"We're dealing with very sick people, Bob, and very sick people often do very sick things. Keep it in the hospital. Call the police on these - what did you call them - villagers. Let the authorities clear them out of the woods. That's not your responsibility. You need to be worrying about that boy in there, why he's so terrified. I admit, I respect your enthusiasm on this project, but chances are some other doctor will soon be dealing with McCoy, so keep a safe distance, okay?"

"Yeah, all right," I said, thinking how I was knowledgeable enough already to handle this case when it went to another city. I'd witnessed the source of the madness at its root - the village and its inhabitants. I'd, yes, risked my life to do so. If another doctor took this case from me, it was only going to happen after a bitter fight.

"Now, let's see what's got McCoy so riled up," he said.

The sentry in the high security wing approached and buzzed us into the ward.

Chapter 12

Stan had remained on duty at the guard's station, and he was the lucky bastard working the night shift who buzzed us in. Following protocol, even though it probably wasn't necessary at this late stage, we dutifully signed the visitor log, and Stan unlocked the last door that led to the hallway of cells. Even before he opened it, I heard the cries and murmuring, the rantings of the enduring cases incarcerated in our hospital. The loudest voice among them was recognizable as Gary McCoy's high tenor.

"...shouldn't have gone there. Told him, I told him, I told him not to go there. Now they know...know where I am, what I done. Oh Jesus, someone let me out. Let me out of here!"

He was screaming so loud he drowned out the others, and many of them were also banging on their padded walls or their doors, repeating his words back to him, a forlorn echo. I wouldn't have been surprised if there were several minor injuries caused by Gary's outburst. Many of these people didn't feel pain in the same way everyone else does, and it's easy to break the fragile bones of your hand when slamming it continuously against a solid door frame.

"This is worse than I'd thought," Carmody said. "We need to get him quiet, or we'll have a whole mess of trouble to clean up when we move these people. All these other poor bastards..."

I turned to Stan and asked, "Didn't you say you gave him Thorazine?"

He nodded. "Yeah. Regulation dose, but it hasn't calmed him down any. Actually, he seems a bit worse for it."

We traversed the long hallway, passing several cells that contained patients who looked panicked at the noise. I saw a few of them huddled in corners, terrified, not meeting my gaze through the glass windows that were lined with chicken wire. Others had their faces pressed against the windows, and even more of them pounded their heads against the doors until the bullet proof glass was streaked with blood.

This was not a good thing. These patients were supposed to be sedated, kept quiet. If agitated, as they were, their ability to harm themselves more than doubled.

Their gibbering swirled around me, a tornado of 'Told them not to go there's and 'Let me out's. In the midst of the cacophony, in the eye of the verbal storm, I knew somehow that I was to blame for McCoy's ravings and, by proxy, the rantings of the neighboring patients.

Finally, we arrived at his door, and I peered through the little window, praying he wasn't in as bad a shape as he sounded. No such luck.

He was rushing around the room, leaping at the walls, pounding against them. He'd managed to tear away part of the padding from the eastern wall, and the floor was lined in the fluff that padded the cell. Some of it was in his hair, sticking to the sweat created by his exertions. His face was a mask of rage. His long, grimy hair spilled behind him, exposing his two different colored eyes, and they were filled to the brim with the worst kind of madness, the kind that screams and flails out at the world with violence. This was not the calm, frightened man I'd seen just the previous day. This was an animal, unleashed and furious with everyone around him.

"Gary," I shouted through the glass. "Can you hear me?"

"Bastard! Told him not to go there. Now they know. They know!"

"We're going to have to open the door and go in," Carmody said, laying a hand on my shoulder. It was meant to be a comforting gesture, a motion to dispel thoughts of blame from my head, but it merely placed more responsibility on me, weighing me down further with its millstone significance. He continued, "We all know the guy needs to be subdued. Jacket's the best way."

Stan held the restraining jacket out, and Carmody, the weakest of the three of us, took it. Putting the key in the lock, he turned it then nodded to us.

"You guys ready?" he asked.

We gestured assent, and he pulled the door wide. We rushed in as one, trying to assert our dominance over the madman with the stuffing in his hair. Before he knew what was happening, we'd cornered McCoy by his bed. He was shaking his head, pointing at me with both his hands and shouting obscenities at me. In an expert, well-practiced move, Stan was behind him, wrapping his arms around Gary's midsection. I ran to his side, grabbing his arms and Carmody slipped the sleeves of the straight-jacket over them. Stan pulled at the restraints, and McCoy's arms were pulled backwards. A grimace of pain spread across his face, but soon Stan had the ties knotted behind McCoy's back, and Carmody and I each grasped one of his kicking feet. Stan held him by his shoulders, and we transported the skinny young man to his bed, where we used leather restraints on his arms and legs to arrest his movement.

"There," Stan said, breathing heavily. "Good and tight. He's not going anywhere now."

McCoy continued to spit and shout, aiming most of his invectives at me. "You bastard, you fucking bastard, you led them ta me, you know. Led 'em right to me, and now I'm gonna *have* to let him through. Gonna be forced to. And yer all gonna die." He started to laugh hysterically. "Now, yer all gonna die."

"Calm down, Gary," I said, and then I looked at Carmody. "You think we could take him down a little? Just another hundred cc's or so?"

"I'd say it's called for," he said. "I'll go get it. You figure out what he's jabbering about. Obviously something caused this episode."

While he left the room to prepare a hypodermic, I turned back to my patient. Gary's head was locked in the vise-like grip of a leather restraint, clasped around his forehead. It drew his skin back a little, making him appear even more wild-eyed than before his restriction on the bed. His skin was full of tiny pockmarks, as though he'd suffered smallpox as a child or severe acne. Even in the bright lighting of the room, his dermas looked sallow and unhealthy.

"Gary, will you listen to me?"

"Ain't listenin' to another word outta yer cursed mouth hole," he said, his lips pulled back in a grimace. "Yer a liar and a goddamned murderer. Don't ya know what ya done?"

"I *don't* know, Gary. That's why I'm asking you."

"Let me outta here, you fucker," he shouted, struggling against the restraints. "I can't be here no more. I need ta get outta here! Now!"

"You're safe here, Gary," I said, trying to calm him. "Nobody can hurt you here. If you knew what kind of security we have-"

"Fuck yer security all ta hell," he said, but his voice was quieting a bit. "Nothin' can keep 'em outta here now they know where I am."

"Who? The villagers?"

"Them too."

Dr. Carmody entered the room, holding the hypo in front of his eyes, checking the dosage. He clicked it a couple of times to get rid of the air bubbles, then he plunged it into McCoy's left arm.

"No," he protested. "Don't give me no more a' that shit. My mind goes all fuzzy. I can't defend myself."

But the result was nearly immediate, and his eyes glazed over a bit, then he seemed to relax all over. I knew I only had a limited amount of time to question him before he completely succumbed to the effect of the Thorazine.

"Gary, how'd you know I went to the village? Who told you?"

"Nobody told me nothin'," he answered, sluggishly. "I knew...knew it when I saw the first of the monsters through here. Went in and outta the walls like they weren't even there, slidin' all serpentine."

"You saw the creatures here? Which ones?"

"Saw the eels. You know which ones, Doc. You seen my pictures in the cave. You know what I'm talkin' about."

Carmody began to speak, but I silenced him with a movement of my hand. I needed this to be quick and succinct with no interruptions.

I continued, "What happened after you saw the monsters, Gary?"

"Well, one of 'em took a bite outta that fat-ass guard, didn't it? Big ole bite, too. I figgered if the monsters knew I was here, then so did Pa. You seen him, didn't ya? You seen my Pa and the village and the cave. You seen it all."

"Yes, Gary, I did. You're a lucky man to have escaped from that place."

"I was till you went there. Now they all know. They all know where I am."

"The villagers?"

He nodded. "And Pa...and the monsters. They move quick ...through the air, so they got here first. Pa ain't gonna stand for me runnin' away like I did. He'll be here afore too long, and he'll take me back...take me back there where I'll have ta do what he says. Whatever he says."

He was fading fast, his words starting to slur under the influence of the medication. I focused, trying to mine for information as he succumbed to the drug.

I said, "He can't get in here, Gary. Trust me. There's no way any of the people from the village can get through all that security."

"You don't know Pa. He'll get in somehow. He'll get in...and he'll take me back...and I'm gonna die and you're gonna die and everyone is gonna die when the Old One comes through me...when the curtains part and the Old One...finds us...gonna...die..."

The fight went out of him, and he started snoring lightly. I backed away from him and looked over at Carmody.

"I'll need you to tell me everything," he said. "And, I do mean *everything* about tonight."

"He's suffering from delusions."

"Was his father a delusion?"

"No," I said. "He was real enough."

"Was the cave a delusion? Was that bite taken out of Rollo's arm a delusion? I don't think so."

"I don't either, but it *can't* be some monster hovering in the air around McCoy. It's not possible."

Carmody motioned me into the hallway, and Stan asked, "It okay to lock him in for the night?"

"Not much night left," I grumbled, looking at my watch. It was almost morning.

"You know what I meant," he said.

"Yeah, go ahead," Carmody said, ushering me back down the long hallway. "Dr. Gaskell and I have to have a few words alone, if you don't mind."

I gulped. Was Carmody seeing what I had seen in this boy? Book deals? A name that rose above the profession? He'd been a psychiatrist for over twenty years, head of St. Mike's for more than ten, but outside of local circles, nobody recognized his name.

Was he going to try to steal my patient? After all I'd gone through the previous day, I sincerely hoped he wasn't attempting a coup. He was a friend, and I didn't want to have to fight him over a lost soul like Gary McCoy.

And I *would* fight if I needed to.

He was *my* patient. He'd remain my patient.

Mine!

Chapter 13

Vicki Hellings was just entering the building and taking up her post at the front desk when we passed her on our way to the east wing. She started to ignore the night nurse's directions, started to wave at me and proffer that big smile of hers. Then she saw the grim countenance of Dr. Carmody, and she relented with a sarcastic roll of her eyes. She'd seen this look of his on previous occasions, and she knew I was in for a long speech followed by seven or eight or nine even longer ones. Holding her hand up to her face as though it were a phone, pinkie to mouth, she whispered the words, "Call me later." I nodded and followed Carmody in silence.

He remained non-communicative until his office door was shut behind us and he was seated at his desk, which had been efficiently cleared of everything that might render it human a week ago. The pictures were absent from his walls, leaving behind ghostly squares where the paint had lightened over the years. A stack of boxes completed his office; everything packed away neat and tidy. That's Steven Carmody for you, king of the anal retentive. I guess that's why he was such a good supervisor.

"This thing going on here, Bob - oh, have a seat, please," he said, motioning to the only other piece of furniture in the room. "This thing - is it too much for you? You don't seem to be handling it very well."

Taking the proffered seat, I fell back into the chair. It felt terrific to be off my feet. They were still throbbing in agony over the long hike and run I'd taken with Deena the night before.

"I think I'm handling it just fine, sir," I answered. "Given the circumstances."

"Oh?"

"Yeah. I inherited this guy with no warning, barely had time to instigate a preliminary examination, and I find out I have a whole treasure trove of psychosis wrapped up in this kid's skull. In case you haven't noticed, his home life makes Billy Milligan's look like *Leave It to Beaver*."

"It's all true then - the strange religions, the insane father..."

"Insane's not the word for this dude," I said, leaning forward, getting excited by the case despite myself. "He's crazier than his boy, and that's saying a lot."

"Hmm...still you shouldn't have gone traipsing off into the woods to investigate his background without the assistance of law enforcement. What if something serious had happened and you'd been killed, or, worse yet, Deena'd been killed?"

"I didn't have time to think," I said, getting up and pacing the room. I was fully caught up in the vagaries of the argument now. "I only have today to make a diagnosis, because they're shipping him off to Pittsburgh in the morning. Wait, this is morning. Tomorrow morning, then. Christ, I need some sleep. Anyway, I want to be the boy's primary when he gets admitted. In order to ensure I get this honor, I'm willing to go balls out and probe deeply. I needed to find out how much of what he told me was true and how much was part of his delusionary Apocalypse scenario."

"And you think you've put your finger on it?"

"Hell, yes. He's been raised by religious zealots, who are also illiterate and delusional themselves. Not to mention incestuous and cannibalistic. His Pa, his father, that is, is certifiably psychotic. The man is dangerous. He's beaten it into this boy that he's some kind of savior, that he's the gateway through which his god, the Old One, is going to enter our world. He's convinced him there are worlds within worlds, and our next door neighbors, these invisible floating monsters, can come and go as they please, moving from their planet to ours through some membrane he calls the curtain. It's all some grand mythology his father's made up, and he's certain it's all true. To the extent that he bit a piece of flesh out of Rollo's arm and got that guard to suspect something else did it."

"You don't believe in these monsters?" Dr. Carmody arched an eyebrow, and I was reminded of Spock on *Star Trek*.

"Of course not. Are you kidding me? There's no such thing as monsters."

"Perhaps the Freudian monsters of our subconscious made flesh?"

"Now you're talking about the Id Monster in that old science fiction movie. This isn't *Forbidden Planet*. Steven, this is real life here."

"You assume this entire thing is a product of a bad upbringing?"

"The worst you could imagine."

"You're a bright young man, Bob," he said, lighting his pipe and puffing on it. "I think you may be on to something, but it's too soon to tell. Why don't you pack up your office - yes, I know you haven't finished - and revisit with McCoy later in the afternoon. Probe a little deeper once he's awake and cogent again."

"You're not pulling me off the case?"

"Heavens, no! You seem to be doing all right so far, even if your methods are a tad untidy. Have someone sit in on the next interview, Deena perhaps. I'd love to hear her reactions. She's very insightful."

"Thank-you, sir," I said, shaking his hand and beaming incorrigibly. "This means a lot to me."

"I can still remember the days when I was young and ambitious, full of piss and vinegar. I wanted it all, the fame, the attention, the money, the gratification of knowing I was helping someone. I'm not too old to recall how that feels. Still, those days are in my past. Perhaps, you'll have a better shot at achieving all those dreams, and maybe you'll keep in touch and let me know how you're progressing. I like you, Bob. Always have, even with all your wild impetuosity - maybe *because* of it. Let an old man share in your dream. Let me live that life, even if it is vicariously through you."

I didn't know what to say, so I just nodded and forced myself to close my mouth. I turned and stepped out of his office and headed to the front desk, where Vicki was finishing up the paperwork from the night nurse. I could hear her swearing.

"Bitch never finishes a damned thing on her own shift. Leaves it all for me to do. Well, look what the cat dragged in. You get bawled out?"

I shook my head. "No," I said, slumping into the empty seat beside her. It gave a hiss as the air whooshed out of the cushion.

"Well, I'm surprised at that. El Capitan had that look in his eyes, as though he was about to start in on the sermons. So, if he didn't talk you to death, what did he want?"

"Just to speak about the new patient."

"The one they hauled in yesterday?" she asked. "Thought there wouldn't be time for much doctoring on that one, seeing how he's being shipped off tomorrow morning."

"Ah, but I'm being shipped off to the same harbor," I said, closing my eyes. "Shit, I'm tired."

"You still need to get that office of yours cleaned out," she reminded me. "Last day to do it or someone's just going to toss it all out in the trash heap. With any luck, it'll be me."

"I know, I know, oh great master," I said, getting to my feet as Vicki picked up the phone's receiver. "I'll get right to it. You'd think you were my mother."

"I wish I were," she said, placing the receiver to her ear. "I'd have thrashed you black and blue when you were young and put a stop to your smart-assed remarks."

"Aw, you love me and you know it."

"Huh," she grunted, clicking the phone a few times. "Phone's out already. Thought they weren't getting to that until tomorrow."

"No connection?"

She listened a moment, tested it, then answered, "Nope. Dead as a Thanksgiving Day Turkey."

"Well, we'll just have to brave it out like the pioneers," I said, heading to my office.

"The pioneers didn't have a ward full of crazy people to deal with," Vicki shouted at my back.

As I walked to my office to fulfill the orders of Mein Fuhrer Hellings, I noticed I was the only person in the hallway. The staff was down to a skeleton crew for this final day St. Mike's would be open - myself, Dr. Carmody, Vicki, and Stan, the guard over at Siberia. Later on, Rollo would be back in the evening to complete his shift if he felt up to it after being chomped on by my wild-boy patient, and I guessed Deena would be in a little later to help with the last transfer of patients when the bus came. They'd have to be heavily medicated for the trip, drugged to the gills to keep them from causing any problems or starting a ruckus while in transit.

My footsteps echoed off the walls, and the hallway was filled with light from two barred windows, a yellowish, pasty light of the sun struggling to disperse heavy, dark clouds. The rain seemed to have let up, at last, but the sky looked as if it wanted to let loose again.

I stepped into my cluttered office. Looking around at the boxes which lined the far wall and the desk, still in a state of disarray. I sighed and started transferring my files from the cabinet to the heavy-duty cardboard boxes Deena'd bought for the occasion. It was dreary, mind-numbing work, and I found myself yawning, blinking the exhaustion from my eyes.

As I turned to retrieve another container for the next drawer of files, I thought I saw something moving out of the corner of my eye. It was pale, ghostly, a wispy thing struggling to weave towards me. When I turned, I saw the empty room. Nothing moved, nothing snaked through the air.

There are no monsters, I reminded myself.

Chalking it up to lack of sleep, I continued with my task - file to box, back and forth. When I finished with the cabinet, I stretched, reaching above my head to the ceiling. Bones cracked in my back.

Just beyond my vision, I thought I saw something flicker and move towards my extended fingers. It looked snake-ish, just like...

...an eel...a lamprey eel squirming through the air towards me.

When I looked again, swiftly pulling my hands down to my sides, I found nothing in the air. No monsters stalking their way towards me, no sharp teeth heading for my fingertips.

Shaking my head, I started on my desk. I took a seat, began removing the detritus of the drawers and putting them in boxes. When I'd cleared out the contents of the desk, I swept the items on top of it - pencil holder, stapler, picture of Deena - all into another carton. It was messy, but it was effective.

I was making good progress, and it was only eleven-thirty. The bare top of my desk looked back at me. Cleared of the rubble, it seemed unbelievably inviting, and I lay my hands down upon it. Then I rested my head on my hands, my fingers forming a rough cushion that felt soft despite their boniness.

And I slept, sinking into a world suffused with squirming eels and things that taunted me just out of my line of sight.

Chapter 14

Something clicked and snapped, and I saw the rows of teeth coming for my face as the snake-creature whipped itself closer. Reaching up, I grabbed at it, but it dissipated in my hands as if made of smoke. I blinked a few times, and the room came back into focus. Deena was standing at the other end of the office with a manila file in her hands, looking at me with bemusement on her face.

"Good morning, sleepy head," she said with a giggle.

"Ugh," I moaned. "What time is it?"

"Almost two-o-clock in the afternoon."

"Been asleep a couple hours then." I smacked my lips together, wishing I had a toothbrush and a big glass of water. I swallowed a few times until my mouth was almost clear, and Deena stepped across the room.

"I got up and did some research on the isolated communities in America. You know how weird we thought it was that a whole village existed just a few miles into the woods in this day and age?"

"Yeah."

"Well, it still *is* unusual, but not unheard of. I found several examples of contemporary communities co-existing with the world around them. Mostly hillbillies and religious groups in the Ozarks and especially in Appalachia."

"Can we get a cup of coffee or something while we talk about this?" I asked, still not quite awake. "I'm bleary."

"Oh, sweetie, of course we can. I think Vicki's still got a pot going behind her desk. I'll bet if you're nice, she'll even toss in a shot of Wild Turkey."

She immediately realized what she'd said, and she raised a hand to her mouth as if to push the words back into her mouth. She knew my problems with drink, and she usually managed to abstain from speaking about it. Every once in a while, something would slip out, and she'd get this apologetic look on her face, as though just mentioning alcohol would bring my old feelings and needs rushing back to me.

She was, actually, pretty right about that. For a moment, I could smell the Wild Turkey, taste the sting of it in the back of my throat, the flush in my cheeks. It took some will-power to shove the desire for a slug of whiskey away from my thoughts, and I managed to smile at her.

"Oh God, honey," she said. "I'm so sorry."

It was important that Deena not see me in such a state of uncontrolled indigence. I couldn't bear for my suppressed needs to be exposed so obviously to her. I bit the inside of my cheek, felt the urge diminish. I tried to return her joke with a volley of my own, feeble as it might be.

"Vicki's carrying a flask of Wild Turkey around with her?"

"You can be so unobservant," she said, opening the door. She knew I needed to move on with the subject, sensed my stupid sense of humor. She'd play dumb now, as if she hadn't just choked on her words. "Haven't you ever smelled her breath after lunch time?"

"I try not to get that close to her," I said. "Besides, I've been really good. You know that. Haven't touched the stuff in nearly two years now. I don't plan on starting again today."

Her face grew flustered, and she blushed. "I'm so sorry, honey. I just meant to make a joke. I didn't mean for you to actually..."

"I know," I said, waving it off. "But, I don't need to be tempted. Especially when I'm so tired and stressed out."

"Okay. We'll pretend she's slurring her words because of a speech defect - a cleft palate or something."

I shivered. "Saw enough of those in the village last night. Come on, let's bum some coffee off the old witch and you can tell me all about what you discovered today."

As I shut the door behind me, I thought I saw another movement out of the corner of my eye, similar to a floater drifting by my eyeball. I hurriedly closed the door, shutting whatever I'd imagined into the office, blocking its tracking of me.

As if that extra inch of wood would keep out a supernatural creature, I thought. *Geez, Gaskell, get a grip on yourself. There's no Easter Bunny, no Santa Claus, and there are no monsters flying through the air trying to eat your face.*

We made our way to the front desk, where we bummed a couple of mugs of steaming hot hazelnut Java from Vicki. Reaching into her desk, she pulled out a bag full of ham sandwiches, each sliced neatly in half.

"You guys want one?" she asked. "I made enough for everyone on the last day. I guess it's a good thing I did, too.

Phone's still not working. They must've cut the line a day earlier than they were supposed to. Stupid, damn phone company. Can't ever get anything right."

I took one of the proffered sandwiches and thanked her. Then, Deena and I walked to the lunch room area, which had once been a bustling cafeteria. In the past few years, everyone had been forced to brown bag their lunches, as the state board had shut down the cafeteria. Nobody complained. The food was pretty terrible. Now, however, the empty tables had chairs stacked atop their Formica surfaces, and conversation echoed off the tiled walls. The light bulbs had mostly burned out, with the exception of a single area, where we tended to eat. It always reminded me of a theater stage, the spotlight shining down upon us, the stars of the show.

As I tucked into the sandwich, which was pretty damn good, I said, "Okay. Tell me about the other places this has happened."

She opened the manila file. "Usually it's in more remote, mountainous areas, like here in Pennsylvania or in West Virginia. Most of the time, it seems the inhabitants of these isolated places seem to be trying to escape from the modern world, a world they think is evil or sinful. Old time religion seems to play a major part in the decision of people to get away from everything they deem sinful. Seems, at least to them, we're all a bunch of sickos and heathens."

"Well, there are days I wouldn't argue with that," I said.

"Me either, but I found several little clusters of people would argue that *everything* about the outside world is anathema. They decide to close themselves off from humanity and all our earthly concerns, separate themselves from the evil, so to speak."

"These are mostly fundamentalist Christians, right?"

"Yeah," she answered. "I didn't find anything resembling the Lovecraft inspired religion of our little village. Still, I saw there were at least three cases in the past five years where someone stumbled across a group of people living in isolation. Once, in the Pacific Northwest, a logging company stumbled upon a group that had been camping there for more than fifty years, living off the land. The place was really set off from the rest of the world, in the middle of hundreds of thousands of miles of forest timber land. Another example...where is it...ah, here it is. In rural Pennsylvania outside Chambersburg, deep in the mountains, a group of albinos were found living in caves. They'd been there so long, generations, protected from the sunlight, only coming out at night, that none of the people could say how many years they'd lived there. In that case, there was also a high rate of incest and birth defects noted. And in West Virginia, in deep, deep Appalachia, a whole community was found that had detached itself from the modern world in 1846, deciding that the world was ending. This happy little group was over two hundred strong, and a single bible was discovered in the main house. A lot of the pages were missing, but they'd based their faith, their whole society really, on what remained."

"Pretty much as the village has done with its cave drawings," I said.

"That's just what I thought. When there's only one, single rationale for the community's faith, they become so inured to it that it no longer seems fantastic. Like believing in monsters and Old Gods."

I neglected to mention to her how I'd thought I'd seen one of the monsters in the air. I convinced myself she didn't need to know; almost convinced myself it never even happened.

"So where does this put us?" I asked.

"I don't know. Maybe it's just more information to add to the pile. Who knows what'll help in the future."

"You're right. And at least I'm not thinking I'm crazy any longer. It's happened before; these isolated pockets of people, even if it isn't as extreme as our group."

"See, I'm that little girl in that shake n bake commercial."

"And I helped!" I shouted with a faux Southern drawl.

I leaned over and kissed her. I'd never dared to do so in such a public place at work, but I decided I didn't care anymore. After tomorrow, we'd no longer work in the same hospital. It wouldn't count.

"That was nice," she said, breaking apart from me. "What brought that on?"

"You did," I said. "I really do love you, you know."

"I know," she said with a winsome smile. "And I love you right back."

"I can't wait until next week. No more St. Mike's, no more restrictions on who I can and can't make out with in the cafeteria."

"It better not be anybody," she joked. "So, do you have your office all packed up and ready for the moving trucks?"

"Well..."

"I knew it," she said and stood with a groan. "Let's go finish it off now. Think how it'll feel if you get everything finished so you don't have to worry about any of it overnight. When the movers arrive tomorrow morning, you won't have to lift a finger."

"Hey, it's a really small office. How long could it take?"

She gave me *the look*. Hands on hips, head cocked to the side.

"You've had weeks to get it done," she said. "If we get started now, we might just finish in time. Plus, there's something I need to tell you, and we may as well finish off one project before anything else happens."

Begrudgingly, I followed her back to my office. She was a lot more chipper than I was, having slept for several hours longer than I had managed. I pressed her about her news, but she waved me off, led me straight to my half-packed headquarters. I watched her from behind, admiring the view.

I hadn't lied. I did love this woman, more than my career, more than my family, more than anything.

I wondered what I would ever do without her.

I prayed I would never have to find out.

Chapter 15

"Okay," I said, lifting one heavy crate onto another in a growing stack. "I'm moving, and the place is getting cleared. What's this mysterious thing you need to tell me about?"

"You have to promise you won't get mad at me," she answered.

"How can I ever get mad at someone as gorgeous as you?"

"How about pissed off? Maybe miffed?"

"That could be an option," I said. I was getting a bit testy with her, impatient for the beans to be spilled. "And it's becoming an increasingly likely option."

"Okay," she said, setting down the paperweight she was wrapping in newspapers. I had bought that little geegaw when I'd still been a student at the university. My desk had been so bare it could've been termed minimalist. The colorful blue and yellow swirlies within the glass still held a sort of fascination for me - how did the glass blowers surround the vibrant tissues with a perfectly circular globule? Often, during my school days, I'd take breaks from writing papers and reading dull textbooks, and I would just stare into the depths of the paperweight. It had calmed me, and now that I was out in the workplace, I still stopped now and again to catch my breath and gaze into the glass. The knick-knack had retained all its calming, meditative power over me.

"So..." I prompted Deena, sitting on the edge of my nearly empty desk top.

"Oh, no, you keep working," she said with a laugh. "You aren't done yet."

"Slave driver."

"Anyway, don't get miffed with me," she said. "But I called the police about what happened last night."

"You what?" I shouted. I couldn't help it.

"Sorry, Bob, but those people are dangerous. You and I both know it."

I was flustered, searched for the right words. "Deena, you...you may have endangered everything we've accomplished so far. What if the police go out there and tear down the village...destroy evidence of that weird culture? God only knows what they'll do with those people."

"The police needed to know what happened to us in case those villagers come after us one day. Plus, there were kids out there that needed help. Medical help. It's just a preventative measure, honey, a practical matter. Just in case."

"What did the cops say?"

"They listened, but I don't think they believed me. I didn't mention anything supernatural, only that there was a sick little Hooverville out in the mountains. I gave them some general directions, but I don't think they took notes or anything. Probably thought I was a crack-pot."

"They going out there to the village? If they are, I want to go with them. I can't have them destroying my whole case I'm building for Gary."

"They aren't going anywhere," she said, shaking her head. "They mentioned they'd probably send someone to

St. Mike's today to take a statement, but they didn't even sound certain about that. They know we close today, and we'll all soon be gone. Probably going to ignore the whole mess, sweep it under the carpet since we - the people filing the complaint - will be under someone else's jurisdiction in another week. I doubt we'll even see one officer today." She took a deep breath, cocked her head, and asked, "So, are you pissed?"

"I have to admit, I'm not happy you informed the police about Gary's case, but I'm sure you did the right thing."

"You need to learn that the wife *always* does the right thing."

"You aren't a wife yet."

"Let's not delve into technicalities," she said with a giggle. "Let's finish up this office. We're getting dangerously close to being done."

Within an hour, we had the whole room packed into cartons, the boxes taped shut and sufficiently labeled so I wouldn't be confused when I arrived subsequent to them at the new hospital. Looking around the now empty room, I put my hands on my hips and smiled proudly at how much we'd accomplished in so little time.

"You bear an uncanny resemblance to the Jolly Green Giant," Deena said, giggling behind her hand. It was an odd habit, given that her smile was so brilliant and contagious.

"Ho, ho, ho," I emulated the big green guy. "Eat your veggies, kids."

"Now that you're done with the packing, what are you going to do?"

"I don't know," I said, moving towards her in what I hoped was a seductive manner. "Maybe we can fool around for a while."

She giggled behind her hand again. "Lock the door."

I did, and we fell upon the couch, Deena on top of me. Our mouths found each other, and I tasted her sweetness, her tongue darting between my lips. I was in the process of unbuttoning her blouse when someone rapped on the door.

"Damn," I hissed. "Maybe they'll go away."

"It could be important," Deena whispered, ever the practical one in our relationship.

"Then again, maybe it isn't."

"Dr. Gaskell," came a voice recognizable as Dr. Carmody from the hallway. "I suggest you find your way to the east wing and check on your patient. He seems to be awake now."

"I'll be right over," I shouted, tucking in my shirt. "Just give me a couple of seconds."

Deena pointed to my crotch and whispered, "You have an erection."

"That's what the few seconds are for," I said, trying to think of very old nuns to dispel the hardness in my pants.

Carmody's voice emerged once again from behind my office door. "And I'd suggest Dr. Bierce should accompany you. That is, if you two are finished with your, ahem, consultation in there."

"How'd he know I was in here?" she gasped.

I shrugged. "How's he know anything. I blame it on telepathy."

She started buttoning her blouse back up, much to my regret. She caught me spying, and she turned bright red through her cheeks.

Deciding it was easier to acknowledge her presence to Carmody rather than ignore him, she shouted, "I'll be coming with him. Just a second or two." Turning back to me, she whispered, "How's that hard-on?"

"Deflated, thanks to Sister Mary Agonies from my second grade religion class."

"I suppose that's good," she said. "Let's go."

She opened the door, managing to look exactly as if she'd been interrupted during lovemaking - which she had - and fluffed her hair. Carmody eyed her suspiciously, then he looked towards me, giving me the old stink eye. I stuck my tongue out at him. It was childish, but the old curmudgeon deserved it for suspending my bit of afternoon delight.

"Shall we proceed?" he asked, ignoring me.

"Sure," I said. "How's he acting?"

"Our friend Stan informs me he's cogent and rather calm," Carmody said.

I couldn't imagine Stan knowing the definition of the word 'cogent', much less using it in a sentence.

We walked down the corridor and turned right, passing by Vicki's desk. She was making another pot of coffee, and the sweet, hazelnut aroma wafted through the hallway like a grace note.

"Telephones are out," she told Carmody.

"Then, we'll just have to somehow manage without them for a few hours, won't we, Miss Hellings?" he deadpanned.

At the end of the hallway, we turned right again, completing the U-shape of the hospital layout. Stan was sitting on the other side of the Plexiglas, and he buzzed us into his room. Then he unlocked the second door. Once we passed this barricade, we started down the Siberian wing. The patients seemed agitated as we moved by their cells, and not by us. Several of them were snatching at the air as though trying to grab something moving by them...

...like the monsters that swam through the atmosphere...like Gary McCoy's visions of hell on Earth... They looked more like the people in the cave drawings than I would have wanted to admit.

I started peering into each cell, watching for this aberrant behavior. It seemed as if every one of the worst-case patients in the wing was suffering from the same delusions, although they greeted them differently. Some of them recoiled in terror from invisible 'somethings' in the air. Others snatched at them, imitating the proverbial fox and the grapes, hopping up and down, reaching for the unattainable. Other patients merely contemplated the air around them in wonder, complacently amazed at whatever they were witnessing.

"Dr. Carmody, look at this," I said. "They're all acting like there's something in the air around them."

"That's curious," he said, his brow furrowing as he took in the various reactions of the patients. "They're all so different, yet they're sharing a similar psychosis." Turning to Stan, he asked, "Has this ever happened before?"

"Not so's I'd notice," the man said. "Weird as hell, you ask me."

"You think it's some kind of mass hysteria?" Deena asked, wrapping her arms around her middle as though chilled.

"Somehow," I said with more conviction that I felt. "Somehow, McCoy's infected the others with his own delusions. I don't know how he did it. Maybe he whispered it to them, convinced them of the monsters he sees, and those whispers took root in their fragile minds. Now, they see what he sees."

"It seems impossible," Carmody said. "But, there it is. All around us."

"Let's check out McCoy," I suggested. "If he's the key to all this, I want to know what he's doing."

We walked to the last cell on the left and peered through the window in the door at the man sitting on the edge his bed. He stared at the floor, his arms wrapped behind him in a restraining jacket. His greasy hair spilled down, obscuring his face. He seemed placid, perhaps a little drugged-up.

I rapped on the Plexiglas. Slowly, he raised his eyes to mine, and I could see the one glowing bright blue. The other was camouflaged by his dark hair. His mouth was set in a straight line, neither smiling nor frowning - an expression of utter passivity.

"Hi there, Doc. I been waitin' for ya," he said.

Chapter 16

Stan admitted us into the room, leaving the door open behind us and taking his station just to the left outside. He had his nightstick ready, but he wouldn't need to use it. Gary McCoy had his foot handcuffed to the bedpost, and the straight jacket would keep him from showing too much physical interest in us. Besides, he did indeed seem cogent and calm, a man with all his senses intact.

"Why, Gary? Why have you been waiting for me?"

"Oh, lotsa' reasons. Mostly 'cause I went all wild and freaky this mornin'. I went a little crazy, but it was just 'cause I was so damn scared. You really oughtn't to've gone to the village. Not after what I told ya. And ya definitely shouldn't have taken her."

He nodded towards Deena.

"How'd you know I took her along?" I asked.

"The whisper whisper whispers in the air tol' me. They gets excited when a woman gets close by. And not the women in the village either - they ain't real sexy like this one here."

Deena wrapped her arms around herself even tighter, as though her arms could restrain his staring eyes from where they'd latched upon her breasts. They didn't deter his gaze a bit.

"Did the monsters tell you that? About me and Deena?" He nodded. "They whisper whisper whisper to me. All the time, I hear it. Don't you? It's pretty loud right now."

"Why is it loud?"

"'Cause they's all around us, silly," he said, and he grinned, his eyes catching sight of something invisible moving past my head. "Ever'where around us. The air's plain thick with 'em."

"More so than usual?" I asked.

"Yep. They's all over, squigglin' past each other, brushin' against one another. They ain't never been so thick as this. Probably 'cause the Old One's comin' through tonight."

"Coming through you? You're the portal?"

"I s'pose. Don't know, really. The drawin's in the cave don't say just exactly how it's gonna happen. Just that it *is* gonna happen."

"Tonight?"

"After dark...when all the villagers dance around me."

"But, Gary, your folks are still far away. At the village. You're perfectly safe here."

"You don't listen so good, huh, Doc? They's on their way right now. Probably be here 'bout sundown, I reckon."

"The villagers will be here?"

"I can feel 'em movin' closer all the time. Can hear them steppin' on the road, tryin' ta be quiet. Oh, they's on their way, all right."

"What will they try to do? Break you out of the hospital?"

"Nah," he said. "They'll probably just wanna be here for the ceremony. They's gonna dance around me, just as the drawin's showed, dancin' all around me. When the Old One comes through, they'll be there to greet him to our world, and he will spare them from his gnashin' teeth and scraping claws."

"Why won't he kill them?"

"They's the promised ones. They's spent all their time tryin' to get him in this world. It's their reward for helpin' him."

Deena asked, "What will they do to all of us? The doctors, the other patients?"

He shrugged. "Don't rightly know, and don't rightly give a damn."

"But, if you had to guess."

"Probably kill you all. Sacrifices for the Old One. Every sacrifice takes us closer ta his side."

"They can't get past the security," Carmody said, mostly to alleviate Deena's obvious agitation, but probably to calm us all down. Gary McCoy's placid, quiescent demeanor made his insane proclamations all the more troubling.

"Oh, you don't know my family very well, do ya, Doc?" he said with a shark-toothed grin. "We been livin' in them woods so long, takin' care of ourselves. We hunt when we need to, fish, forage, even steal sometimes. We're - what's that ten cent word - oh, yeah - resourceful. They can get in and out of damn near anywhere, and this place ain't gonna stop 'em. Not with me in here and the Old One a'comin'. "

"Would it be better if we let you go?" I asked. I wanted his perspective, wanted to know if the boy still wished to be saved.

"Hell, no," he answered quickly. "I keep thinkin'...what if all this ain't real? What if it's all somethin' Pa made up, and he believes it hisself now. I mean, really thinks it's gonna happen to me, to the village, to all the world. And what's gonna happen to me when it don't work? I seen him mad before. Seen him kill men when they don't do what he says the drawin's tell us to do. I'd be lucky if he don't smash in my skull at midnight. At least in here, I got me a chance to get away. That is, if the Old One don't come through me. If it all don't happen like Pa said it would."

"Gary, this is important," I said. "Do you really believe in this whole mythology?"

"This what?"

"That the Old One is using you as a gateway to our world, that you've been breeding in that village to get someone like you, the Preacher, who can see the monsters."

"The monsters are real. I see 'em now. All around us. You don't see 'em, Doc? Not even a little bit outta the corner of your eye?"

"I..."

He grinned, exposing moss-brown teeth. "Yeah boy! You seen 'em, haven't you? That's why you're so damn interested in what *I* can see."

"No, Gary, I need to know what you really think is gonna happen."

"I 'spect Pa's right," he said, lowering his eyes to the floor and fidgeting his hands within the confines of his straight jacket.

"You think that a god's moving through parallel universes to get to ours. Why? Why would anything so powerful in its own world want to travel to someplace new?"

"I dunno'. Maybe to see the sights? Pa said it wants to spread its reign over every world it can find, or that maybe it began in this world but was banished to that other world, sent away by the new, weak Christian god."

"If the Christian God is so weak, how'd it overcome this Old One?"

"I don't know, I don't know, I don't fuckin' know! All's I know's what the drawin's show, and you seen 'em already. And what Pa told me. I'm the preacher. I'm more important than any other villager there is, because I'm gonna be the path through which our god flows. I'm the one who's gonna let him loose on all of you. Only, sometimes, I don't wanna let him through."

"Why not, Gary?"

"There's some good things in the world I don't wanna see destroyed. Things like the trees and some birds. There's a girl named Sue Ellen I wanna talk with, but I ain't never had the nerve. I gets all blustered when I try. Still, even if I could just talk at her, she'd never see me. She'd only see the Preacher."

"Then, why do this terrible thing?" I asked. "Why let the Old One through at all?"

"You're actin' like I got a choice. I ain't got no choice. He's comin' through me no matter what. It's been prophesied by the drawin's. Nothin' can change that."

"Gary, I think you can change it."

"Bullshit. You seen those pictures."

"If you're so important, then, think about it, just how essential are you? How long did it take to get a Preacher?"

"A long ass time. Years and years and years."

"Right, so think about what that means. You're more than important to your people. You're indispensable."

"I'm what?"

"They need you. The Old One needs you. Even the monsters you see need you so that people realize they're here and what they look like. If you never explained them to the villagers, they'd never even know the creatures exist as more than pictures."

"I guess they do need me."

"If you refused to let the Old One through the curtains, I think you could stop him from coming."

"He's a god. You can't stop a god. Pa always said so."

"I think you can, Gary. I think you've got the power within you, created from years of correct breeding. You're nearly a god, yourself, if what you say is true."

I looked over at Deena and Carmody and was gratified to see they had figured out what I was trying to accomplish with this line of questioning. If I could get Gary to realize he could stop the Apocalypse from occurring, I would have empowered him to make his own decisions, to see that his Pa and the villagers were all wrong. With such empowerment comes a sort of courage. Perhaps, he could begin a new life, in the world he believed he had saved from extinction.

"They always said I was special, but I don't think I'm a fuckin' god. Ya don't mess with your gods. Don't make 'em mad or play act to them or nothin'."

"You wanna save Sue Ellen, maybe one day marry her? You're going to have to stop this thing from happening. You're going to have to put an end to all the madness."

"You really think I can?"

"I do, Gary. I believe the Old One's met his match, and you'll be able stop him and save the whole world in the process."

The boy was beaming, and I was feeling pretty damned good about myself, as well. If I could get him to first see how foolish all this talk about other worlds and monsters and gods was, then I could, perhaps, get him to see his other delusions for what they were - delusions, hallucinations, artistic fucking license.

And the book advances in my imagination just kept getting larger and larger. The zeroes multiplying like farm rabbits.

Chapter 17

A few hours passed uneventfully, with Deena and I relaxing a little in my office. Carmody had mentioned he wanted us to stay on duty through the evening, until the night guards clocked in and took their stations. The patients had all been fed, and I'd even managed a little shut-eye on a mattress in an empty room for about a half hour. My thoughts, as I drifted into a somnolent state, were on Gary McCoy and his wild delusions. My dreams were suffused with semi-invisible creatures, biting holes in my body. Deena awakened me with a kiss, but I swatted out at her, flailing against my unseen enemy. She laughed and stepped back a bit from the cot.

"Sleeping Beauty," she said, kissing me again. Then, she made a face and continued, "Only with five o clock shadow. Ouch, razor burn."

"Been a while since I had a chance to shave," I apologized, rubbing my whiskers. "Man, I can't remember the last time I let them get this long. I'm going to end up looking like George Michael."

"Promises. promises," she said. "Say, what time are we allowed to leave anyway? Carmody can stick around all night if he wants to, but I still have that jack-o-lantern to carve and a whole evening's worth of horror movies to watch."

"I'm too tired for horror movies and wholesale pumpkin slaughter," I complained.

"And maybe a little monster sex afterwards?"

I was all ears. "Well, in that case, hand me a knife and I'll carve that sucker in seconds flat. It'll be a massacre," I said. "It's just got to be close to quitting time. How long's the old guy expecting us to stay here?"

"Let's go check with Carmody," she suggested. "We've put in more than a full day."

"More like two or three full days. I'm wiped."

"Me, too."

As we moved towards the door, a dark shape loomed in the frame. Lit from behind, it looked huge, as big or bigger than Rollo, and I have to admit my heart leaped in my chest and I let out a scream that would embarrass any ten year old girl. The shape took a step closer, and the dim light from the room spread over its form.

It was a cop, wearing the dark gray uniform of the Pennsylvania Police Department, the one which so many newspapers were writing editorials regarding the similarity to those worn by state constables. His hair was short and blonde beneath his gray cap, and his muscles pushed at the strained buttons of his shirt. Standing about six foot four inches, the guy was huge, looming over me and Deena, but his brown eyes looked kind, like those of a bear cub. He held a notepad in one hand and a pen in the other, the writing instrument appearing tiny in his massive paw.

"Jesus Christ," I shouted. "Warn a guy if you're sneaking up on him in a half-abandoned asylum!"

"Sorry," the cop said, and he actually blushed, his cheeks turning a rosy pink. "Didn't mean to scare you."

I saw he was little more than a freckle-faced kid, twenty three years old tops. He removed his hat and wiped his forehead. "Hot in here," he muttered as his complexion paled again.

Crazy people in the woods threaten us, I thought, *and they send Ron Howard to help. Some cavalry.*

"You Deena Bierce, ma'am?"

She nodded to him then looked at me with a grin. "Yes, but, please drop the ma'am business. Makes me feel old."

Was it my imagination, or was Deena actually flirting with this strapping, muscular, handsome police officer? I glanced down at my small yet expanding pot belly, deciding I needed to start jogging again.

"Fine," the good-looking bastard said with a grin that showed off his perfectly white teeth. "Says here you made a report about some threats. My chief told me to get a statement from you."

"You drove all the way out here just for that?" I swear, she was batting her eyelashes at him.

"Yes, ma'am. Uh, sorry about that. Habit, you know?"

"There's worse habits."

Stepping forward, I said, a bit louder than necessary, "I was there, too. Robert Gaskell. I'm Miss Bierce's fiancée."

"Oh, yeah, of course," the boy stammered, and to his credit, he did look as though he'd been caught with his hand in the cookie jar. That'll teach him to make goo goo eyes with *my* lady. He continued, "If either one of you could tell me exactly what happened and where, I'll take it back to the station and type up the report. Then, you'll have to come down, read it, approve it, and sign it. Whenever it's convenient, of course."

"Of course," I said, sarcasm dripping from my thin frame.

Sensing the waves of insecurity beaming off of me, Deena reached over and did the best thing she could have possibly done. She took my hand in hers and squeezed, and I let go of the jealousy in a heartbeat. She was asserting she was my lady, that she would always be mine, and I had no recourse for worrying. It alleviated my anxiety, and, suddenly, this cop looked astonishingly young and non-threatening to me.

"I'm Ron Justice," he said. "Please, no cracks about the last name. I get enough of them at the station."

"This is how it happened," I began to rattle off the story of how St. Mike's was closing and the remaining prisoners locked up in the east wing. I told how Gary McCoy was brought in for transfer tomorrow morning, how I'd follow him to Pittsburgh. I described his diagnosis, how he'd told me about the village in the woods and drawn a map. Justice wrote down every word in his little notebook. As I finished, I wondered if he was using shorthand, because he'd easily transcribed fifteen pages.

"And that's the threat?" he asked, his brow furrowing.

"The guy's family seems to believe they'll come after Gary if we leave him in the asylum, and there's no chance we're setting him free."

"Well, I honestly don't know what we can do for you folks," he said. "This threat seems kinda vague."

"Well, at least check out the village," Deena suggested. "There has to be some law being broken by them. Squatting rights or something. Child abuse or sexual abuse?"

"Yeah, well, probably is something we can do there. You still have that map the crazy fellow drew up for you?"

I nodded. "Yeah. I need the original for proof in my diagnosis. Would a copy be okay?"

"If it gets us there without falling down the mountain, it'll be fine."

"Then, let's get the map out of my office and we'll copy it for you."

The hallway was quiet as we moved from the low security ward where I'd napped to my office. My briefcase was set on the floor beside my desk, and I'd placed all of Gary McCoy's files in it while packing up the rest of the room. These were too precious to leave in the hands of unknown movers. They contained my future.

"Here it is," I said, rummaging through the paperwork.

I took a seat at my empty desk, removed a plain piece of paper from a box with the words 'Office Supplies' written on the side in Deena's neat script. I copied the map by hand, and the basics were the same, but I had far less artistic talent that McCoy. My map looked off-kilter, the scale all screwed up.

"Thanks a lot," Trooper Justice said, tipping his hat. "I'll take this to the station with me, file it with the report."

"Sounds good," Deena said. "When did you need us to visit and sign the statements?"

"Oh, well, shucks, ma'am," he said, and I almost slapped my forehead at the word 'shucks.' Did people still spout such archaic cusses? He continued, "Maybe I'll get it all written up and bring it on back here in the morning. That'll be the end of my shift."

I knew he just wanted another look at my scorching hot fiancée. I moved closer to her, put an arm around her shoulders. If it wouldn't have been over-the-line, I believe I would've started necking with her then and there.

"That sounds great," Deena said. "It'll save us a trip to town." She turned towards me, adding, "Won't it, honey?"

"Yeah, sweetiekins," I said in a gritted-teeth whisper.

"All right then. I'll see you two in the morning."

He tipped his hat at us again, then he moved back out into the hallway. He looked huge as he ambled slowly away from us. Like a big old friendly bear.

"You were flirting with that boy," I said.

"I was doing no such thing," Deena protested. "I was trying to get him to take the whole thing seriously. Maybe they will go investigate the villagers, take them all downtown or into some other hospital."

"I still think you were flirting."

"Please, hon, don't get all green eyed on me."

"These eyes aren't green, they're just open wide. You want to see if we can blow this popsicle stand yet? Carmody might be in his office. I mean, now that we have to be back so early in the morning to see Trooper Studmuffin."

"Listen to me, Bob," she said, taking my chin and directing my gaze into her eyes. "You are the only man I love. You're the one I'm marrying, and that counts for a hell of a lot. You stick with me, and I promise you a Halloween night date you'll never forget."

"Oh yeah, monster sex."

"Monster sex it is."

"I think we'd better find Carmody and see if we can clock out for the night. We're overdue and I'm getting overheated."

"Amen," she said, and I discovered her hand in mine again. Squeezing, just to let me know she was there for me.

Chapter 18

We walked down the hall to Carmody's office and knocked. When there was no answer, I peeked inside the door. The room was empty save for a desk shoved against the far wall, a chair flipped upside-down on top of it, and a stack of four boxes. Not a very big legacy to be moved. It made me a bit sad, all those years my boss had toiled away at St. Mike's only to have it stashed into four pathetic boxes.

"No one here," I said, closing it behind me.

I thought I heard his voice. I pulled Deena with me until we arrived at the front door, where Carmody was talking to Vicki. She was doing her best to shout over his mild protestations. She looked royally pissed off, her face redder and puffier than usual. He remained stationed on the opposite side of the desk, leaning forward slightly, his fingertips resting on the barren surface. He was sweating.

"I have a kid at home," she said. "And I need to get there before the baby-sitter starts charging overtime. I can't afford it. You realize what those punks charge these days?"

"You must wait until the night nurse arrives," Carmody said. "I'm asking you, no, begging you to stay a little longer."

"How do you know if that bitch is even going to show up? She's late half the time, doesn't give a good goddamn about this place. I'd put a hundred bucks on her not even coming to work for her last shift. Probably already has another job."

"Please, Miss Hellings..."

I thought he was actually going to drop to his knees to beg her to remain at her post. But, knowing Vicki Hellings, even that wouldn't have appeased the goddess of the front door.

Vicki noticed us and waved. "Hey guys," she said. "Limp dick here was just trying to get me to stay later on account of little miss tardiness herself is, surprise, late getting here. You have Rollo, don't you? He can run this desk as well as anyone, considering there's no phone to answer."

"Rollo made it back?" I asked. "I guess that means he's feeling all right after the bite?"

Carmody said, "I suppose so. I didn't ask. But, he's downstairs, relieving Stan from his post right now. He'll be here for the duration of the night, so you can ask him yourself."

Leave it to Dr. Carmody to be more worried about staffing issues than the health of someone whose shoulder was bitten by something or someone during work hours. I bet he didn't even have Rollo fill out his workman's compensation forms.

Carmody continued, "If he's down there sequestered in Siberia, then who will man the desk, Ms. Hellings? He can't be in both places at once."

"What purpose does it serve, for Christ's sake? If all the damn patients are locked up in Siberia, who needs someone to buzz the front door? Prop it open with a piece of wood or something," Vicki shouted. Her face was getting blotchy, a sure signal that her blood pressure was rising. I took a step back to further myself from the nearing explosion of volcanic fury. I noted Deena did the same.

"There may be an emergency."

"Like what? Nothing's happened all day. Nothing's going to happen tonight. We aren't getting any more deliveries. It's dead in here."

"Please, Miss Hellings-"

"You going to pay me overtime? I want double time for any hours over and above my usual schedule - which ended, let me see, fifteen minutes ago."

"Done. Double time's no problem."

I raised my hand. "Um, I want to get double time, too."

"Tough luck, Gaskell. You're salaried."

"Hey, can't blame a guy for trying."

Vicki said, "Okay, I'll stay, but not all night. I need to somehow notify the baby-sitter. She's going to want extra pay. Damn her withered, black, teen-aged soul."

"You could use a pay phone down the road," I suggested. "At the gas station. It's only about eight miles away. You'll be back in fifteen minutes."

She looked at Carmody, who was fidgeting. "Oh, may I, sir? Please, sir, may I notify my sitter?" She batted her eyelashes like a silent screen vamp.

"I suppose it's okay. I can watch the desk in the meantime, but, please, hurry up. I still have things to pack in the storage areas."

"Watch that desk," Hellings said with a gum-popping grin. "It might run off and join the circus."

She put on her coat, while Carmody took a seat behind the big desk. As she zipped herself up, Vicki looked into the glass of the front doors. It was already dark outside, and she had a good reflection of herself, so she primped her hair a bit. Nothing she did to that frizzy mass of red curls could tame its wildness. It was a hirsute alien blob, trying to take over the planet one head at a time.

"I think we'll go have a look-see at Rollo," I said. "See how he's feeling."

"What?" Carmody asked, startled. "Oh, yes. Good idea. Let me know how he is."

"Sure," I said, starting to walk down the hall towards Siberia.

Deena nudged me in the ribs. She whispered, "What about going home? Pumpkins? Monsters? Lustful demonic forces?"

"Oh, yeah," I said. "I forgot in the excitement."

"If you think this is exciting," she purred "just wait till I get you back to that apartment."

Vicki finished messing around with her hair and reached for the door. "I wonder what's keeping Johnson? The bitch is always late, but there has to be a... What the hell is that?"

"What?" Carmody asked, standing again. "What's what?"

"Something out there in the dark. I thought I saw something. Hell, I should wait. Could be Johnson dragging her late ass into work, and I won't have to stay after all. I still want that double time for the fifteen minutes if it is her."

"What *is* that out there?" Carmody asked, peering into the darkness.

A body wearing a nurse's uniform smashed into the glass near the front doors, startling everyone. Deena shrieked, and Vicki, the bravest of us all, moved forward to get a closer look. I ran to her side, telling Deena not to move.

"Don't worry," she said. "I'm staying right here."

"It's Johnson," Vicki said as I arrived at her side.

The body had smacked into the window at about chest level then slid to the concrete sidewalk, leaving a trail of blood smeared down the glass. The dead woman's nurse's uniform was immaculately white, except for several areas of blood stains blossoming like chrysanthemums on a summer's day. The body lay very near the front door, twisted at an unnatural angle, one leg obviously broken, the tip of a white bone poking through the skin near her knee. One arm lay across Johnson's eyes, and, forgoing the bloody uniform, she looked as though she had swooned.

I said, "Deena, buzz the door open. I have to see if she's still alive." She scurried to the desk and pressed the button, popping the door open a quarter of an inch with a slight whirring noise.

I looked into the darkness and, seeing nothing lurking nearby ready to spring at me, opened the door. Deena protested behind me, calling out my name, but I was damned if I was going to just let Nurse Johnson lie outside, limp against the cold cement. Even if she was a bit of a bitch. I grabbed her arms and dragged her into the lobby. A trail of crimson streaked the ground behind her.

Once I had her inside, I put my fingers to her throat, feeling for a pulse. There was nothing, and her skin was growing cold and clammy to the touch. She'd been dead for some time.

"Is she...?" Carmody let the question hang in the air. Remembering himself, he rushed to the door and locked it after me.

"Yeah," I said. "She's gone. For a while, too. Looks as though someone bashed her skull in with a blunt object, and her back looks broken, too."

"Who could've done it?" Vicki asked, looking back out into the dark night outside the hospital. The night obscured any sign of a murderer.

"Someone really strong," Deena said. "Had to be. She was hurled a fair distance before she hit the glass. And she hit it pretty high up."

"But, why would anyone kill Johnson?" Vicki whispered, pressing her face against the window to look further out. "I mean, I didn't like her, don't think anybody did, but, come on!"

"I'd get away from that window if I were you," I said to Vicki. "If they can throw her that hard, who knows what else they're going to catapult against the glass."

"They? Who's they?" she asked. "You know about this, don't you? You know something."

"I think it's the people from the village," I said with a resigned sigh. "Gary McCoy's folks, come to spring him out of what they think is a prison so he can lead their god into our world."

"This is not the Twilight Zone," Vicki shouted. "This is fucking Pennsylvania!"

"You didn't see the way these people live," Deena said. They were animals, worshipping weird monsters, building pagan statues to them. They said we'd better release him, or they'd come and get him themselves."

"But I never thought they'd actually do it," I said. "They're so primitive. So archaic. I can't imagine how they even got all this way from the woods. Could they have walked? So many of them didn't even have functioning legs, they were so deformed. And how'd they know this was where the hospital was located?"

"Hold on a minute," Carmody suggested, waving his arms. "We don't even know that this is who's out there. We don't know they killed Nurse Johnson. It could've been anyone. A random serial killer."

I shook my head at him. "You weren't there. You didn't see the way they threatened us. You did hear McCoy this afternoon, though, didn't you? He said they'd come for him. He said they wouldn't let anything get in their way. They think this is holy work they're doing."

"I think we should call the police," Carmody said, picking up the phone. When he didn't hear the dial tone, he gave a single, defeated, "Oh." Resigned, he hung up the receiver. "That's right. The phone's out. Fine night for it to happen."

I examined Johnson's body a little more, checking out the fresh, wet dimple in her head, the glistening blood in her hair, and I knew in my heart the villagers were out there. Probably all of them, watching us through the big, bullet-proof glass doors. It was so bright in the hospital and so dark outside by the woods, we probably offered them quite a brilliant view - something like a television screen set into the wall of St. Mike's. It wasn't a very comforting thought.

"They're watching us," I said. "I can feel it."

"Where are they?" Vicki asked, looking at the tree line by the road that led up to the hospital. "I don't see them. Just the branches of the trees in the wind. It's going to storm again. I just saw some lightning off in the distance."

"Just what we need for Halloween," I said. "It always storms in the scary movies."

Deena tugged my arm and said, "I'm worried, Bob. Let's get out of here."

I nodded over to Carmody. "Alert the guards about the situation." I'm taking Deena home. Maybe if we aren't here, they won't bother hurting anyone else. They were pretty fixated on me last night. Or maybe we let Gary go free."

"I am not letting a patient as disturbed as Gary McCoy loose," he said, determined. "He's my responsibility. I signed for him, and now I have to make sure he doesn't harm anyone, or anyone harms him. Who knows what he'd do out there? He already took a bite out of old Rollo's shoulder."

"I don't give a damn," I said, pulling Deena to the doorway. "We're out of here. Come on, honey."

And then, with no warning, the lights went out, and we were plunged into a despairing darkness.

Chapter 19

Deena clutched my arm and shoulder when the inky gloom enveloped us, and I flinched at her touch, despite feeling somewhat comforted by it. The room was suddenly as dark as the woods outside, and with the cloud cover of the encroaching storm, it was as black as pitch. We stood a moment in silence, letting our eyes adjust to the murk.

"Great," Vicki finally said, breaking the stillness. "That is all we need right now."

Soon, I could see enough to stumble around a bit. I walked Deena back over to the desk and guided her into the chair behind the big, oaken piece of furniture. Carmody put a hand on her shoulder, and I liked him immensely for the gesture.

"I'm going out for my car," I said. "I'll be right back, and I'll pull around in the front. I'm going to keep the doors locked on the car till I'm right here, and I suggest you all lock down these doors while I'm gone. When I get back, you can all pile in, and we're heading straight for the police station."

"What about Johnson?"

"She isn't a problem. She's not going anywhere. I can't be burdened down by her when I'm running for our escape vehicle."

"And I, for one, don't want to sit next to a corpse in a compact car," Deena muttered.

"What about the guards? Rollo and Stan?" Carmody asked.

"Shit, I forgot about them," I said. "Well, while I get the car, you fetch them and get them back here. We can all fit in one vehicle for the journey into town. It'll be cramped, but at least we'll all be safe and far away from any danger."

"And the patients?" Carmody reminded me.

"They're locked in their rooms, right?"

He nodded. "The bolts automatically latch in the case of a power failure. But, anyone can let them out from the other side of their doors as long as they can get to the Eastern Wing."

"Dr. Carmody," Vicki wheezed in her harsh, smoker's voice. "Who in the hell's going to come into a mental institution on Halloween night during a thunderstorm and a power outage to let the scary people out of their cells? That's creepier than almost anything I can imagine."

I knew who would want to let them loose, but they would have to get through so many locks they'd never achieve their goal. The villagers were a crafty bunch, but unless they were experts at picking locks, they'd never get McCoy out of his cell before we returned with the police.

"Don't worry about the patients," I said.

"That's my job, worrying about those poor souls," Carmody argued.

"Then you stay and watch over them," I suggested, and even in the darkness, I could see his face turn white. "I'm grabbing my car and taking off with my fiancée and Vicki."

"And the guards," Deena reminded me.

"Yeah. And the guards."

By this point, Carmody was really looking flustered. "They won't leave their posts," he said. "They're too dedicated. Rollo even came in with a wound today to work his last hours at St. Mike's. He loves this place."

"I love the paycheck," Rollo said, stepping around the corner from the hallway to Siberia. He was wearing a loose shirt, and I could see padding and white bandages where the bite had been. "The job, not so much. Why'd the lights go out?" he asked. Then, he got close enough to see Johnson's corpse on the floor. "Whoa! What did that?"

"She was thrown against the window," Vicki said.

Stan hurried around the corner to the front desk, his shoes clicking on the hardwood floors as if he were wearing tap shoes.

"What the devil's happening?" he asked. "The lights are out."

"No shit, Sherlock," Vicki said, lighting a cigarette. I wondered where she kept the three packs she must go through for every shift at the hospital.

Carmody protested, "You can't smoke in here. Not during a black-out."

"Watch me," she said, and she blew a perfect smoke ring. It wafted in the air over towards the doctor, as if the smoke itself was defying his orders.

I explained to the newcomers what seemed to be happening, and they took it in seriously, not doubting a word of my testimony. Rollo scratched at the wound on his shoulder every few moments, but Stan stood straight-backed and attentive, his pale eyes shining behind his spectacles. They made quite a pair, both rather large, but one looking like a line-backer turned college professor and Rollo resembling a thug from a gangster flick from the thirties.

"And I plan on driving my car back to the front of the hospital, letting everyone get in, and high tailing it out of here," I said, completing my tale.

"I don't think you should be out there alone," Stan said.

"Amen to that," Deena piped in.

"I could come with you; sort of watch your back while you're walking out to the parking lot." He took off his glasses and cleaned them on the front of his shirt.

"To be honest," I said, "I wouldn't mind the company. God only knows what they're planning out there. Does that gun work, or is it only there for decoration?" I gestured to the hand gun on his belt. I couldn't say what it was, having never really paid any attention to guns in my life up to this point. They'd always been something other people needed, but I could tell it was a pistol. There was a clip, not one of those round thingies the bullets get fed into.

Sliding it out of its holster, he spun it on his forefinger cowboy style. The sleek, black metal of the thing shined in the meager light from the moon behind the clouds. If anything ever glinted, this gun did.

"Sure does, and I'm the best shot in the county," he said.

"Second best," Rollo mumbled from across the room. He was holding his shoulder as though it ached, rubbing it.

"That's a matter of personal opinion," Stan said. "Come on, let's go get the car and we can all get the hell out of Dodge and argue marksmanship later."

"And leave behind your patients?" Carmody shouted in wonder. "What'll happen to them?"

"Who cares? They're locked up tight as a drum in Siberia. Somebody would need either my key ring or Rollo's to get in or out of the checkpoint," he said, jangling the big batch of keys at his waist. "Takes two keys for each door, two to get into the guard station and two others to get into the hallway past the station."

"Then they should be fine. Let's go," I said, leaning over and kissing Deena's cheek.

I heard the sudden pounding of the rain against the outside of the building. It sounded really heavy, and I knew it would be leaking into the third story, soaking the third floor even worse. When I glanced outside, I shook my head at the drenching water I'd soon be running through.

"It just figures," Stan said.

Deena looked at me petulantly, then grabbed me by the collar and planted a real kiss on me that sent electric jolts through my body. When she released me, I was practically panting.

"Just in case," she said. "Not that anything's going to go wrong. Nothing's going wrong out there. Just know I love you."

"I love you, too."

"Be careful."

I nodded, and Stan and I moved to the front doorway. Vicki took her keys from a scrunchy around her wristband and unlocked the glass door leading outside. I stepped into the cool night air, instantly soaked by the rain, followed momentarily by the husky security guard. He had his little revolver smashed in between his big hands, held out in front of himself, emulating his hero, Dirty Harry. Somehow, I didn't think he needed both hands for such a small gun, but maybe it made him feel more secure. He glanced around then gestured with his head towards the parking lot, two hundred yards distant. I nodded my assent, and we took off, keeping fairly low to the ground.

By the time we reached the far side of the hospital, where a grassy lawn extended to the tree line on one side and the parking lot on the other, I was feeling the chill of the night air. The rain was freezing, so the temperature had to have dipped down into the low forties at least. I wished I'd brought my coat. In the distance, thunder boomed, sounding like kettle drums.

As we started across the lawn, I heard, or maybe just sensed, something whiz past my left ear. Turning, I saw a rock hit the side of the hospital, taking a small chunk out of some of the bricks. It wasn't a very big rock, no more than two inches across, but it had been hurled with near-lethal force. I was lucky as hell it had missed me.

"That's just a rock?" Stan asked. "Jesus, what're they using to fire it at us? A cannon?"

"Probably slingshots," I said. "They aren't into the whole modern weaponry scene."

"Good thing we have old Bessie here for protection," he said, waving the gun.

Why do men name their weapons? I wondered as I tried to move again.

There was a loud ping and Stan's little revolver dropped to the ground. He swore, shaking his empty hands. Bessie had been tossed somewhere in the darkness at our feet.

"Bastards hit me in the fingers," he swore, shaking the walloped digits. "If they're using slingshots, they're better shots than I am."

He searched the lawn for a moment then retrieved his gun, and we snuck across the grassy area, passing white wrought iron benches and a basketball court that hadn't been used in years, the hoops rusted and missing their nets. On our left, the forest loomed. Tall evergreen trees swayed in the increasing breeze, as though in collusion with the villagers, whispering to them, encouraging them, covering up any sound they might accidentally make as they stalked me. I peered into the trees, and I thought I saw something or someone moving in the darkness, but the foliage was so thick I couldn't be sure. It could've just been the wind. Then again, it could've been an inbred maniac with farm implements.

Or some eight foot long lamprey eel waiting to attach itself to your throat, I thought. I knew it wasn't rational, but the world of science seemed to take a back seat when it came to the close proximity of the primeval woods. In between the swaying conifers and the thorny bushes, superstition reigned supreme over reason. And I was standing on a lawn somewhere between the world of the hospital - the rational - and the world of the villagers - the deep, dark woods. It wasn't a very comfortable feeling, nor was it a safe place to be - mentally or physically.

"What are you waiting for?" Stan asked from several yards closer to the parking lot. He was carrying his revolver daintily, between three fingers on one hand, and he was still shaking the other.

"There's something in the woods," I said.

"Of course there is. Animals, trees, bugs, and probably a lot of crazy-assed bastards wanting to kill us. I don't intend on ending up like Johnson in there. Ow!"

The gun went skittering across the pavement and under a blue Chevy pick-up truck. Stan hissed and started shaking the fingers of his other hand as though trying to dispel a sticky substance.

"Another rock?" I asked.

"Got me right on the middle knuckle of the middle finger. Ow! Goddamnit!"

I saw the next assault when it came, and I rushed forward to try and bat it away from him. Another rock, at least three inches around with sharp, angular edges, hit him in his right temple. Blood oozed from a two inch cut, and I saw, during one of the brighter lightning flashes, that he was sliced pretty deep. It might even need stitches, and I told him so.

"Little ignorant shits," he screamed at the woods. Another volley whizzed past his head, then one caught me in the side, stinging much worse than I'd expected. Looking down, I saw the rock had torn my shirt, leaving a hole I could slip three fingers into.

"Let's get the damn car and get out of their target area, somewhere they can't hit us," Stan shouted, then cursed when another missile smashed into his neck.

"Mine's the red Civic," I shouted over the wind, hearing another stone fly by my head, too close for comfort.

He started for the car at a run, but I stopped when I heard something from the woods, a voice calling my first name. I trembled a little with the recognition of Pa McCoy's dulcet tones, but I stopped for a moment, effectively distracted. The attack with the rocks stopped, as well. For a moment.

"Gaskell!" came the voice from the woods, echoing between the white birches. "I can see you. I say, I can seeeeee yoooouuu."

His voice bounced off the solid trunks of the trees, so I couldn't get a fix on where it was coming from. The evergreens swished in the developing wind, whispering to me.

whisper whisper whisper...

"Ignore it," Stan said. "Let's get the damn car. "A large stone smacked into Stan's temple where he'd already been wounded once, dropping him to his knees. It made a crunching sound as it hit him, and I was afraid the villagers had broken his skull. He clutched his head in his hands, moaning as I ran over to him. When I saw the rock on the ground, the one which had struck him, I whistled. It was at least five inches long, and it had to weigh a pound and a half.

Who was strong enough to use a slingshot with something that big?

The answer came to me - someone who's insane. Someone with an agenda. Someone on a mission from his imaginary god.

"Oh, my fucking head," he groaned, trying to get to his knees, but slipping on the wet ground. "What'd they hit me with? A cannonball?"

"Just a really big rock," I said, helping him to his feet. "Are you okay?"

Blood was trickling from a wound near his right eye, and a second laceration at the side of his face was leaking at a steadier rate. Bruising was already darkening the skin to a rich plum color at his temple, where his hair went gray.

"Hurts like a son of a bitch, but I can still make it. You realize, they're just playing with us?"

"This is playing?"

"Hey, if they wanted us dead, they could easily kill us," he answered. "You see where my gun went?"

I remembered it clattering across the pavement, and I got on my knees, searching for it. It had fallen under a pick up, and in a few seconds, I spotted the revolver three lanes down.

"There it is," I said, handing the keys to my car to Stan. "That's my car right there. You start it up, and I'll get the gun. Something tells me we're going to need it tonight."

"Oh, doctor," Pa's voice taunted from the tree line. It wasn't echoing so much, so he must have moved closer to the pavement, away from the tallest of the trees. Closer to me. "Where are ya goin', doctor? Just where the hell do ya think you're gonna run to? Ain't nowhere you can go."

Getting on my hands and knees, I reached under the truck, stretching far enough to grab the gun and pull it close to me. I'd never been a gun person, never owned one in my life, but it sure felt good in my hands at that moment. The steel was cold, even though Stan had been gripping it tightly for several minutes. It hadn't taken long to cool down.

I saw something slide from shadow to shadow within the pine trees at the edge of the woods, and I backed away from the movement. Quickly spinning, I took off for my car. I could see Stan behind the wheel, turning the ignition.

Only there was no sound of an engine roaring to life, no turn-over symphony. Not even the dead clicking sound I always dreaded hearing on cold winter mornings.

I hopped into the passenger seat and slammed the door shut behind me. Pushing down the lock (I was too poor to afford automatic locks, and it was a rare luxury in cars those days), I watched as he pumped the gas and swiveled the key again and again. Nothing.

"Is it dead?" I asked.

"Looks like it," he answered and popped the hood.

I hurried out of the car and looked under the hood of the Honda. Even to my untrained, un-mechanical eyes, the engine was a mess. Belts had been torn from their moorings, filters were slit, several wires had been cut and dangled uselessly, and a rather large puddle of oil was accumulating beneath the front end of the car.

Slamming down the hood, I heard laughter from the woods - not Pa McCoy this time, but several high-pitched voices. The forest rang with the echoes of hysteria, the frenetic giggling of madmen. Or of children. Or of mad children.

"Think that's funny, do you?" I shouted, and the tittering ceased for a moment, only to resume much louder than before five seconds later.

Stan walked around the decimated engine block and clucked his tongue at the damage.

"This isn't going anywhere tonight," he said. "Maybe not for a long, long time."

"What about the other cars?" I suggested. "Have they been vandalized, too?"

We moved to the next car and opened the door. I was leery, because people didn't leave their cars unlocked. Especially, not at the parking lot of a mental institution. Stan pulled the lever, and the hood opened enough for me to slip my fingers into the crack. Exposing the engine, I immediately saw that the villagers had ripped cables from this one, too, and spark plugs lay white and exposed against the top of the battery.

Stan went from car to car, opening them, checking for signs of trouble. After seven cars, the laughter from the woods had grown downright raucous, and we still hadn't located a serviceable vehicle yet.

They want to keep us here, I thought. *They're stopping us from leaving the only way they know how. By disabling all the vehicles.*

And how the hell am I going to explain this to the others, that we're stranded here until someone comes looking for us. No phones. No car to drive away from St. Mike's. No easy escape. Only the woods and the wild people who inhabited them.

"We're not going anywhere tonight, are we?" Stan asked, leaning against a station wagon with four flat tires. "We're trapped here."

I nodded. "Looks that way. Let's get back and tell the others."

While we loped back to the front entrance, I watched the silhouettes of my companions on the other side of the glass. They moved around, shapes with very little form. One of them lay stiff on the floor.

All the way back, I heard the crazed, mocking laughter coming from the woods on all sides of us. The villagers had spread out, surrounding the mental hospital. Now and again, one of them would give a big hooting noise, and the others would crack up at him.

Cutting through it all like a newly sharpened knife, Pa McCoy roared, "Where ya gonna go now, doctor? Where ya gonna go to save yer lily white ass?"

I wanted to shout something witty back to him, return the volley of insults and derision. But, I merely walked back to the front of the hospital, across the lawn, and was let into the building by Vicki. Her keys clinked against the locks as she turned them.

"Where ya gonna go now, ya fuckin' quack?" Pa's voice was muffled by the closed door, but it still chilled me.

And deep inside, I knew he was right. They'd cut off all possible escape routes by disabling the cars. They'd surrounded the building. There were a lot more of them than there were of us, and who knows what kind of weapons they possessed.

I knew that Pa McCoy was right. There was no place else to go.

We were trapped.

Chapter 20

Stan and I shook the rain water off of us canine-style in the foyer, and Deena provided us with paper towels stolen from a bathroom so we could dry ourselves. I hadn't really noticed the rain much while outside, while the villagers spied on me from the safety of the woods. Now, in the relative warmth of St. Mike's, I was beginning to shake, tremors caused by a chill from the rain, the wind, the cool air. Maybe even shock. I dropped into one of the chairs, listening to the air squoosh out of the leather cushion.

"What happened?" Carmody asked. "Where's your car?"

"God, you're bleeding," Vicki said, futzing with Stan's forehead. She whipped a handful of tissues from the vicinity of her bra, and she dabbed at the still-oozing blood. Something in the manner in which she tended to Stan gave away the fact the two had had a prior relationship of some sort. There was a concern in Vicki's eyes as she cleaned the man's face, an emotion that shooed away all the usual sarcasm and grit. Her hardness seemed to melt, and I wondered if they were an item on the sly, akin to Deena and me.

"It's nothing, really," Stan said. "Cavemen bastards are throwing rocks at us."

"You're lucky it wasn't an inch to the side or you'd have lost an eye," Vicki said. "It's still a pretty deep cut. I think you might need some stitches."

"Aw, just plaster it down, and I'll be all right," he said, reaching out and squeezing Vicki's hand. He gave her a patient smile, the smile of someone accustomed to such fawning.

"What happened out there?" Deena asked, wrapping me in her warm arms. I never knew so much heat could emanate from such a small body.

"They've destroyed the cars," I said, shivering. "Cut the lines, slashed tires, tore off belts. We aren't getting out of here in any of those vehicles."

"But, how'd they get into the cars to hurt them? Weren't they all locked up?"

"No. In fact, they were all unlocked. We just got into them and popped the hoods."

"I know for a fact I locked mine," Carmody said, squinting. "I always do. It's a habit from when I lived in the city."

"Same here," Rollo grunted.

"Yeah, well I locked mine, too," Stan said. "It isn't locked now. They got in somehow, some skeleton key, maybe."

I said, "In any case, the movers are due here tomorrow morning, right? To pick up all the boxes and stuff?"

"Yes," Carmody said with a curt nod. "At nine a.m. The price gets lowered if they're late, so I expect them to be on time."

"Well, this isn't going to be a popular idea," I began.

"Oh please tell me you aren't going to say we have to spend the night in this place?" Vicki moaned. Turning to Carmody, she stated, "I think we've just entered triple-time territory."

"I think there's more to worry about than our paychecks," I said, and Carmody nodded. "They're acting vicious, and they're all through the woods. We could hear them out there."

"All fifty of them?" Deena asked.

"Probably," Stan added. "At least, it sounded that way, bunch of crazy bastards."

From the corner of my eye, I thought I saw something in motion by the front door, and I spun, looking out into the darkness. A thin laugh emerged from behind the doors, but the mirthful crazy was nowhere to be seen.

But I did see something for a moment.

A monster.

A ten foot long lamprey eel with rows of teeth ringing its open mouth.

"I am not staying overnight with crazy people on the inside *and on* the outside of this creepy old place," Vicki stammered. "I mean, it isn't fair. I was supposed to have been long gone by the time Johnson here got killed. If I'd have left when I'd had a chance..."

"...you would've probably been killed as well," I finished for her. "These people live by a single mode of thought. They want to bring this Old One, this ancient god they've developed from cave pictures, into our world. They're single-minded in this mission, and I doubt they'll stop at anything to get their preacher back for the ceremony. Whatever it entails."

Vicki glanced down at the corpse on the floor. Someone had draped a white table cloth over the figure while I'd been trying to start my useless car, and blood stains had seeped through areas where she'd been attacked.

"I don't want to end up that way," Vicki said, pointing to the bloody shroud. "Like her. I have kids. They need me. Hey, you think the baby-sitter will get pissed off at my lateness and call the hospital. She wouldn't get an answer, so she'd probably call the cops, right?" When no one answered her, she repeated, "Right?"

"How old is this baby-sitter?" I asked.

"Sixteen."

"Hell," Stan said. "You'll be lucky if she hasn't robbed your house and sold your babies on the black market. Teenagers don't have any ethics when it comes to how they work."

A figure stepped up to the front door, and we watched it limp through the rain. It looked wrong, somehow, but I couldn't put my finger on why until a burst of lightning illuminated the area.

The woman had a regular body, but her arms were missing. Tiny hands sprouted from her shoulders like sea anemones or exotic flowers, the fingers opening and closing, grasping at the air. Her eyes were wild, and her long, untamed hair was plastered to her head, covering the left half of her face. The right half was stained with a dark, wine-colored birthmark.

She pounded on the door a few times with her head, turned to her side and started tapping it with her fingers, her hand squeaking as the fingers scrambled for a grip on the glass.

"She can't get in, right?" Deena asked.

Rollo, who'd been sitting quietly in the corner, scratching at his shoulder wound, stood up and said, "Naw. That whole area's made out of bullet-proof glass. Takes a hell of a wallop to get through that stuff. Plus, it's locked on the outside and on the inside glass door."

"Kind of resembles an aquarium," Deena said.

Lightning burst again, and the woman shoved her face against the glass door, dragging it across the glass, distorting her features. Drool spilled from her lopsided mouth. Her eyes seemed very small, a rodent's uncaring gaze.

Eventually, she moved away from the front of the hospital, stumbling towards the lawn, while rain pelted her head and body.

"What the hell was that?" Vicki asked.

Something made of glass shattered down the hall towards Siberia. Then, silence descended again on the hospital. We waited a second, looked out at the lawn beyond the front doors.

"I think it was a diversion," I said. I was still holding the gun, and, yes, it still felt damn good in my clutches. "They're trying to get in."

"That noise came from the high security ward," Carmody said.

"Where their favorite preacher's being held," I said.

Something thumped above us, then a series of muffled thuds. I looked at the ceiling, and saw tiny cracks forming in the old plaster, cracks that followed the path of the footfalls, opening a little wider with each step the intruder took. Plaster dust rained down upon us.

"They're inside," I said. "Upstairs. Probably came in through the second floor where the ceiling's collapsed."

"At least, one of them is," Deena said.

"Give me back my gun, Doc," Stan said. "You know I can shoot better than you."

I hated to admit it, but he was right. I put the safety on and handed it back to Stan - cowboy style, with a flourish at the end. It was damned impressive, if I say so myself.

"Are you sure that's a person up there?" Deena asked, drawing closer to me. Her eyes followed the crack as it opened across the ceiling.

"Yeah, has to be," I said. "Those damned holes in the roof, where all that water damage is located. They're dropping down from the third floor, and they don't care that we can hear them."

"Oh, they care all right," Carmody said. "They *want* us to hear them. They need to scare us, so we let Gary McCoy go free. Well." Then, he cupped his hands around his mouth, and he screamed, "It isn't going to happen! You hear that, you little shits? I'll never let your preacher loose. He's mine."

Everyone looked at Carmody as if the man had put on a clown suit and broken into a Barbara Streisand medley on a xylophone. Realizing he was overreacting to the intrusion, he looked sheepish.

"Guess I'm a tad overexcited," he said.

"Oh, I guess," Vicki said. "I also suppose you've gone halfway round the bend and all the way past the damned curve. What's wrong with you? You want to take out advertising to show them where we're hiding? Personally, I don't like this place. Too much glass in front." She gestured towards the front entrance and the big windows on either side.

"Nothing can get through that glass," Rollo said, wincing at the pain in his shoulder. It seemed to be getting worse. "Not even a bullet."

"You want to take a chance on that?" Carmody said, sarcastically. "You want to take chances on our lives?"

"Why don't we just hand the little creep back to his people so they can all just get on with their little rock and roll ceremony," Vicki suggested.

"He's a patient of ours," I replied. "Of mine, particularly. We need to protect him from harmful influences, and his father's about the most unsavory character I've ever had the displeasure to meet. They don't get more harmful than that."

"He was scary as hell," Deena said. "Full of righteous indignation and completely convinced he's right about everything."

"So, we need to lock ourselves up somewhere in the hospital they can't access?" Carmody said, steering the whole conversation conveniently back to where it had started. "That's right, isn't it?"

"Yeah," I said. "Someplace that locks really well. Someplace tight."

"No place tighter than Siberia," Rollo said. "No way out except the double doors, and you need locks for both of them. If these bastards get into the building..."

The thumping above our heads from the second floor increased in volume and number. I pointed towards the ceiling.

"Sounds like they're already inside."

"Yeah, well, they won't get through those two doors at the guard station in Siberia. You need our key rings and both keys to get in or out. Pretty damned secure, if you ask me."

"But, we'd be so close to all those...well, scary people," Vicki stammered. "Isn't there one broad who killed her kids with a back hoe? I mean, how safe are you around someone like that?"

"Safer than out here in front of all this glass," I said with a shrug.

"Bullet proof glass, remember," Carmody said. "Supposed to withstand a whole volley of ammunition."

"Have you tested it?" I asked.

"Well, no."

"Then I second the high security ward," I said. "They don't call it high security for nothing, and I'm not comfortable sitting out here on full display for them to see. You all weren't hit with those rocks."

Carmody fussed a bit. "I still don't enjoy the idea of one door being both exit and entrance. What if it gets blocked? We'll be trapped."

"Only till morning," Stan reminded him. "The movers will be here then."

"Maybe we should run for the highway. We could be pretty fast. I still can't believe we're trapped here," Vicki said. "Isolated. Like rats."

Deena added, "I'm not particularly happy about it either, Vicki. But, it looks as if there's no other choice. You want to go out in the dark woods and walk down that road to the highway with all those villagers around you?, You want to step outside surrounded by a bunch of jeering, deformed people who know their way around the forest?"

"Well, if you put it that way-"

Another sound from upstairs - someone dropping to the floor from a height. Then, the villager got up and rushed across the floor, running in several directions, one after another, searching for a way out of the room in which he or she had landed.

" They're coming through that opening in the second floor, some spot just above our heads."

As if in answer, more plaster dust puffed from the widening crack in the ceiling. I was growing leery of that fissure. It looked as though the ceiling could collapse down upon us with the next falling villager.

"That sounded like the third or fourth one," Rollo said. "Intruder, I mean."

"At the least," I affirmed. "How many got through quietly, without drawing our attention to them? How many are already roaming the corridors? What are they doing?"

"Hell with this," Vicki said, turning on a heel and walking towards the high security wing. "I think double locks sound good. I'm heading for Siberia."

There were more noises from the floor above us, random bumps and knocks. A few times, we heard obvious footsteps, running or limping or slapping their way across the upstairs room. Once, when we readied ourselves to move to the high security wing, we heard one person, a child perhaps, giggle hysterically. They were soon joined by several other voices, laughing and braying along, and I knew we didn't have much time before they streamed into the lobby and found us.

"They're getting ready," I said.

"For what?" Deena asked.

"Hell if I know, but it sounds as though they've been preparing something and it's done and they're about to move to the next step. I'm a little afraid that next step is going to involve doing something to us. I'm not about to wait for them to come down and cut our damn throats or whatever their plans involve."

"We're going now?" Carmody asked, looking at the paperwork still laid out upon the desk top. "And we're just leaving everything unboxed down here?"

"Screw the boxes," Rollo said, and I noticed he was still rubbing his shoulder. On some level, that disturbed me as much as the invasion of the hospital. "Stan and I have the keys. We're heading to the west wing. You all can either come with us or wait out here."

"I'm with you," I said.

"Me too," Deena said.

"I was just saying..." Carmody began.

"Look," Rollo explained. "You are with us or not. It's that goddamn simple."

"But, maybe we should..."

"Then stay here alone. See if I care," Rollo continued, and he started down the hallway. "Fucking doctors."

Carmody opened his mouth to argue, but thought better of it. Shaking his head at the mess Vicki had left at her station, he joined us as we moved down the hall, away from the offices and the front door.

We could hear the shouting even before we reached the double locked doors, angry and frightened shrieks coming from the patients in the high security wing.

"What's going on?" I said, speeding up my pace.

The others moved swiftly behind me, keeping tempo with my quickened stride. As we reached the doors, Stan and Rollo whipped out their keys and started unlocking the first glass door. When they opened it, the cacophony increased in volume - desperate cries for help, terrified screams from beyond the second door. It sounded exactly as you'd imagine old Bedlam would have sounded during its most notorious days.

"They're scared to death," Deena said. "Haven't they been medicated today?"

Stan nodded. "Yeah, exactly like usual. We didn't alter anything in the least."

"Then they shouldn't be so disturbed," Carmody said. "They should be quiet and sedate."

The screeches grew louder, almost animalistic in their fury. Some of them were pounding on walls or throwing themselves against the padding.

We stepped, as a group, into the cubicle between the two doors. Deena sat on the corner of the guard's desk. Rollo and Stan locked the first door behind us and moved to the next one, using two different keys to unfasten the bolts. We were cramped in the small, empty guard station, with all the accouterments and electronics cartoned up and stacked in the corner.

When they opened the second door, the one leading into the hallway of the eastern wing, the caterwauling magnified into a symphony of horror - loud, desperate cries, gibbering, phrases shouted over and over again, each sound piled atop the others until I could barely hear myself think.

I shouted at the others, "Follow me. Something serious is happening to our patients in here."

"No shit," Vicki screeched back, lighting a cigarette. "I thought it was a party."

"Stay close to me," I said as Rollo and Stan pulled their weapons.

And we stepped out of the guard station and into an aural Hell.

Chapter 21

With the two guards leading the way, the rest of us followed. I held Deena under my arm, and Vicki fell in behind us, cigarette trembling in her red-painted fingers, a last grip on reality, and Dr. Carmody pulled up the rear. We were a motley group, and we probably would've looked ridiculous to an observer.

But there were no observers, except for the screeching men and women locked in their cells. The sound was as loud and invasive as a hurricane, whirling around us, surrounding us with chaos and horror.

At the first door, I peered through the window, staring at the woman in the room. She was ancient, at least seventy years old, with long gray hair and sagging, wrinkled breasts. She wore no clothes, and she was trying to claw her way through the padding of the wall. Her fingernails were broken and bleeding, smearing crimson across the white leather we used to enhance the safety within cells of the violently disturbed. Her mouth was a black hole, without a tooth left in it. She was shrieking, slobbering down her chin.

And she had a six inch piece of flesh missing from her shoulder.

"Jesus Christ," Carmody cried.

The woman saw us, and she spun to the door, screaming for help. As she got closer, I could see that the wound was ragged around the edges and almost perfectly circular - just as though she'd been bitten by a giant lamprey eel and the muscles of her shoulder torn loose and devoured. A knob of bone gleamed obscenely white in the center of the bleeding orifice.

"What did that to her?" Vicki asked.

Deena looked at me, and I could tell she was thinking the same thing I was - that this woman was another victim of the floating monsters from Gary McCoy's imagination.

But, *imaginary* beasts don't chow down on people, leaving bleeding, oozing wounds.

I moved hurriedly to the next cell and peered through the window. A man stared back at me from where he was sitting in the corner, Indian style. Long claw marks had gouged out flesh from his left cheek, down his face and neck, and trailed off along his shoulder. Blood pooled beneath him, and he mumbled some soft mantra to himself. He was definitely in a state of shock, blindly attempting to protect himself from whatever was attacking him.

"This one's hurt, too," I said. "Something clawed him in the face."

Deena had moved to the cell across the hall, and she nodded back to me. "This one looks bitten, only in his leg. He's limping around his room, holding it, but there's a lot of blood smeared everywhere."

Carmody walked to another cell, and he saw the woman inside of it. "Good Lord," he whispered. "Look at this."

We clustered around the little window and watched through the interlacing chicken wire. A young woman, no more than twenty years of age, lay on her bed. The sheets and mattress were suffused with blood, soaked through to the dripping point, and there were bite marks of varying sizes all over her naked torso. Something had taken its fill of her, eating most of her stomach, leaving a gaping hole through which it had pulled her intestines. As I watched, several drops of blood fell from the soaked mattress and spattered to the floor. It looked as though every inch of the uncarpeted floorboards were obscured by gore.

"Is she dead?" Rollo asked.

"Of course she is," Carmody grumbled. "Something's eating her."

"Oh, Christ...look!" Stan said, and he covered his eyes, turning away from the sight of her.

I shined my flashlight into the room, and I could see the woman's body lurch to the left, and dozens of holes appeared in her white flesh. The holes grew larger, and something tugged on her corpse again, dragging it to the edge of the bed. Then, the flesh in the center of the rings of holes tore away, and I realized I was watching some invisible creature taking a bite out of the woman. Something else grabbed the end of her exposed colon and yanked it further from her body.

"It's eating her while we watch," Deena said.

"I can't understand..." Carmody said, shaking his head. "It's not possible."

Another ring of punctures appeared on the woman's throat, almost a foot in diameter. The shape of these new wounds was very different from the others, as though the invisible mouth was set on its side, a long slit an inch across but several inches long.

"See," I said. "The holes are teeth marks in her flesh. Soon, it'll bite down, separating the flesh from her body, eating it..."

That's exactly what happened. The bite of flesh disappeared into something's indiscernible gullet.

We pin-balled between each of the small rooms down Siberia's hallway, looking through the windows in the doors, watching the people trapped inside their cells being consumed by Gary's dream monsters. Some only had a few scratches, the marks of long, thin claws. Others had entire pieces of their anatomy missing. One man had had the top of his head bitten off, and, as we watched, his brains were disappearing - wolfed down by another invisible creature.

"I believe we can say that Gary McCoy's been seeing something real," I said. "This is no hallucination."

"McCoy!" Deena shouted. "What about him?"

She took off for his cell, last on the left, and she slid on the freshly mopped floor when she reached his window. Peeking through the glass, she motioned for the rest of us to join her, but we were already nearly there. I put my head next to hers, and our ears touched as I looked into the room. I felt Carmody anxiously watching over my left shoulder.

Gary McCoy sat on the edge of his bed, his head in his hands, hair falling forward over his long fingers, apparently unmolested. His shoulders were quivering, as though he was laughing or crying - I couldn't tell - but there didn't seem to be any wounds on his body. There was no pond of crimson on the floor.

"He's okay. They aren't touching him," I said, sighing with relief. "Can we get him out of there?"

Carmody warned, "You can't let a dangerously schizophrenic patient out of his cell as though he was joining a tea party."

"Hey, Steven," I said. "In case you haven't noticed, the monsters are real. We aren't dealing with hallucinations or delusions any longer. These things are feeding upon our patients like this whole hallway is an all you can eat buffet, and we might be next. So far, everything that young man's told us has been truthful - the cave, the village, the monsters. Maybe, he knows how to put a stop to them. Maybe, he knows how to protect us."

"I don't know if I want to take that chance."

"Well, you don't have a lot of say in the matter, doc, 'cause I'm freeing him," Rollo said, and he and Stan unlocked the door with their two necessary keys. "He's the only one I see in here who hasn't been bitten, so obviously he knows something."

"Or the creatures are staying away from him until he gets the Old One into our dimension," Deena said. "Some kind of an understanding between two parties in a contract."

Rollo swung the door open, and Gary looked up at us. His eyes were limned with black circles, and I could tell he hadn't slept well, despite the drugs we'd pumped into him. With as much Thorazine as he had circulating in his bloodstream, he should be lethargic, at best. As a matter of fact, he looked wired, antsy, and scared half to death.

"They're here," he said softly. "The invisible swimmin' monsters are all around us."

"Why haven't they bitten you, Gary?" I asked.

He laughed, looked up at me with a glassy stare. "Because," he said, as though explaining something to a small child. "I'm the Preacher. I'm the chosen one."

"What about us?" Deena asked. "Will they harm us?"

"You're not the Preacher, so, yes. Of course they's gonna hurt ya. They's gonna feast on yer bones, taste yer eyes, squirm in between yer organs."

A scream erupted from the next room, which ended suddenly with a disgusting gurgling noise. I looked into that cell and saw a man pulled from his bed by something hidden from my view. His skin was being flayed from his body by sharp, invisible claws.

Carmody shouted, "I want to get out of here. Right this goddamned minute!"

"And get killed by one of the villagers?" I asked.

"Well, at least I can see them," he answered, and he made a lot of sense. "At least I won't be fighting some supernatural invisible monster. How do you fight something like that?"

"Gary," I said, kneeling next to him. He smelled of body odor and halitosis. "Gary, buddy, how can we protect ourselves from these things? Is there something we can do to stop them from biting us? Some potion or incantation?"

He shook his head. "No siree Bob. They's gettin' stronger all the time, gettin' closer and closer to this world. Have ya seen 'em? Just outta the corner of yer eyes, have ya seen 'em?"

I nodded. "Yeah, I think I have."

He looked me up and down then smiled a crooked, sardonic smile. His teeth looked even browner than the day before, if that was possible. He shook his head knowingly at me.

"Aw, you seen 'em, and you know it, too. Surprised you didn't see 'em even better, many as there are floatin' around right now. Like they've all come out for a party."

"You see all three kinds of monsters?" Deena asked. "The eels, the fox things, and the bats?"

"All them and more besides. There are things 'round now that I ain't *never* seen before, and the worlds are leakin' into each other - leakin' good, and all sorts of critters are swimmin' into this one. I think they're here to meet the god when he comes through."

"Groupies for the Old One?" I asked, chuckling despite the tension. Or maybe because of it.

A scream erupted behind us, and when I turned, I saw streams of blood pouring out from under four of the doors in the hallway. Then, the hallway was silent, and more crimson trails oozed from under the doors of the rest of the rooms. The floor in the middle of the hallway was becoming one huge sanguine puddle.

"I think they're all dead," Deena whispered. "Every one of them."

"Poor bastards," Rollo muttered. "Didn't have a fucking chance."

The silence was terrifying. None of us moved, watching the gory remains of our patients seep across the hallway, the blood of one patient intermingling with that of another.

"Is anyone else here disturbed by the fact that we're still okay while all those poor people are dead?" Vicki asked. "I mean, what's stopping the sons-a-bitches from eating us? Not that I'm complaining, you understand."

Turning back to Gary, who met my gaze with a sort of ferocious audacity, I asked, "Yeah, why aren't they attacking us?"

He giggled like a child, put his hands over his off-color, rotten teeth.

"Why?" he asked through his stained fingers. The word seemed to ooze between them.

The blood in the hallway had covered nearly the entire tiled floor behind us, and Vicki and Deena moved closer to the brick wall that terminated the hallway, trying to keep their feet out of it.

"Yeah," Rollo said, and I saw he was rubbing that shoulder again. I wondered what the wound looked like now, if it was infected with some inter-dimensional virus, red veins of septicemia networking across his skin. "Why?"

"'Cause," McCoy said, looking straight into my eyes, "they just ain't started on you yet."

"Oh, my God, look!" Deena screamed, pointing to the lake of blood in the center of the hallway.

I turned, and I saw what she was pointing towards. Something was moving through the red liquid on the floor, probably many different things by the profusion of activity in the blood. Footprints, disturbances, and trails could be seen moving through the layer of gore, evidence of the imperceptible creatures' presence, of their direction and intent. The movements through the blood headed closer to us.

"They're coming this way," I shouted.

I saw oblong footprints stomping down the hallway towards us, surrounded by slithering tracks, as though snakes were winding their way through the carnage.

"That's 'cause they *just* noticed ya," McCoy said, and he started that horrible, high-pitched laughing again. "It's feedin' time!"

I searched for an exit, but, as I noticed earlier, the hallway ended in a dead end of a brick wall. There was only one way out, and it awaited us on the other side of the blood and the monsters. I saw the footprints of something huge ambling closer to us through the beam of my flashlight, something with three legs that moved in jerky, twisting actions.

"I think we're going to have to run through them," I said, pointing back to the guard station. "That's our only hope of getting out of here alive."

"Not much of a hope," Carmody mumbled.

"Then, you come up with a better idea," I shouted, getting angry with his pessimism. "Or do we just wait here to die like all those poor bastards locked in their cells. They didn't go anywhere. They couldn't, and look what happened to them. You want to just wait here and get eaten?"

"Screw this noise. Let's roll," Stan said, and he took off, hurrying through the tacky spillage on the floor. His sneakers made squelching noises in the blood. I was a little surprised by his abrupt action - the man was all forward momentum with no thought behind his initiative. I didn't know whether to admire him or condemn his lack of reflection.

"What about him?" I asked, pointing to Gary, who still scrunched himself in the corner of his cell, his eyes darting about the room madly. "Are we going to leave him to the same fate as the others?"

"Hell with him," Stan said. "Those things aren't going to hurt him. He brought them here."

Deena warned, "They're getting closer."

A quick glimpse of the hallway showed me the disturbances in the layer of blood were, indeed, approaching us quickly. A squirming writhing thing, making multiple tentacle-like trails through the blood inched nearer. Crimson splashes spattered the walls with little red dots, evidence of the monsters' determination.

"Okay, then this is it," I shouted, and I grabbed Deena's hand.

I had expected to feel something when we ran through the corridor, through the unseen bodies of the things lurking on the opposite side of a thin inter-dimensional wall - a cool wind fanning on my face, a chill in the air - but the atmosphere seemed undisturbed. Looking behind me, I noted the others moving slower, with a lot more trepidation, and I shouted out a few words of encouragement to them.

"It's okay. I don't think they can reach us while moving."

I saw Gary McCoy's face get close to the window of his room, his breath fogging against the cool glass. His unmatched eyes gleamed beneath the beam of my wavering flashlight, and his teeth were exposed in what appeared to be a snarl. I turned the light around and rushed for the guard station.

Deena and I arrived together, stopping next to a panting Rollo, and we had to wait a few seconds as Stan reached us. Keys rattling in his hands, he shoved us rudely aside and fitted the metal into the locks. Rollo was at his side in an instant, matching the other guard's motions. Behind them, I could hear Vicki and Carmody hurrying, then a loud splash as Vicki slipped in the blood and fell jarringly to the floor.

"Shit!" she cried, and I saw Carmody attempting to haul her back to a standing position. "Oh God! God! This is disgusting."

Rollo pushed the door open and held it as Deena and I entered the small station that separated Siberia from the rest of the hospital. I turned, offered them more light, and I was in time to see Carmody push Vicki in front of himself. She stumbled into the little room, the entire lower half of her body covered in gore from where she'd stumbled. Her face registered disgust and the advent of shock, her eyes starting to glaze over. Her small hands flicked at the red stains on her uniform, ineffectually trying to erase them from her person.

Stan stepped into the station, and Carmody started to follow him, but the older man was yanked back into the hallway as though he had a chain tied around his middle that was jerking him backwards. He made a small sound, not quite a scream, and he fell in a pile onto the floor in the hallway. Blood splashed around him, rippling with his impact. Climbing to his knees, he looked up at our group, his arms and legs suffused with the bodily fluids of his former patients.

"Help me," he shouted, pushing himself up on his arms.

Rollo started for him, but a hole abruptly appeared in Dr. Carmody's back, and he arched like a cat as cloth and flesh was torn from his trapezoid muscles. The flesh disappeared, but I thought, just for a moment in the faint light, I saw it disappearing down the gullet of some great eel, teeth spinning as though on rotors, its lips divided into five separate petal-esque appendages. The beast faded as quickly as it materialized, and I wondered if it had just been my imagination.

Carmody fell back to the floor, his spinal column exposed to the beams of our flashlights.

He screeched, high and inhumanly loud. A chunk of tissue was scooped from his cheek, revealing his back molars and the gleam of his white jaw bone. His head crashed to the floor, and something pulled on his feet, dragging him through the blood of his worst patients, until he was almost out of the beam of our flashlights near the brick wall.

Realizing I'd been holding my breath during the entire assault, I gasped. I heard several people screaming. Stan was slamming the door shut, the only person with enough self-control to get something solid between us and the things eating our friend and boss.

Pieces were sliced from Carmody's body, but it was mostly obscured by the darkness. We could still witness, however, his corpse jerking and quivering with every bite and slash the creatures made in his flesh. I also heard the sound of tearing muscle and gristle, just before something came flying at the bullet proof glass that had been locked between us and the terrible scene we were watching.

"Oh God, oh my God," Vicki cried.

"It's an arm," Rollo said, pointing to the crimson streak on the glass where the thrown object had made contact. "Fuck me, it's Carmody's arm."

"They're real," Deena said in a low voice. "They're all real. This whole damn thing is really happening, isn't it?"

I could tell she was getting close to the precipice that would drop her into a night of sheer madness, and I shook her by her shoulders. Her head bobbed back and forth, but when she looked back at me, her eyes seemed to be focusing again. I clasped her close to me, feeling the security of another warm body next to mine, a familiar body, a reassuring body.

Vicki, however, was visibly shivering, clutching her arms across her large breasts. Her gaze was locked to the scene of carnage at the other end of Siberia, but her eyes glazed over with a thin membrane of hopelessness. I went to her and tried rubbing my hands along her body, and Deena saw what I was doing and emulated my motions. Vicki didn't seem to notice the two of us.

"You got a blanket in here?" I asked Stan. "She's going into shock, and we need to get her warm again."

"There's some in the hallway closet," he answered, cocking his head in the direction we'd just left. "Sheets and stuff, too."

"We'll have to fetch some to get her warm," I said. "Open the door."

"Over my dead body," Rollo said. "We're safe now - safe here. Always liked the feeling I got in the guard station. It's very secure in here. We're staying, not letting those things inside."

"They'll come in if they want," I explained, trying to keep my voice low and controlled, even though I wanted to let loose with screams of fear and anger. "They got into every patient's room here, even though they were locked."

"Maybe, maybe they went in before," he said. "Maybe they were already in there. Hell, even if they can get in here, we aren't gonna help them gain access. If you try to open that door, doc, I'm going to have to kill you."

He removed his revolver from his belt. I tried to recall how many bullets he'd already used, but I had no idea. Deciding to cut my losses, I moved back to Vicki, rubbing her arms and shoulders, laying her down on the floor. Deena glanced up at me, and her look told me not to take any unnecessary chances. She didn't want to be alone during this ordeal.

"They're tearing him to shreds," Stan said, pointing his gun at the hallway leading to Gary McCoy's room. "Carmody, the poor bastard. Not my favorite guy in the world, but no one deserves to be ripped apart like that while they're still alive. If it comes to that, I'm popping myself. I'll save a bullet for the job. Anyone else want to join me? I'll save ammo for anyone else who doesn't want to go the same way."

"No," I said, and Deena shook her head.

"I don't know about you all," Rollo said. "But I don't plan on dying. I met those things once, and I came out alive." He rubbed his shoulder and a grave look shadowed his face. "They aren't going to finish me off."

"Anyone have any ideas?" Deena asked, rubbing her way down Vicki's leg. Her hands were sticky with blood, but she was maintaining her composure like a real trooper. I was incredibly proud of her at that moment..

"About getting out of here?" Rollo asked.

"What else? Yeah."

"Let's see," I said. "We have invisible monsters eating everyone on one side, crazy religious fanatic rednecks on the other side. I don't know which is worse."

Rollo looked down the sights of his gun. "I can see the rednecks. They make better targets than those invisible bastards."

Vicki's body was starting to react to our machinations, and a bit of warmth started spreading through her limbs. Her eyes, however, remained closed, her breathing shallow.

"I agree with Rollo. I say we take our chances with the villagers," Deena said.

"Second that," Stan said, watching as another piece of Steven Carmody flew at the window and splatted against it. This time, the red and white flesh was unrecognizable as any specific part of him. It was just a large chunk of flesh and fat.

"I think I'm going to throw up," Deena said, gagging at the disgusting sight.

"Don't you dare puke in my station," Rollo warned. "I gotta work here."

"Well, not anymore," Stan said.

"Take our chance with the villagers? Sounds good to me," I said. "Any bright ideas where we can hole up and hide until morning when the movers show up with vans? That's really all we have to do - make it till morning when transportation out of here arrives."

"How about one of our offices?" Deena suggested. "Mine's closest past the front door."

"I don't know. I still say we're pretty safe here," I said. "We should sit still, nice and quiet."

"Hell no," Rollo grumbled. "Too close to those invisible things for my comfort."

"And I really think it'd be better away from all that blood," Deena said. "And the sound of them eating. The chewing - it's making me nauseous."

"Are we all agreed, then? Head for Dr. Bierce's office?"

Vicki mumbled something. I slapped her cheeks a few times, not too hard, but enough to sting. Her eyes opened, and I saw a bit of the old fire still encamped in there.

"What the hell are you doing to me?" she asked. "Copping a feel?"

"She's back," I said, and Deena laughed, leaning back against the desk. "How are you feeling, Vicki?"

"Shitty, as if I've been diced, sliced, and pureed. I guess I didn't bite the big one, huh?"

"Still in the land of the living," I said.

"And Dr. Carmody? He was right behind me. I don't see him in here. Oh, don't tell me..."

I nodded. "They took him apart. What's left of him is back there in the hallway."

"Steven, you stupid little shit," she said, and the tears started dripping from her eyes. "Had to stop and save my fat ass, didn't you? Couldn't just get to a safe place."

"We're going to try to get to my office and hole up there until morning," Deena explained. "Away from those things."

"And away from that crazy piece of shit who started all this," she said. "That little fucker isn't dying, is he? I hate him. I hate him for bringing all this here to us." She looked over at Deena. "Your office? Sounds all right to me."

"Then, let's do it," Deena said.

Rollo and Stan slid their keys into the respective locks and positioned themselves against the door. They had their guns in their hands, prepared for violence. Rollo nodded once, and they flung the door wide and removed their keys, shoving them back into their pockets.

Behind us, down the dark hallway of Siberia, something slammed against a wall with a loud crashing sound. Focusing my flashlight beam, I saw Gary McCoy walk out of his now open room. His door had flown open and slammed so hard into the brick wall that it had shattered several of the bricks and lodged itself at an angle in the mortar. Dust swirled around in the air, and McCoy looked directly at me, an evil grin on his face.

"You city folk think you're so damn smart," he said, and I could hear him as plain as day through the door, through the bullet proof glass. "I'm the Preacher. I can do more 'n you ever put a mind to."

"How'd he get the door open," Deena asked.

McCoy stepped slowly towards us, his bare feet sinking into the drying blood on the floor. Passing Carmody's remains, he kicked at the corpse. Several ribs broke loose and skittered across the hallway towards us. Nothing attacked him. No monsters even seemed to be moving through the drying viscera, as though they'd all flown away and disappeared into their own worlds.

"I'm the goddamned Preacher," he shouted, the veins standing out on his forehead and neck. They seemed to throb in the meager light from our flashlights. "I do what I want. I get what I want, and I want out of this fucking place right now!"

As he moved towards the guard station, stepping closer to us, the locked doors to the dead patients' rooms swung open with fury, clanging into the brick walls, raising more mortar dust. Our flashlight beams could barely pierce the swirling motes. After a few more steps, the doors on either side of Gary swung open.

"He's going to open this one," I said. "Get moving. Now! Now!"

Stan and Rollo took off down the dark hallway towards the front desk, their lights bobbing with their motion.

I leaned over and kissed Deena, listening to McCoy's booming laughter behind us.

"Come on," I said. "Let's barricade your office."

"I love you."

"I know," I said, starting to run. "I love you, too. So much, Deena."

I don't know if she heard me. She was holding Vicki's hand and running by my side.

The door behind us flew open, and the hospital was filled with the stench of new corpses and congealing gore. It filled my head like thick paint filling a canister, only dizzying and sickly sweet.

I never ran so fast in my life.

Chapter 22

It was extremely dark in the hallway, and I followed Rollo and Stan's bouncing flashlight beams. My own light mostly caught flash-capture images of their backs and their pumping arms as they ran. A lot of the time, all I could see were the painted plaster walls, a sickly green almost hidden in the darkness.

When we arrived at the front desk, I saw the storm was raging full blast outside, replete with lightning brightening the desk area so much it seemed like daytime. Thunder rumbled deeply, ominously, and I wondered how long this cacophony had been going on. How long had this storm been blowing itself against the hospital? I hadn't heard anything - no thunder, no pounding rain - since we had arrived in Siberia. I'd forgotten all about it, truthfully.

But in the reception area, the place seemed to vibrate with electricity from the thunderclouds. The frequent blazes of lightning gave the whole thing a sinister quality, and I saw something at the front doors, illuminated by the crackling in the sky.

Four people, sodden, barely clothed, and each terribly disfigured, pressed their faces against the glass windows. One of them was gesticulating with his / her / its left arm, which didn't seem to have any bones in it. The appendage flapped wildly in the wind like a gigantic earthworm. All of the little audience were silhouetted against the glass, their eyes long, dark patches beneath protruding brows.

One of them, a child of about seven or eight by all appearances, reached down and picked up a rock. As more of the deformed villagers joined the initial four, the child began slamming the rock against the bullet-proof glass. It didn't break, but the action did manage to give a similar idea to all of the other people arriving at the doors. Soon, they were all clutching stones and slamming them into the glass. I knew it was safe, the glass didn't break when shot with a bullet, so a bit of a pounding wasn't going to crack it.

But how long can it sustain against such a barrage? I wondered. How long until it shatters and they all began creeping or limping or crawling in here on their diseased, broken limbs?

"Come on!" insisted Deena, pulling me away from the desk.

Vicki seemed to be taking in the way her work station appeared in the thunderstorm. The shadows of the front door's assailants were cast over the room by the insane lightning behind them, skinny and elongated, arms reaching as though to snatch something off the desk top. She looked around, disturbed, her eyes flitting this way then that way.

Deena yanked her along with me, the sound of rocks smashing against the (please God) impermeable glass. "Come on," she said, and Vicki started running again, looking over her shoulder at where she used to sit every day and welcome guests.

I knew what she was feeling. The hospital wasn't the same old St. Mike's without the lights brightly illuminating the passages. It fell back to being Saint Michael's Mental Hospital, a creepy old building with feeble Bedlam aspirations. Things looked more dangerous, and they also, oddly, appeared emptier. Our footsteps echoed louder than in the daylight, and my thoughts were never so jumbled or suspicious.

Not that the situation was helping my ruminations. I could feel the blood pumping through my ears, loud and full of adrenaline. My heart felt as though it would burst.

"Wait a second," I shouted.

Deena stopped with Vicki. "We don't have time, Bob. Come on."

"There's whiskey hidden at your desk, isn't there, Vicks?"

She nodded. "Yeah."

"This isn't the time for a drink," Deena warned. Rollo and Stan were getting farther away from us. The pounding on the glass grew louder as even more monstrously deformed villagers took up positions outside of it.

"Oh, I think if there was *ever* a time to drink, this would be it," I said. "Where's the bottle?"

Vicki turned and rushed back to her desk, reached behind some folders and retrieved a fifth of Jack Daniels. She shoved a few binders aside and pulled out a bottle of Southern Comfort.

"Nice," I said with a grin.

"Hold on," she said.

Digging deep behind the files in the bottom drawer of her file cabinet, the nurse produced a half-full quart of

Bacardi Rum, 151 Proof. I looked at her in admiration. She'd been drinking alcohol this powerful and had managed to still do her job. She had to have been soused.

With a shrug, she said, "It gets me through the day."

She held the rum while I clutched a bottle of whiskey in each hand. I could almost feel the delicious tingling of the drink through my fingers, as though I were soaking up the alcohol by osmosis. I was sure I could smell it, even though the bottles were capped.

In that moment, holding two bottles of whiskey close to my chest, I forgot to hold Deena's hand. It was as though some other part of me, some primal core of myself that needed that drink more than it needed *anything*, was dictating my movements. It told me to hurry to Deena's office, to lock the doors, and to start gulping down the liquor as fast as I could. That was my only way of escaping the horror of the situation around me. That was the only way I could take flight.

And Deena was no longer quite so important in this other person's plan. She'd been relegated to someone who could help carry more bottles, someone who was behind me in the dark hallway, someone who could help if things ever went more askew.

She was no longer *my* Deena, no longer *my* fiancée.

She was merely a woman with more booze for later.

I stopped for a moment, realizing where my thoughts had been running. I knew it was the alcohol doing my thinking for me, allowing my conscience to be soaked through with its influence. Within only a few seconds, the booze had changed me back into that pre-Deena lush, the guy who put his drinking ahead of everything else.

The bottle seemed very heavy in my hand now. Looking over at Deena, I saw her helping Vicki away from the desk, but the woman was too heavy for her. Still, she was trying to support the nurse under her arm, straining with the effort.

"Jesus Christ," I said, and I almost tossed the bottle away from myself.

It had enough of a grip on me to prevent me from doing so, but I'd come to some of my senses. I moved to the other side of Vicki and put her arm around my shoulder. The fifth of Jack Daniels was in her left hand, temptingly close to my mouth. I wanted to lick the glass in case some of it had spilled and left a residue.

I didn't. I supported my friend and caught Deena's eye. She smiled at me, and I was certain she knew exactly what intoxicating drama had just unspooled within my stupid brain. Together, we moved again, away from the desk, into the dark hallway.

As we rushed away from the front entrance area, we were once again enshrouded in complete darkness. The lack of windows added to the claustrophobic feeling, and every so often, the corner behind us would be illuminated briefly by flashes of lightning.

Deena's hand in mine was reassuring, and I wondered how she was holding up so well under all the pressure. I was on the verge of hysterics, of uncapping all three bottles of alcohol and chugging them down like a maniac, and Vicki appeared to have passed that point hours ago. Rollo and Stan were big, tough guys, so I expected them to be brave and level headed under violent conditions, but I was surprised by Deena's self-assurance. Of course, it could've all been an act, a false face to propel me and Vicki to our destination where we could be safer.

But, I didn't think it was. She was my rock. She was a rock for all of us.

Within seconds we'd passed the stairwell, blocked off so people wouldn't wander into that dangerous area, and arrived at the office. I was the last one inside, pushing Vicki ahead of me, and Rollo slammed the door shut after I entered. Vicki lay down on the leather sofa at the other end of the room, putting her hands over her eyes.

"I can't believe this is happening," she said. She was sounding dangerously close to hysterics again. "I just can't believe it."

"We'll be all right," Deena said, scanning the room with her flashlight.

The rest of us did so, as well. We didn't see anything, but the place was full of ominous shadows that blocked out whole corners. Without getting on our hands and knees to search every crevice, we were assured the place was empty.

Stan started hauling the file cabinet towards the door, and he shouted, "Hey, someone give me a hand with this."

I helped him, dragging the heavier than expected empty cherry wood cabinet and placing it in front of the door. Next, we grabbed Deena's desk, a big mahogany monster, and we placed it next to the cabinet. Before long, we'd stacked most of the heavy furniture in front of the door, blocking entry from the outside. I wished we had some boards so I could nail us into the room, ala *Night of the Living Dead*.

After all the activity, we rested. I sat next to Vicki and took a quick reading of her pulse. It was extremely rapid, no big surprise, but it didn't seem abnormal given the circumstances. I'm sure my blood pressure was raging.

I had placed the three bottles of Vicki's on top of the desk, across the room from me, and my eyes kept drawing towards them. Deena squeezed my hand, informing me that it was all right. I was doing fine without a drink. I didn't need it as I had believed.

But, Christ, she didn't know how much I wanted to taste that whiskey's burn in my stomach.

"Are we safe in here?" Deena asked.

There was a long pause before Stan answered, "As safe as anywhere in the building, I suppose. After seeing what's waiting outside the front door, I don't relish being outside, either."

"I don't know about anyone else," Vicki said, standing and walking over to the desk. She picked up the fifth of Jack Daniels and spun the cap off in a well-practiced single motion. "But I could use a slug or two."

She put her mouth to the opening of the bottle and drank deeply - two, three, four swallows. Then, she pulled it away from her lips, wiped them with the back of her hand, and gave a sigh of utter, resigned satisfaction. I could smell the whiskey, could nearly taste it in the air, molecules of the stuff tempting me.

"I could use a shot," Rollo said, and Vicki handed him the bottle. Stan also took a sip, wincing at the searing liquid as it hit his stomach.

"Whoo," he grinned. "Haven't had decent whiskey in a long time. That'll bolster up the courage."

"Give me another bolster, will you?" Vicki asked, holding her hand out. She took another slug and glanced over at me. She waved the bottle at me. "You want some, Bob? I think even A. A. would understand."

I wanted that drink so badly I was practically licking my lips. The waving motion Vicki was utilizing only seemed to tempt me more, and it took everything I had not to reach out and swallow the contents in a single, long gulp.

But, Deena squeezed my hand again, drawing me back into myself. I wondered if that little trick would always work for me - a distraction from the devil's liquor.

"No thanks," I said. The words were hard to pronounce, and I could tell by Vicki's face she realized she'd gone too far. "I'm okay. Don't want to lose my sharp edge."

"All right, then," she said, recapping the bottle and walking back to me. She took my hand, patted it with her other. "Guess you know what you're doing."

"How did you know I was in A. A.?" I asked

"Please, Doc, everyone knows. There's nothing more annoying or sanctimonious to a drinker than an ex-drinker."

I nodded, not certain if she was joking or serious.

"How long is it until morning?" Deena asked. "I didn't wear a watch today."

Rollo checked his wrist. "Two and a half more hours or so. It gets light pretty early."

"I just hope they don't kill the movers when they pull up," Vicki mumbled, uttering the words all of us had thought and none of us had dared to say aloud. "We could be stuck here forever. Or, at least until they figure a way in."

Suddenly, something banged on the window, and we turned. Rollo and Stan leveled their guns on the single pane of glass covered in chicken wire. Vicki clutched my hand as I watched, holding it tightly. Deena was almost breaking my other one in her grip.

In the dim light from the cloud-covered moon outside, I could see a single silhouetted shape. I couldn't tell if it was a man or a woman, but it had a big rock in its hand and it was pounding it against the glass. Soon, it was joined by another, then more were huddled around it, casting swiftly moving shadows across it.

"That the same bullet proof glass as what we had in the guard station?" Rollo asked, edging closer to the window.

Vicki was grasping, clawing at my hand, almost hurting me with the pressure she was extending. I hadn't thought she was that strong.

"I don't know," Deena said. "Carmody would know, but..."

"Yeah, well, he isn't giving out much information right now," Rollo finished.

Vicki was really starting to hurt my hand, and I was developing a headache from the incessant pounding on the window. Thankfully, it looked as though the glass was somehow reinforced, and it wasn't shattering. I couldn't tell how many of the villagers were outside the window, they kept moving around so much, but there were at least five rocks whacking the glass. You could see them, jagged, random shapes, when they made contact.

Vicki's long fingernails were starting to break the skin of my palm. I loosened my grip on her, and she dug in further.

"Christ," Stan said, eye-balling the pile of furniture blocking the door. "If they get in here, we're dead meat. There's nowhere to go."

I tried to let loose of Vicki's hand, tried to shake it off, but the hand-clasp was too strong. Where did she get the strength? Had she been lifting weights?

Then, Vicki stood and walked over to Deena, who put her arm around her.

And there was still someone clutching my hand.

I reeled, spun off the sofa, but I didn't break free of the clutches of the hand that extended from a skinny arm behind the couch. A man moved from his hiding place behind the furniture, painfully, skeletal thin, with white skin and only one eye. The other socket was empty, puckered skin emerging from the hole. He tipped the sofa over, as he scrambled out from behind it.

During this moment of distraction, I shook his hand from mine, brushing the offending appendage against my pants. The man hissed like a snake and climbed on top of the overturned couch where he squatted, letting his long, bony arms hang loose. He resembled some albino, reptilian monkey.

"Jesus Christ!" Rollo said.

"I was holding its hand," I said. "The son of a bitch is strong."

"Do something," Vicki shouted.

Rollo and Stan raised their guns into position, and I could hear them clicking off the safeties.

214 ~ William D. Carl

The skinny villager shrieked and leapt from his crouching position. In an instant, he was on top of Vicki, clawing at her throat, his feet scrambling to insert themselves between her knees. She fell over backwards, her skull slamming against the hardwood floor.

Rollo fired as the man jumped, but missed, shattering a watercolor landscape's frame that had been propped against the couch.

The thing raised its fingers over Vicki's screaming face. Its fingernails were long and sharp, jagged at the edges. It plunged its fingernails into the nurse's eyes, pushing until it was well past the knuckle and Vicki had ceased her squirming. Her screaming stopped, too.

The deformed people with the rocks outside our window hooted in delight, as though they were watching a hilarious comedy. They began banging against the glass again, the same incessant rhythm.

"Oh God," Deena cried. "Kill him. Kill it!"

As the man raised his head, he withdrew his long fingers from Vicki's bloodied eye sockets with an extended squelching sound. Looking down at the black vitreous humor on his hand, he flipped the disgusting stuff off his fingers and turned towards Deena. Hissing, he stood. I should say *it* stood. I couldn't think of this obscene thing as human.

And Rollo and Stan each shot the man in the chest. Rollo actually shot him twice.

The scrawny man/thing fell to the floor, the leer still frozen on his/its lips.

"Okay," Rollo said. "I don't know about all of you, but I'm checking every goddamn inch of this place before I put this gun away again."

Nobody disagreed, and we spent more time than was probably necessary to discern the place was devoid of other villagers. The racket coming from the window and the undeterred assailants didn't seem to pause for a moment, and it wasn't doing anything to help my headache.

Looking down at Vicki's body, I checked for a pulse. I realized it was futile, but I needed to be sure. I nodded up at Deena, who yanked one of her curtains down from the window and covered the nurse's face with the cloth. It was a bit more comforting not to have her staring up at the ceiling with those empty, bleeding sockets, the black and red gunk streaming down the sides of her face, dead cancerous tears.

"Now what?" Stan asked. "We wait until morning and try to flag down the moving van drivers?"

"It's a long wait," I said. "Especially with McCoy working some kind of hoodoo on the doors of this place. How'd he accomplish that, do you think?"

"Hey, I'm not even going to try to guess," Stan said. "So far, everything he's said has been a hundred percent true, right?"

"Yeah," I said.

"Then, this probably has something to do with some other dimension. Maybe, as a result of genetic manipulation through all that inbreeding, he's accumulated some kind of powers he can use. Telekinesis," Deena suggested. "Or, the membrane between this world and the next is getting thinner, and that's giving him some of the Old One's powers. It makes as much sense as anything."

"I just wish they'd stop with the banging," Rollo said, pointing towards the windows. "Making me crazy in here."

"Better to hear it from that side than from this one," I said with a shrug.

Stan moved over to Vicki's side. Two pools of blood had soaked into the curtain where her eyes had been, and it looked as if she were still staring up at the ceiling through the material.

Putting a hand on Stan's shoulder, I said, "I'm sorry, man. I know she meant something to you."

He tried to shrug it off and act all macho. "We went out a few times. Nothing serious. But, I liked when she was here in this place. I liked having her around."

"I'm sure she knew that."

He nodded and moved back to the bottles of booze on the desk. Without another word, he started drinking the Southern Comfort, taking several long drinks, gasping between each one.

"Don't get drunk now," I said, taking the bottle from his fingers.

Oh God, I have an open bottle in my hands. I'm touching the glass, can feel the label beneath my fingertips. All I have to do is lift it to my lips...and...

Drink. Drink. Drink. Drink

I put it back on the desk. "No, we don't need you drunk, Stan. Stay sharp tonight. When we get out of here in the moving vans, we'll stop off someplace dark and scummy and get seriously shit-faced drunk."

He looked at me, then he nodded and ran a hand through his thinning hair.

Something moved overhead, a padding sound traversing the length of the second floor. Someone was running from room to room, the footsteps heavier than usual. Then, a second set of footsteps, limping this time, lighter than the first. The second foot dragged across the floor, scraping it, evoking images of fiercely long toenails curling from the foot.

"You hear that? They're all over the place," Stan said.

I moved over to Deena and wrapped my arms around her. "How are you holding up?"

"About as well as can be expected," she said. "I just wish this was all over and we were home in bed after watching TV and carving those pumpkins I bought. Halloween will never be the same after this."

"Hey, we get out of this alive, and I swear we'll take Halloween off work every year. Make it a holy day of obligation, and we can carve as many pumpkins as you like."

"I'd love that," she said. Then she pressed her face into my chest in a warm embrace. "You know, I love you."

"Love you, too," I said. "Always will."

The pile of furniture began to scrape across the floor, moving on its own power away from the door and into the room. When the desk and cabinet were far enough away for the door to open, it swung wide, nearly flipping off its hinges when it impacted against the wall. Screws flew through the air. Plaster dust swirled in a cloud from where the door-frame battered into the barrier, imprinting its rectangular shape and the circle of the door knob.

"Aw shit," Rollo said. "This won't be good."

Gary McCoy stood on the other side, in the hallway, framed in the entrance and surrounded by the swirling dust. His face had the glow of someone caught in the throes of religious ecstasy, his arms spread out to his sides. His limp hair was blowing in a breeze, although I had no idea where the wind was coming from. It just seemed to envelope him, and it smelled of birch tree sap and pine needles - the smell of outdoors.

"Hello everybody," he said, and he started to laugh.

Chapter 23

We stood still, stunned by the impossible events surrounding us. McCoy hadn't pushed the door open by shoving against the heavy obstruction of our blockade. He had moved the furniture from the other side of the door, *then* he'd opened it, using only some power of the mind. No hands were involved. It looked as if Deena's telekinesis theory was panning out.

"Is this some kinda party? Ain't you gonna invite me?" he drawled.

"Of course, Gary," Deena said softly.

Rollo flashed her a look. "Are you nuts, woman?"

Gary took a step into the room. The lightning outside flashed at an opportune moment, showing his bloody shoes and stained and spattered pants legs. His hair was mussed more than usual, but those unsettling eyes fixed right upon me. They seemed to pull me towards him, and I had to stop myself from taking a step forward.

"How ya doin' there, Doc?" he said.

The pounding outside the window ceased abruptly as the villagers caught sight of Gary moving into the room. The silence was disturbing after so much raucous noise, leaving me with the feeling I had suddenly gone deaf. I could hear a low buzzing, a vestige of the incessant screaming and pounding.

"Now, that weren't nice, you leavin' me like that back there," he said, leaning against the wall and blocking the exit with his tall, thin torso. "But, I guess I can understand why you done it. You see me, and ya see a monster. Only, I ain't no monster. They's all around us, watchin' all the time, sometimes creepin' into our world fer a little taste of what we got ta offer. You can vouch for that, can't ya, buddy?" he asked, glancing to his side at Rollo, who grazed a hand across his wound. It was bleeding again, a wet spot darkening on the shoulder of his uniform.

"I'm what'cha might call a victim of my birth. Ain't no easier way to put it. I am the way I am because of what went into me - all them people breedin' just right, just like the drawin's say. Like they preach to us. Hell, I don't want nobody hurt. You understand? That's why I come to the city in the first place. I wanted to warn everybody 'bout the Old One and what he intends. I wanted to help, so you got it all wrong, Doc. I ain't no damn monster."

Rollo said, "Speaking of monsters, do you see any of them around right now? Just curious, you know."

McCoy made a big show of scouting out the room. His gaze lingered a bit on the window, where the other villagers lay in waiting. They held his eyes for a moment before he continued. He finally shook his head side to side.

"Don't see none in here," he said. "But they's close. I can feel 'em movin' around, lookin' for more meat. They's always hungry."

Deena shivered under the feeble protection of my arm.

"Preacher," someone from outside called, slurring the words as though they had a cleft palate. "Preacher, we's here. Preacher! Preacher! Preacher!"

The others took up the chant, repeating the nickname over and over again, demented fans at a football game in Hell rooting for the home team. Gary McCoy looked a bit nervous for the first time since he'd ambled into Deena's office, moving heavy furniture as though it was nothing. The corner of his eye started to tic, and his shit-eating grin faltered.

"Preacher, preacher, preacher, preacher..."

The mantra increased in volume, and then the villagers outside began to pound on the window with their rocks again, keeping in syncopation with their chant. It was as though they were the percussion section, accompanying a rather monotonous song. They didn't have much rhythm, as their syncopation was off quite a bit with their repetitive invocation.

"They want me to do this awful thing," McCoy said, pointing towards the silhouettes at the window. "They want the Old One ta come outta me, ta destroy ever'thing in his path."

"And what are you going to do, Gary?" I asked. "Whose side are you going to take?"

"It ain't about sides, Doc. It's all about power. Ain't no choice in the matter if somethin' has a power over ya."

"You can beat the Old One, Gary," I continued. "You can stop the whole thing from happening. You can single-handedly save the world you seem to love so much."

"I ain't strong enough." He pouted like a petulant child, actually kicking at the corner of the door, which was enough to release it from its single remaining hinge. It slapped to the floor with a loud crash, but I barely heard it over the clamor outside.

"You looked pretty damn strong to me when you scooted that desk across the floor. It took two of us to move it against the door. It has to weigh three hundred pounds. Solid mahogany."

"Don't matter. The Old One's gonna' do what he wants. I couldn't get away from the monsters by leavin' the woods. I can't get away from a god. No way. No how."

"You can, Gary," I insisted, hoping it would give him the strength to stand up to his father and the other villagers. And, if there happened to really be some kind of god traveling from dimension to dimension, ready to invade our world and force us to our knees, well, maybe he could actually stop it from entering.

"They's gonna' get through that there window 'ventually. Ya oughta find some other place."

A booming sound started in the hallway, and McCoy spun to look.

"What is it?" Stan asked.

"I cain't see nothin'," Gary said. "Someone come here with a light so's I can see."

At first, nobody budged, but then I drew up my chest and moved to the doorway. Gary nodded at me, as though we were co-conspirators in some television show about the French Resistance.

"It's comin' from down the hall. That a way," he said.

I pointed the flashlight down the darkened hallway, and saw something fly from the wall. I adjusted the beam, and I witnessed the boards which covered the door to the stairwell leading to the second floor popping off and clattering to the floor. Someone was pushing them out from the other side, smacking at them until they exploded from their moorings. I knew it was more of the villagers. They'd penetrated the hole in the roof and made their way down to this level. They must have become bottled up in the stairwell, because there was a lot of grumbling sounds emerging from that area, the sound of flesh slapping flesh and something beating against the wooden barrier.

"It's the village," Gary said. "They's after me, and Pa's probably in the lead. The old man's spent his whole dang life gettin' ready for tonight, and he ain't about ta let me go."

"Just don't forget what I said about you, Gary. You can stand up to him."

"I know I can," he said. "He's an old man. Nothin' else. Me - I'm more worried 'bout that Old One who's comin' later."

Another board fell off the door to the stairs, rattling to the floor. The door inched open, creaking on rusted hinges. Several fingers of varying size and arthritic deformity snuck around the side of it, hungry grubs in search of soft food. The door opened a bit more, popping the last board off.

"Reckon I'll be seein' Pa pretty soon," Gary said, smiling over at me. "Hope he ain't too mad."

I felt exactly the same way. I looked over at Rollo, who had drawn his weapon, and I picked up the bottle of rum Vicki'd had stashed at her station. It wasn't much in the way of defense, but it felt good and solid in my hand.

Chapter 24

The villagers spilled out of the stairwell, as though a shaken bottle of champagne had been uncorked. With Pa McCoy in the lead, they positioned themselves in the hallway, blocking the way to the front desk, just on the other side of the door to the office. Many of them carried crude torches, and it lent the hallway a weird, glimmering glow. Pa's face, however, remained shadowed in darkness, his eyes shimmering brightly in the gloom. He held his arms outstretched on either side of himself, blocking the forward movement of his followers and relatives. I aimed my flashlight on to his face, but he didn't seem disturbed by the beam of light. He merely blinked a few times and stepped forward. It was show time.

Gary stepped out of the room, nonchalantly, arms stretched out in front of his body. He walked up to his Pa, stopped just in front of him. He ran a hand through his dirty hair.

"Well, lookie what we got here," he said. "How ya doin' Pa?"

"You ready to let the Old One through? It must be tonight." The older man sounded manic, the words almost tripping over each other in their rush to escape from his mouth. He was breathing heavily, panting in between phrases, the exertive toll of breaking into St. Mike's.

"We have ta go back to the village, don't we? The drawin's show the village, don't they?" Gary asked. "If we don't follow the pictures, the whole thing ain't gonna work."

"We'll just have ta make do here, is all. You gonna be a good boy and let the Old One through? You gonna do like yer Pa told ya?"

"Pa," Gary McCoy said, and he paused, taking a deep breath. It was a hell of an effort to stand up to his father, but it looked as if he was actually going to do it. "I ain't gotta let nothin' through. Why you wanna do this anyhow? What's so bad about the world you gotta make damn certain that it's all destroyed, that there ain't nothin' left?"

Inside, I cheered as Gary stood up to Pa McCoy, but I could feel Deena and the two guards getting antsy behind me. They wanted to move, to get out of the room where we were trapped and away from these crazy people with their insane belief system. There was real danger here - Vicki's bleeding corpse on the floor behind us attested to that terrifying fact, and I think we all wanted to remove ourselves as far from this damn drama as possible.

Only, they were as entranced as I was with the conversation. We slowly moved forward, listening to every word, watching Pa McCoy's eyes shined like a cat's as he talked about the Apocalypse with his son, who was rebelling against his old man for the first time in his life, striking out for his own beliefs. I wanted to pat myself on the back, but, instead, I inched forward with the others, heading for the doorway that led to the now empty stairs to the abandoned second floor. Many villagers had filled the hallway, quietly watching Pa and Gary argue back and forth. By my estimation, there were very few, if any of them, remaining on the next floor. We could make it to the stairs on the other side of the building, and maybe escape.

"You sassin' me, boy? You tryin' to say somethin' back to me?"

"I'm askin' ya why ya gotta kill ever'one. This ain't a perfect place, but the world ain't that bad."

"It's full a' sin and degradation."

"How would you know, Pa?" Gary asked. "You been makin' trips to the city to look at all the sin they got there? You been trapped in that village in the woods for a long time, Pa. Longer 'n me, even. At least I made me some trips out ta see stuff. How you know all them people deserve to die?"

"The drawin's say so," he answered, standing firmly with his arms now crossed in front of himself.

"The drawin's say a lot of things, Pa. It don't always mean they's gonna come true. Maybe it's supposed ta happen way off in the future."

"You're the holy one, Son. You're the Preacher, so it's time. The Old One's only been awaitin' you, awaitin' this very night."

Our little band of hospital employees was getting close to the doorway to the second floor. Deena accidentally kicked a board, and it made a noise like a gunshot. Pa McCoy looked over, caught sight of us, and he took hold of his son's shoulder.

"Them's the ones what brought you here," he said.

"Yeah, but they didn't know what they was doin'. They can't see the monsters. Hell, Pa, they think I'm crazy."

We edged a bit closer, but now that Pa and his followers had spotted us, they didn't look away for a second. They swiveled with our movement, slow, attuned to our exact position, and it felt as if they were taking sight of us down a rifle. I didn't know how we'd get up the stairs and away from them without a pretty good head start, and they were mere yards away from us. I took another step. Their heads turned a bit.

"We need ta get ya back with ta' brethren," Pa said to his son, though his baleful gaze never left us.

"Not really, Pa. I can do it right 'chere if I have ta. Ain't no difference where. The monsters done followed me here. Started ta get more solid-like, too."

"They're here?" Pa asked, and he looked around the torch-lit hallway. "They around us now?"

"They're ever'where," Gary said.

I thought I saw something out of the crook of my vision, a movement sharp and twisting. Maybe, I didn't actually see it, but I sensed motion in the torch-illuminated, half-dark hallway. Pa McCoy must have felt it, too, because he spun around on his heels as though something were swiftly approaching him from behind.

"Go," I whispered to Deena, and we rushed for the stairwell.

But, we weren't quite fast enough.

One of the villagers threw a spear (where had they been hiding such a weapon?), little more than a sharpened tree limb, really. I shouted, tried to warn the others. Everyone turned, their attention drawn by my call.

The world slowed down from my perspective. The spear traversed the length of the room. It made a soft swishing noise as it sliced through the air, heading for our little group. I ducked, my eyes instinctively moving to where I saw Deena spinning to face this new danger. Her hair billowed out from her head. The arrow passed her.

And it pierced Stan's throat. The crude instrument went all the way through his neck in a burst of blood, sticking into a cork-board of notices on the wall. The thrower must've been extremely strong, because Stan remained impaled on that board like some gigantic butterfly, his feet dangling, crimson fountains exploding from torn carotid arteries. His gun slipped from his fingers, clattering to the floor. His hands reached up for the spear, but they couldn't get a good hold on it. At least, not good enough to pull it from his flesh. His hands, covered in slippery blood, slid along the pole, twitching.

He was a few steps behind me, but I headed back for the weapon he had dropped. Deena shouted something after me, but her words were obscured by the shouts that had started to emanate from the crowd of villagers and the gurgling death throes of the guard. I slid in Stan's blood, but I managed to grab the gun and his key ring as my head hit the wall. I didn't let myself think about the pain; I couldn't, for I knew I didn't have much time. Stumbling to my knees in the slippery puddle that had once coursed through this man, I put a hand to the wall, grasping the corner of a door frame. I pulled myself to my feet, head throbbing. In one hand, I held the weapon and in the other hand I grasped the bottle of rum. I knew I'd need one or the other or both before the night was over.

As I shook the stars from my eyes, I heard murmurs from the villagers. Then, shouts. Then, screams of unadulterated terror.

I made my way back to the door, and I saw the villagers running around in a disorganized chaos. They were flailing their arms - some waving only flippers or boneless appendages - some of them swinging their torches against an unseen enemy. Others dropped the torches and fled.

In the dim light, I saw those deformed, inbred people swatting at the same invisible creatures which had overrun the east wing earlier in the night (had it really only been a few hours ago?). Pa McCoy was in the front, standing completely still, but several bites had been taken from his face and hands. He was missing a thumb. Remaining motionless wasn't a very effective tactic when dealing with the beasties. Others fell, spurting blood from torn bodies. As I watched a woman fall to her knees, I realized she'd lost her legs to one of the monsters, and she was attempting to walk on kneecaps devoid of skin or tissue. The bone chinked against the floor with every futile step. A large bite appeared in her throat, and she fell to her side.

Pa McCoy looked at Gary, and he dropped his torch to the ground. Then I realized something had bitten through his arm, and his wrist and hand were still gripping the flaming club. He screamed, bodily fluids shooting from his stump across the green plaster walls.

Then, in a flash, his face was gone, replaced by a skull with two bright eyes staring out of the sockets. The skin and muscles that had covered this skeletal visage had been eaten by something that was making huge, three-toed footprints in the tacky puddles on the floor.

And his torch had set fire to a pile of boxes which had been stacked neatly along the side of the hallway.

"God damn it, give me a break," Rollo moaned.

And I had to agree with him. Seemed some higher power was actually determined to make every bit of progress we made a Sisyphean joke, placing more and more obstacles in our paths.

Out of the frying pan...

Chapter 25

"**C**ome on," Gary shouted at me. "Get outta here while they's still busy with the monsters."

I pulled my eyes away from the nauseating sight of the villagers being devoured alive, and I launched myself at the stairwell. Deena and Rollo were already up the first flight of stairs, and they waited for us at the landing. Deena's eyes were filled with questions.

"The monsters came," Gary informed her. "They's all over them, eatin' everyone of them."

"Did you call them?" I asked, needing to know the extent of his power. "Did they come because of you?"

He shook his head as we entered the second floor's hallway.

"Naw," he said. "I dunno' why they come and go like they do. They's different from us. I don't understand 'em. But, I do know they ain't gonna hurt me, and I'm with you now. So, I dunno. They might not be hurtin' you fer the same reason."

I looked at Stan's gun in my hand, setting the bottle of liquor aside for a moment.

"Let me see that," Rollo said, and I handed him the weapon. Flipping it open, he tossed it aside. "Used up all the bullets already. This thing isn't going to be any use at all."

I heard the gun drop into a rain puddle several yards away, and I held on to my bottle. It was getting tougher and tougher not to pop the lid and start chugging away, to lose myself in intoxication.

But, the weight of the bottle made me feel braver when it was clasped within my fingers. I swung it a few times, practice swings at the bat.

"Well, let's get to someplace safer," Rollo yelled from farther down the hallway. "This second floor is falling apart. Almost as bad as the third floor."

I saw he was right. It had been a long while since I'd made a trip to the second floor, and the place had plunged into a ruin of its former self. The leaking water, especially from this furious storm, had soaked through much of the third story, and the ceilings had collapsed in several places, crumbling to the flooring in piles of brick and water-saturated mortar and plaster. Rain dripped through the holes, soaking the floor, which consisted of peeling yellow linoleum from the sixties. Furniture was rotted, ridden with fungus. Paint flaked from the sodden, water-logged plaster walls, drifting into puddles where the chips floated - dark green boats on a sea of neglect and putrescence. Bats flitted over our heads, and I saw several large sewer rats making their way brazenly down the passage. The stench of rot pervaded everything.

"This way," Rollo cried.

We followed him, wondering where he was leading us, but confident in his capabilities simply because he projected such an impressive image. He'd become the man in charge simply because of his raw physicality.

"Where are we heading?" I asked, helping Deena over a pile of bricks.

"Back to the guard station," he said, waving away a giant cobweb. "Last place I felt safe. I guess since Junior here isn't going to hurt us, we can all stay there, safe as pie till morning."

I was dubious about exactly how safe anyplace was at the moment, remembering the blaze started by Pa McCoy's torch. Had other fires started on the floor below us? How long until they reached our feet?

"Is the guard station fire proof?" I asked.

"Christ, why?"

"Pa McCoy dropped a torch when those things attacked him," I explained. "Set some boxes on fire, but I don't know if it'll spread."

"All those hardwood floors downstairs," Deena muttered.

"Aw, shit..."

Undeterred, Rollo pulled himself through a hole created by a fallen eaves resting atop a book case. Volumes lay open, wet, and crawling with bugs at our feet, the spines bulging with moisture. Water dripped all around us at this point, falling from the hard rain outside the hospital. Some of it caught me in the face, and I was shocked at how cold it was. Then I realized I could see my breath in the air, and I knew it must be truly frigid outside if the chill had crept into the corridors of the hospital. Then again, I could look up through a hole and see the sky through the ceilings, exposed directly to the elements.

"You see any of the monsters, Gary?" I asked to the man following me as he stepped over the bookcase.

"Uh-uh. Probably too busy eatin' downstairs. That was a lotta people down there. Lotta family, too. Not as I'm gonna miss many of 'em a lot. Never helped me none. But their feast should keep 'em busy for a while."

Rollo called back, "The guard station was built to withstand almost anything, as a place we could go if there was a riot or all hell broke loose on St. Mike's."

"I'd call this Hell," Deena said, pushing aside a spider's web. Something furry with a multitude of legs crawled away from us.

"It's supposed to have the strongest bullet-proof glass, double locks and electrical locks. Not that they'd do us a lot of good now. If you noticed, the floor wasn't hardwood. A fire might burn around it, but I doubt it could get inside that little area."

"But what about smoke inhalation?" Deena asked.

"I don't know," Rollo answered. "Let's just hope it doesn't get too bad, or we'll have to go outside and wait for those movers, who are probably going to be late anyway. Movers always are."

I said, "I wouldn't want to be out there right now. Who knows how the villagers outside are going to react to Pa McCoy's death, the killing of all their friends and relatives."

"I can tell ya," Gary said. "They ain't gonna be happy. There's about twenty five of 'em gettin' eaten now, so that still leaves, maybe, twenty-five or thirty more of 'em."

"Then let's get back to the guard station. We can leave later if we have to," Rollo said.

Gary stopped, putting his hands on his knees and breathing hard. He shook his head a few times, like a dog shaking off water from its ears.

"What's wrong?" I asked.

"I dunno'," he said. "I feel kinda funny inside. Somethin's crawlin' through my guts."

"Is it the Old One?" I asked.

"Dunno'," he said. "Hurts, though."

"Come on," Deena said, hauling him forward by his left arm. I took the right, and we pulled the young man along with us, his feet spasming on the ground, kicking up water from the puddles of rain.

"Here's the stairs down," Rollo said, pointing with his flashlight beam.

We descended to the first floor, half way between Siberia and the front desk area. The stairs creaked beneath our tread, and I prayed they wouldn't give in to age and years of wear. Some of the wood felt spongy.

I thought I could see a faint orange glow coming from down the hallway, but I wasn't certain.

Gary started thrashing, as though caught in the throes of an epileptic fit. He shook so badly, Deena and I lost our grip on his arms and dropped him.

"Only a few more feet, Gary," I cried out. "You can make it, buddy. Come on."

"Oh Go-o-o-o-od," he cried, and I saw tears of blood run down his cheeks from the corners of his eyes.

Rollo rushed forward, grabbing the keys I had snatched from Stan. He set about unlocking the door to the guard station just as I saw the flames begin to steal around the corner, long snakes of fire creeping along the hardwood floors, eating their way towards us.

"I see...circles..." Gary stammered as Rollo opened the door. "Circles and circles within circles..."

His eyes rolled back in his head. I tried to force a piece of cloth between his teeth, but several of them had already shattered during his fit, slamming together with such quivering force it broke the enamel. Blood dripped from his lips, gnawed raw from the jagged teeth.

"I can...see 'im...Old One...coming..."

Rollo grabbed one of his feet and I took the other. We dragged him across the hallway, away from the approaching fire. When Rollo saw the flames, he dropped the young man's leg. I set the bottle of rum on the guard's desk to free up my hands.

"This is too much," he said. "Spreading too fast. The smoke's going to be really bad."

"You don't think we should stay here?"

He shook his head. "No, I think we'd be better off taking our chances outside."

Gary McCoy's thrashing was becoming increasingly alarming, and the blood from his eyes told me something more was occurring here than your typical grand mal seizure. I put his foot down at the edge of the door that led to the guard's security station. We looked down at the suffering man, wondering what to do next.

"Do we take him outside with us?" Deena asked.

"I don't want to just leave him here," I said. "After all he's been through."

"Fuck him," Rollo said. "Guy's dead anyhow. I don't know what's causing that seizure, but it can't be good."

At that moment, McCoy started coughing up blood in small, watery spurts. His eyes were rolled back into his head, exposing only the whites, tinged with the crimson liquid seeping out of them.

"What the hell's going on with him?" Deena asked.

"I don't know," Rollo said, kneeling next to the young man's trembling body. "But, we need to get out of here before that fire completely blocks the entrance. We also..."

Rollo's words were interrupted when a black claw erupted from Gary's chest, followed by a long, insectoid arm, bent at awkward, impossible angles. Fingernails sharp as knives raked across Gary's forehead and down to his throat, pulling skin away from the bone, and tossing the young man's left cheek into the corner. The arm extended a bit more, slashing out at Rollo. The guard fought back, grabbing the long appendage emerging from the boy's chest cavity, and he tried valiantly to aim the sharp claws in another direction. The thing had two elbows, and the arm reached out of Gary's ruined thorax at least five or six feet.

Gary sat up, and we could see the arm coming out of his chest, but nothing reached from behind him. The thing was being born out of Gary, just as if the hole in his chest was a porthole.

"Oh no," I said. "The Old One. He's coming through. He's real."

"Gary..." Deena cried.

The boy looked over at the noise, seeming much younger than his years, and he reached out a single hand to us. The other didn't seem to be working properly, and it just hung there by the tendons. A second black limb snaked out of his chest. I could hear the sound of his bones cracking as the beast parted his ribcage and peered out of Gary's still living body with glowing, red eyes.

Chapter 26

A sense of power emanated from Gary and the beast emerging from him. I could feel it rolling off of the 'birth' in waves, and it brought tears to my eyes. The organs in my own chest and abdomen shifted uncomfortably, and I prayed nothing was going to be tearing its way into our world through my own torso.

The second arm reached out as far as the first, and Gary (or what had once been Gary) began to slide backwards as the beast shoved a long, wrinkled snout out of the boy's ribcage. It stretched out one of its eighteen sharpened, skeletal fingers and gutted Rollo as if he were a deer, opening him up from throat to nuts, allowing his innards to spill out onto the tiled floor. The motion seemed to be little more than the merest gesture, but it effectively mutilated Rollo with a single swipe. The guard gasped, choked up some bile and blood, and fell face first to the floor where he lay still as death. His leg hit the desk, knocking the bottle of 151 proof rum to the floor.

I didn't know what to do, and I reacted on pure instinct. I shoved Deena backwards, out of harm's way, and I followed her into the guard's station where I locked the doors behind us. Looking through the window, I saw Gary (or the thing clawing its way out of Gary's shell) stumble to his knees. The hands clamped themselves around each side of his chest and started to shove at the skin and tissue that refused to slough off its new form. With a snapping of bones, the hole in his gut opened wider, and several horns emerged from the young man's body.

I was reminded of a butterfly escaping from its cocoon, at the effort extended to rid itself of the delicate webs surrounding it. Only, flesh and bone weren't as malleable as a cocoon, and Gary's body was torn to shreds.

"What are we going to do now?" Deena screamed. "How do you stop a god?"

"I...I don't know," I said.

"It's coming through," she gasped, pointing.

Even though I was already staring at the monstrosity, I couldn't peel my eyes away.

The horns shoved aside Gary's guts and intestines, some of which clung to the top of the beast's head.

It was growing easier to see the terrible scenario playing out in front of us. The glow of the fire became brighter around the corner, reaching closer with its tendrils of flame.

I wish I could've closed my eyes. I wish I hadn't seen the face of the Old One, its long snout and mouths of teeth and tendrils growing out in every direction - I wish I hadn't witnessed the birth of the thing.

When the head finished shoving its way out of Gary's lifeless body, it shook its snout, opened its six mouths, and screeched with the pain of a newborn. Its long arms attempted to clear away the bits of human anatomy that still adhered to its thorny head, but its movements were awkward, like those of an infant. It blinked its red eyes at us, as though trying to focus.

"It can't see us," I said to Deena.

And I saw the gun, Rollo's revolver, lying two feet outside the door of the guard's station.

"It isn't ready yet," I said. "Or it's not strong enough to move well."

"What are you doing?" she screamed as I opened the door to the hallway. "Are you crazy? That thing'll kill you. How do you kill a god, Bob? How?"

"You close the portal," I said, and I flung the door wide open.

Scrambling for the gun, I saw the beast lower its head, following my motion. In a second, I had the gun in my hands, and I knelt to the side of the monster, this god that had invaded our world. From my vantage point, I could see Gary McCoy's ruined body, little more than his skin with a few bones and red organs spilling from it. The Old One had shifted out of its mortal coil, discarding Gary as easily as a cicada and its outer membrane.

It howled, a sound I can only describe as unnerving in the extreme, something that battered at my innards.

"Got to destroy the portal," I said, aiming at what remained of Gary's forehead.

I fired. There was little chance I would miss, as the remains were only four feet from me. A hole appeared in his face, and his carcass skipped backwards a foot.

The Old One shuffled towards me on clumsy, cumbersome legs. I laughed, reminded of the opening of *Bambi*, in which the titular Walt Disney character attempted to stand after his birth. I guess even gods aren't immune to weakness after such a strenuous activity.

And if it was weakened, it could be killed.

I shot at Gary's emptied husk of skin again, hitting him near where his heart would've been had it still been ensconced in his chest. Pulling the trigger a third time, I heard a dreaded *click*, as the hammer fell on an empty chamber.

No more bullets.

And the creature still stood in front of me, trying its best to coordinate its limbs in an attempt to get at me. One of its ugly arms bent and swiped at my mid-section, but I easily stepped aside, closer to Gary's sloughed off skin.

I had been so certain that if I destroyed the portal - Gary's body - it would close the inter-dimensional passageway this Old One utilized, sending it back to whatever Hell it had escaped. With the portal gone, the beast would either be sent back or be trapped here with us. I didn't even want to consider that second option.

Deena shouted behind me, "Come on, Bob. What the hell are you doing?"

The Old One quivered for a moment, then dozens of appendages started sprouting from around its neck like some obscene collar. They grew longer so swiftly, I almost forgot myself and watched the show.

I reached out and grabbed Gary McCoy's foot. Well, his shoe, at least. Yanking, the shoe came off, exposing a flat-looking foot. I grasped it, wincing at the empty feel of it, and I heaved the surprisingly light-weight body to myself. It was little more than his dermas, and I grabbed it around where the waist would have been. His other shoe fell to the floor.

The appendages around the Old One's throat had extended to a point where they became whipping tentacles.

Tiny mouths formed on the ends, and they opened and shut, exposing sharp, snapping teeth.

Grasping the skin, I backed up into the guard's station. Gary's pants slid off his empty body, and the belt clattered on the floor.

One of the gnashing mouths, a good two inches across, bit me in the shoulder, removing a small hunk of skin and muscle. I screamed, hurrying into the station. As Deena slammed the door and locked it behind me, I could see the maw on the end of the tentacle chew and swallow. My flesh was visible as it made its way down the tentacle to the throat of the god. The Old One heaved a bit.

"Jesus," I said, dropping what I thought was the portal. "Bastard got me."

Deena peered at my wound, worry on her face. "Looks red already, like it's infected."

"Where's that bottle of rum?"

She looked around until she discovered it under the desk. Opening the top, I poured a bit of it on my arm over the bite. The liquid bubbled and spat. I let it go for a few more seconds, then I soaked the wound again. This time, the effervescence was minimal, even if the sting was just as bad.

Without really thinking, I upended the bottle to my lips and felt the rum warm its way down my throat and into my stomach. The sensation spread through my body and I choked, coughing on the strong alcohol. I was about to raise the bottle again for a second gulp, when Deena took the container from me.

"I need you sober," she said. "If we're going to make it out of here alive, you need to have all your senses about you."

"Have you looked out there," I asked, motioning to the beast, which seemed to be acquiring its sea-legs pretty well as the minutes passed. "What the hell are we supposed to do against that?"

"We get out of here," she said. "Why did you want Gary's corpse?"

"I thought if we could destroy it, we could close the portal and send this bastard back to his other world. Crazy, I know..."

She shook her head. "No, Bob. It makes sense. At least, it fits with the rest of this messed up mythology."

The monster god raised itself on muscular, black-skinned legs and shoved itself against the guard station. Everything rocked, and I fell to the floor next to Gary's corpse.

His eyes were open, staring at me through his face with no skin covering it, and, as I tried to get to my feet, I saw his eyeballs roll so that they gazed upon me.

"Holy Fuck!"

"What?" Deena asked, helping me up.

The Old One rammed himself against the door again, and I could see the hinges buckling.

"He moved his eyes. He's still alive."

"That's impossible," she said, but, as the words left her lips, Gary rolled his eyes again and then opened his mouth.

Though his lips were gone, along with the rest of his face, he whispered, "...Elp...Eeee..."

"It can't be real," Deena said.

I motioned to the battering ram of a god in the hallway. "Oh, and this is reality we're messing with?"

"...Elp...Eeee..."

Deena looked at me. "This explains it, Bob."

"What are you talking about?"

"The Preacher. The portal. It's still alive."

The Old One shoved into the door again. I was shocked it still held under the attack, but I knew it was only a matter of time before it gained access. I searched the room for an escape hatch.

"Well, if that doesn't kill Gary," I said, motioning to the moaning skin on the floor. "I don't know what the hell will!"

Tentacles whipped at the safety glass of the guard station, and tiny mouths opened and shut, trying to bite into the window. They smeared the glass with trails of lime-green spittle.

The Old One lumbered back to its feet. It stood almost twelve feet tall, hunched over, its bumpy back and spiked head scraping the ceiling.

It rammed the door at the same moment I saw the ventilation grill over the desk. I leapt on top of the surface and pulled with all my might. The grill popped off the wall easier than I expected, and I nearly tumbled ass over elbows off the table. The heating vent system lay exposed.

"Can we fit through there?" Deena asked as I helped her up on the desk. As if in answer, she squirmed into the ducts. In an echoing, hollow-sounding voice, she hollered back, "There's plenty of room. Come on!"

I didn't know where the ducts led to, and I didn't have much time to think. All I knew is they'd take us someplace other than this guard station, which was on the verge of being torn apart by the Old One.

I jumped up on the desk.

"...Elp..."

Reaching down, I grabbed Gary's skin, heard him make a gagging sound. He folded neatly over himself, and I tried to mold him into a manageable shape, maybe something I could tuck under my arm or roll in front of me.

I know how terrible this sounds; he was still a human being, after all, still alive and sort of breathing. There wasn't a lot of time to stop and consider his feelings, and it's pretty difficult to be mindful of someone's emotional well-being when that someone can be folded. He'd become less than a man to me. More like a commodity. Still, I wasn't about to let him lie around, waiting to succumb to the flames. I wasn't that heartless. Plus, I somehow felt he could be useful in the future, even if there was no way this guy was going to ever play the piano again.

The Old One smashed through the door as I shoved the bundle of flesh ahead of me into the heating ducts. He didn't roll very well, but it would have to do. His skin skidded against the tin of the little passageway.

Please God, I prayed. *Please let this take us someplace safe.*

Chapter 27

Deena was five feet ahead of me, scurrying on her hands and knees, her back almost touching the top of the ventilation shaft. Her ass was twitching side to side, and I would've found it funny if we weren't being attacked by some tentacled creature from beyond. I pushed the balled-up skin in front of me, and I heard it emit groans and sighs every once in a while.

Someplace, along the line, this had ceased to be a *him*, transforming into an *it*.

I was bigger than Deena, so I naturally had a tighter fit, and the claustrophobic tin interior of the ducts pressed against my spine and my sides, forcing me to slow my progress. I had to hunch myself down, elbows tucked into my stomach in order to make any headway at all.

Behind me, I heard a scuttling noise, and I flipped myself onto my back to look through the space between my spread legs. I could push myself with the bottom of my feet, scooching along on my back, the skin of Gary McCoy batted forward by the back of my head.

The tentacles of the old one were whipping their way into the passage, banging against the sides of the tin. The fanged mouths on the tips of the pseudopods chewed and bit the air, snapping and gnashing their fangs in frustration. The nearest one was at least six inches from my feet, but they seemed to be getting closer, as if the tentacles were still growing longer from the beast's neck.

Driving myself backwards with the soles of my feet, I shouted up to Deena, "Hurry! The thing's trying to get in."

"I am hurrying," she replied, sounding annoyed.

One of the tentacles latched on to my left shoe, biting into the leather. It sank its needle teeth deeper, until I could feel their points against my toes. I kicked and several more of the tentacles snapped at my other foot, trying to catch it in their open, saliva-dripping jaws.

The one that had hold of me started pulling me back to the ventilation hole in the wall, back to the guard station, back to the Old One and its gaping, tooth-filled maw.

Pushing the heel of the left shoe with my other foot, I slipped it off, and it was snatched away from me. I knew I'd lost a form of protection, a layer of leather armor, so I started moving faster, hurling myself onto my stomach and crawling through the duct. I weaved on my stomach like a lizard, lugging myself forward with my elbows.

"Are you okay?" Deena shouted back at me, her voice reverberating off the metal walls.

"Just dandy," I replied.

"This is no time for sarcasm, Bob."

Seemed as good a time as any.

I was making pretty decent progress, and the tunnel of ductwork was turning a corner ahead of me, probably towards the front entrance, when the entire structure wobbled with the force of a huge earthquake. Looking back to where we'd entered the shaft, I saw the Old One trying to thrust its way after us. The thing was far too large to fit into the gap, but it seemed to be pulling the metal ducts from their moorings, shaking it and therefore us, with its attempts.

Deena called back to me, "What's that?"

"It's trying to follow us."

Something above me snapped, and the entire duct slipped to a forty degree angle down towards where the Old One was still trying to squeeze its enormous bulk into the vent. When I started sliding toward it, the thing raised its massive head, opening its multiple sets of jaws on its biggest mouth, placing it over the hole so it might catch me as I glided backwards.

Jerking my arms out and catching myself with my one shoe on my right foot, I stopped myself from slipping right down into the thing's gullet. The bottle of rum in my hand clinked against the sides of the tin walls, and I nearly lost it. Gary bumped against my head.

It was a lot harder crawling, now that I had to do so at a forty degree angle upwards. I heard Deena calling after me, saying something about heat, but I couldn't hear her. Blood was whooshing through my ears, my heartbeat so loud I would never have made sense of what she was saying. Besides, the Old One was pulling itself out of the vent, and the sound of metal against metal screeched so loud, it almost covered the beast's angry screams. Almost.

"It can't get in," I shouted as I propelled myself forward. "I think it's giving up."

Glancing back, I saw that the entrance to the shaft was empty, a cold, orange light exposing its vacuity. The beast was gone. At least, for now.

Orange light. The fire.

Shit.

I maneuvered myself so I could inch my way forward, pushing the disgusting mass of skin ahead of myself. It made soft sounds of pain and apprehension. I tried not to think about what it...he...it must be feeling.

The bottle of rum slammed against it, and I realized I could see awfully well considering I was inside the heating system of a hospital. It should have been pitch black. Orange and yellow light from behind me cast long shadows, and I could see Deena about ten feet away from me, where the duct was still nailed securely into the walls, running parallel with the roof. She was motioning to me, but I couldn't take my eyes off the bottle, the way it caught the glow of the light, the way I could see right through it and into the collapsed eyes of Gary McCoy.

He was staring back at me, wrinkles of loose skin surrounding the exposed, nearly flat eyeballs. He hissed air, and the other side of the bottle fogged up. Something about the juxtaposition of the glass and the rum and his collapsed, ruined face nagged at me.

"Goddamnit, Bob! Look at me," Deena screamed, snapping me out of my reverie.

Yes, I could see her fairly clearly. I shouldn't have been able to.

"Oh shit," I said, and I started feeling a tingle in my fingers.

The guard station was on fire. That was why the Old One had left, not because it had given up on us.

And my fingertips were getting increasingly warm.

Deena said, "The whole first floor must be in flames by now. This metal's getting really hot."

I scurried to her side, pushing the gibbering ball of skin ahead of me, ignoring its protestations. I gave her a quick kiss, then looked around for an exit.

"This tin's acting as a conduit for the heat," I said. "We've got to find a way out, or we'll be fricasseed like fish in a frying pan."

"Not a nice metaphor," she said.

Deena put her hand down, and she hissed and winced, drawing it to her chest. I heard the sound of sizzling, smelled burnt flesh.

"Use your shirt," I suggested, pulling mine off and placing it under my hands.

Deena removed hers and used it for protection against the hot metal. Wearing only a black bra, she slid forward, crying out every once in a while when a shoulder or an elbow touched the tin. I had it even worse, being so much larger. Any time my skin made contact with the duct, it burned and blistered.

What was left of Gary McCoy was starting to turn black on one side, so I flipped him over, like a hamburger getting too well-done on one side. He moaned.

Just ahead, I heard a sputtering sound. Deena reached it first.

"Rain must be pouring in through the roof," she said. "It's hitting the top of this vent."

"Can you see where it leads?" I asked, grimacing as I burned my left shoulder again. "Can we fit through it?"

"It's all rusted. Must've been exposed to the elements for a long time. Hold on a second."

I didn't want to tell her, but the heat was now reaching through the material of my pants and shirt, and I was starting to feel my skin blister. Gary was sizzling and popping, but he still managed to remain conscious. He must have been going through hell.

Deena shoved against the top of the shaft, quickly withdrawing her hands when they encountered heat. Covering her fingers with her shirt, she pressed upwards, and I heard something give way with a metallic shriek. Then, Deena's half-naked body was squirming upward, and water was falling into the duct, evaporating when it hit the hot metal with a crackling noise.

I shoved Gary forward until I arrived at the hole Deena had made. She reached down and hauled him up to where she was. Rain fell on my face, and I reveled in its coolness for a moment, letting it run down my burnt shoulders and chest. Then I stood, looking into a room on the second floor.

Stepping out of the ventilation shaft, I squirmed into my wet shirt and took a quick look around. The damp material was invigorating against my baking skin.

It was an office with a sofa, ruptured and covered with pustules of mold. A desk was set against the wall, under a hole leading to the third floor. Rain streamed from the three foot gap in the ceiling, hitting the desk and trailing down to the floor in a little river. On the opposite side of the room, the wallpaper was curling, on fire in thin, finger-like runnels.

"We can't stay here long," Deena said, eyeing the smoking wall.

"Let me catch my breath," I pleaded.

"...Elp...Eeeee..." McCoy begged.

"We can't go down," Deena said. "This place is burning from the ground upwards. This floor's definitely next. It'll probably drop right down onto the first story."

"You think it's safer if we climb up?"

"Better than being on fire."

"We could get trapped on the roof."

"Why're you still carrying that bottle of rum?" she asked, pointing.

I shrugged. "I don't know. Something...don't know what, but something tells me I'm going to need it."

"Grab Gary," she said. "Let's go to the next floor up. The stairs should be just past that doorway. If we can-"

Her sentence was interrupted by the door being smashed in and the Old One lumbering into the room on its long, multi-jointed legs. It shoved its horned head towards us, and I grabbed Deena, pulling her back. Opening one of its mouths, it exposed layers of needle-sharp teeth, and it roared - a howl of triumph I will never forget.

"Can't use the stairs," I said, yanking Deena back to the desk in the corner. "Go up through the hole to the roof."

Rain smacked her in the face, but she didn't protest when I grabbed her by the waist and raised her to the ceiling. Wrapping her fingers around an exposed board, she hauled herself to the third floor, her legs scissoring until she scrambled to her feet above me.

The Old One growled from several of its mouths at once, sounding like a whole herd of predators, and it launched itself at the desk.

Deena's hand emerged from the gap in the ceiling, and I handed Gary up to her. She tossed him aside, reached back for me.

The monster shoved the sofa across the room with its massive, clawed meat hooks, and I heard it smash into the far wall as the beast marched closer.

I grasped Deena's hand with my right, and I flung the bottle through the hole to the third floor. Then I grabbed the exposed board with my left. She began pulling, and I felt air beneath my feet, especially through the unshod left one.

The thing was at the desk. I could hear its talons scrabbling for a purchase to tow itself to the surface beneath my dangling feet.

Flinging out an elbow, I felt the floor beneath my forearm. Deena was pulling on the back of my shirt, and I was moving my legs to grab hold of anything solid so I could squirm my way through the sodden hole.

Tentacles snapped and wriggled at my twisting torso. Something nipped at my pants leg, tearing off a shred of material.

And Deena had me by the collar of my shirt, pulling me into the room.

A tentacle emerged from the hole, and I swear it stared at us and smiled with its fanged choppers. Attaining my feet, regaining my balance, I stomped on it, pleased with the crunch as its teeth shattered beneath the sole of my shoe.

On the floor below us, the Old One screeched, withdrawing the wounded pseudopod and bellowing for all it was worth. It leaped, grabbing at the exposed boards with its gnarled, black claws.

"This way," Deena insisted, pulling me to the door on the opposite side of the room.

We hurried to it, and she made to open it. With a hissing sound, she pulled her fingers back to her chest. Shaking it, she explained, "It's hot. Really hot."

I wrapped my hand within the folds of my rain-soaked shirt and turned the metal doorknob. The moisture whistled at the heat, but I managed to pull the door open.

The Old One wrenched a board loose, and it fell down to the second floor, its claws not achieving a grip on the rotten wood. It reached again, tearing out another hunk of the hardwood flooring.

I looked into the hallway of the open door and sighed in defeat.

It was filled with flames. Most of the floor was gone, consumed by the fire from below, and the walls had already turned black from smoke and heat, wallpaper falling like bark peeling off a birch tree.

"We're going to have to go up to the roof," Deena said.

"Are you crazy?"

"We got monsters below us and an inferno out that way. What would you suggest?"

Gary McCoy mumbled something unintelligible through his lipless mouth. "...orta..."

"What's he saying?"

"That we're fucked?" I suggested. "He's *skin*, Deena. Skin can't make suggestions."

The Old One got leverage on the floor and tried again to wrestle itself up through the wet aperture. It pulled a good three feet of flooring back with it. If the monster continued shredding the place from underneath us in this manner, it wouldn't take long before there was no floor at all.

"...orta..."

I nodded to Deena, and I said, "Okay. Let's get up on the roof. But if we get through all this shit just to get struck by lightning, I'm tearing God a new asshole when we get to Heaven."

She nodded, determined. "Okay, let's do it."

We shoved the small desk over to a position near the ever-widening hole. I didn't particularly enjoy being so close to the Old One's deconstruction, but we had to get near the rupture in the ceiling. Grabbing my bottle and Gary's limp bundle of flesh, I stood beside Deena on the desk's top, trying not to slip in the rainwater and plunge down to become the monster's next snack.

The Old One reached through the hole in the floor again, and claws extended from its fingers, long, white, and thin. The perfect tools to grab some wood and get a purchase on them.

"Come on," Deena said as the Old One bumped the leg of the desk.

I heaved her upwards, through the opening in the ceiling. My hair was plastered to my head, and I heard the rumble of thunder from the storm raging outside the hospital.

After passing Deena the bottle and Gary's useless form, I grabbed hold of a beam just as the Old One expanded his hole enough to pull the desk out from under me. It toppled backwards, clattering through the floor below us. With any luck, it smacked the damned monster right between the eyes.

I pulled myself onto the roof, feeling shingles slipping beneath my weight.

And I heard Gary call in the night. It must have taken every ounce of effort he could muster to make that single word sound audible to us in the throes of the rain and wind, the destruction caused by the creature at our feet.

"Portal!" he screamed.

"Oh," I said. A light bulb had gone off in my head. "Oh!"

I knew what I had to do.

Chapter 28

"Where's Gary?" I shouted at Deena, who was sitting on similarly slippery tiles a few feet away from the hole in the roof. "Or at least what's left of him?"

She shrugged, and we looked across the slippery roof for him. The night was dark, the moon obscured by heavy, water-laden clouds. The rain came down in torrents, as though intentionally trying to keep us blind. The trees at the edge of the woods beyond the hospital waved wildly, swept back and forth by the wind. Some of them nearly made contact with St. Mike's, their upper boughs swept by the hurricane-strength gales.

The weather wasn't the only dangerous thing, either. All along the roof, holes were visible, leading to empty, glowing spaces, where the fire beneath us devoured the place where we'd worked for so long. It had reached the third floor, and it was continuing its progression skyward. I knew it wouldn't be long before the roof, as drenched in water as it was, gave up the ghost and collapsed into the fiery ruins of Saint Michael's.

Within the hole through which we'd climbed to this point, I could see the Old One stretching to get its long white claws into the tiles of the roof. It made several leaps before it scratched into the edge of the hole, pulling several loosened tiles down upon its head.

"There!" Deena shouted, pointing her finger down to the rain gutter. "I see him."

Following her direction, I caught sight of Gary's balled up remains stuck in the tin gutter at the edge of the roof. His head and arms were mashed into the space, water sloshing behind it, dammed by his malleable flesh. His legs dangled over the side, flapping in the violent wind like flags on top of the turret of a castle.

I laughed aloud, but felt as though I'd probably go to Hell for finding humor in something so pathetic.

Beside Gary, a few feet away, the bottle of Bacardi 151 floated down the gutter, carried along by a stream of water.

"Catch that bottle!" I shouted, sliding down the angled roof on my ass.

I halted myself at the edge with my foot, feeling the gutter give a bit under my weight. Making my fingers into claws, I dug into the space between tiles, holding on for dear life. The bottle floated past me, moving faster on the current. Cursing, I scrambled to my knees and took off after it.

I peeked over my shoulder. Behind me, the Old One got a grip on a wooden beam and started hauling itself into the rain-filled night. Its horns emerged first, then its eyes, shining bright red in the night.

Or was it morning now? I'd lost all track of the hour.

I didn't have time to think about anything at that moment with the exception of retrieving that bottle of alcohol. It was moving pretty fast, quicker than I could've gone on my knees. I knew I'd have to stand and run on the wet roof, over unsecured tiles that could come unmoored at any moment, with lightning still flashing in the sky.

The Old One fell back to the third floor, taking with it a three foot hunk of roof and several tiles. It screamed in rage.

I stood and started running before any more doubts could enter my racing mind. Beneath my feet, the roof tiles shifted with the pressure I put on them. My shoeless foot actually gripped the wet surface better than the one with my Florscheim, which skated over the smooth shingles.

I was never really much of an athlete, some high school triumphs that were long forgotten and closeted, along with the accumulated cheap trophies. Still, that night, I ran like I was a starving man and someone had opened an all you can eat bacon buffet on the other side of the building. The roof crunched beneath my footfalls, and I tried not to think of all the holes surrounding me on the roof - a new one could open at any moment under me.

Out of the corner of my eye, I saw Deena holding fast to Gary's skin, her hair haloed by a burst of lightning, and she was probably wondering if I had a death wish. I made a desperate final dash, leapt, and grasped the cold bottle in my hands.

Only to have it slip out again when I stood.

I performed a neat juggling trick, hitting and spinning the bottle several times, praying I'd catch it again. It fell to the roof, and I dropped on top of it, a less than graceful linebacker on a fumble. Snaking my hands beneath me, I grabbed hold of the neck and held tight.

I turned in time to see the Old One hiking up a leg, trying to get a foothold to the roof. It had its head wedged in between two beams, and I heard them snap, cracking in half and dumping the monster - and another couple of feet of rooftop - back where it had started.

Deena, noticing the way the roof was diminishing before her very eyes, started towards me, holding Gary's flapping skin wrapped around one of her arms. It looked like she was talking to it, holding a conversation, but the storm blocked any sound from reaching my ears.

"What are we doing?" she asked me, getting close.

"I have a plan," I said. "I think it'll work."

Something whizzed past my head, striking and shattering several bricks in a chimney behind me.

"What was that?" Deena said.

Another missile flew through the air, nailing me in the shin. I fell to the rooftop, clutching at the area of contact. Glancing down, I saw a rock the size of my clenched fist roll down to the gutter where it was swept away by the steady flood of water.

"Rocks!" I shouted. "The villagers are out there with slingshots or something, and they're shooting rocks..."

Another one hurled past my head, coming too close for comfort.

"...at us! Bastards!"

Behind me, fire whooshed out of one of the holes in the roof, as though a gas line had burst, exploding shards of tiles and chunks of brick into the air. They landed on and around us.

"Close your eyes," I shouted, holding Deena close. I could feel Gary's corpse between us, empty and hollowed out.

A rock smacked into Deena's side, and she moaned at the sudden burst of pain. Below us, on the lawn, I could see figures darting about in the light of the inferno of St. Mike's. They were hooting, taking position, and letting loose with their arms swinging about their heads. It appeared as though there were about fifteen of the villagers down there, moving in and out of the tree line closest to the hospital.

And, lest we forget about all the other damn problems we had, the Old One made another try at getting up to us. Arms flailing, it was using its tentacles to bite into the roof's tiles in order to secure itself.

"What're we going to do now?" Deena asked.

"One thing at a time," I said, grabbing Gary from her. He was lighter than before, as though some life force was flowing out of him as well as his bones and organs. "One thing at a fucking time."

A rock careened past us. Another one thumped me on my hip. Their aim was getting better.

The Old One seemed to gain a steady grip on the roof, and it pulled itself up through the hole, stepping out into the rain. Tentacles lashed around its neck, relinquishing their hold on the tiles, and I noted with pleasure the one that dangled uselessly from the swarm of others. It padded slowly towards us, cautious of its precarious foothold.

"Bob," Deena said. "If you're going to do something, this would be a damn good time to start."

From the front driveway, I thought I saw colored lights blinking on and off, and I had to ask myself, *Now what?*

Chapter 29

The stones were hurtling from the lawn at an even faster rate, with several scoring direct hits to my body. Thankfully, I hadn't been struck in the face or eyes, so I could see the huge Old One making its way across the roof towards us. Deena hadn't been so lucky, had taken a rock to her chin, and the area of contact was already bruising and swelling.

"Hold Gary out," I said, and Deena pushed him forward. I could see his eyes rolling in their flat sockets, his mouth continuing to whisper words I couldn't understand.

A gunshot rang out on the front lawn, and Deena and I both flinched, hurling ourselves against the roof. Peering down, I saw several of the villagers high-tailing it for the protective tree-line. Some of them weren't so speedy, what with useless limbs and flipper-hands and spines bent into nearly impossible positions from Spinal Meningitis.

The colored lights came into focus as a police cruiser drove up onto the green lawn, digging tires into the mud. Before the car had stopped, I saw Ron Justice hop from the driver's seat, gun held confidently in front of himself, firing off more blasts into the woods. His determined face was illuminated by the alternating blue and red flashing lights from the top of the mounting rack.

"It's whatshisname," I said.

"Ron Justice," Deena said, and I had to grit my teeth over the fact that she remembered his name so speedily. "Thank God."

I started pouring the rum over Gary's desiccated body, ignoring the baffled look I was receiving from my fiancée. Using my body, I tried to block as much of the rain as possible, thoroughly soaking the skin with the alcohol. Gary seemed to realize my intentions, and he closed his eyes, resigning himself to his fate.

Then again, what fate could be worse than existing as a living corpse while a god from who knows where trashes your world?

"What are you doing?" Deena asked over the gunfire from Officer Friendly.

"Closing the portal," I answered. "For good."

The Old One hulked ungracefully closer to us, until we were nearly within reach of those hungry tentacles.

"Come on," I said, grabbing Deena's hand and pulling her with me across the roof, away from the creature. I headed for one of the holes in the hospital, one through which flames were spouting. The beast couldn't move as quickly as we could, its bulk actually working against it.

Our friendly, neighborhood police officer must have looked up at our motion and caught sight of the Old One. "Holy Mother of Fuck," I heard him scream as he reloaded. This was followed by a volley of bullets that sank into the black flesh of the god without seeming to do a bit of damage. Tiny, pink holes appeared in its skin, but it persisted in its pursuit of us, oblivious to the pain - if it could even experience such a sensation.

I arrived at a hole with more than its share of fire burning within its interior. Looking into it, I saw an entire room, an old cell, unused for years from the looks of it. The floor below it was exposed through flaming support beams. The fire raged, an inferno of heated energy and destruction.

"Sorry about this, Gary," I said, looking into what was left of his face.

He sighed once. I took it as an agreement, as permission for what I wanted to do.

I tossed the skin into the opening. It fluttered slowly into the flames, like a sheet of paper on a gentle breeze, turning end over end, so I could witness his unmatched eyes staring at me. I prayed the expression on his face was one of relief, of gratefulness.

The Old One screeched, high pitched, a tea-kettle shriek.

Ron Justice took a rock to his forehead while he was distracted and watching the horrific scenario on the roof, and he dropped to the ground next to his car. So, the villagers were still on the attack, still determined to - what? Free the skin of Gary McCoy? Aid the beast that had suddenly stopped in its tracks on the roof, not twelve feet away from us?

He wiped at the blood on his forehead. Something in the woods giggled, and Justice fired twice at the shadows. He was rewarded with a grunt of shock and pain. He'd nailed one of them. I wanted to applaud his marksmanship, even if he had been hitting on my fiancée earlier that day. He fired a few more times.

The Old One remained still as the smell of burning flesh wafted up from the opening in the roof. A quick peek down showed me Gary's skin was turning black, curling in upon itself as it roasted in the fire. I could no longer tell what was a leg or an arm or even a head on the crispy corpse. It was merely a lump of charred meat.

A ruined portal.

Please God, I prayed. *Let this work.*

The Old One made a noise, similar to a belch, and then it collapsed onto its bulky mid-section. Tentacles writhed frantically, as if trying to pull free of the monster's neck and run off independently. With a gurgle, the beast started wavering, its black flesh trembling. Something within the creature was boiling and bubbling under its skin. It turned its accusatory gaze upon us, rows of angry, bitter eyes damning us for what we had accomplished. A few of its gnarled horns twitched, and it blinked. The eyes opened and closed in a wave of confusion, staring us down. I knew the beast was realizing it had been vanquished; mere humans had halted its eons-long attempt to return to Earth and rule over us. It seemed stunned by this knowledge. The light burning within those eyes slowly faded. The blinking increased. An acknowledgement of defeat suffused its muscular body as it drooped further.

Below, on the lawn, Ron Justice called out, "Are you all okay up there?"

"Give me a minute and I'll tell you," I called back.

The Old One seemed to sink in upon itself in several spots. Its mass was dissolving from within, and gray and ochre colored liquid started dribbling out of its six mouths.

The spikes on its head wilted, folded into themselves. The beast moaned, and it seemed almost human for a moment.

Its portal was gone, destroyed, as was its tenuous life on our world. By destroying Gary McCoy, I had cut off its life support system, like someone taking an ax to an air pump, stopping the flow of oxygen to a skin diver. Its fragile cord that sustained it in our atmosphere was dead, burnt to ashes so that even on a molecular level, the Old One's air pump was gone.

I had hoped it would work. The first clue I had was when Gary'd shown signs of life after losing his organs and skeleton to the birth of the creature. Then, the beast had tried awfully hard to get Gary back, to have him close to its side. Deena and I had assumed it wanted to eat us, and maybe it had, but I was almost certain it desired Gary's husk for some reason.

Turns out, at least in my diagnosis, the Old One had assimilated many of Gary's internal organs, had used them to develop its own body. While the shell survived, so did the newly-hewn organs created by the birth. When Gary was destroyed, completely obliterated, he took his missing organs back with him.

Or something like that. I'll never know for certain.

The creature exploded, spattering bits of black and purple flesh and half-formed innards all over the rooftop. Deena and I were covered in some sort of slimy goo. Shards of bones lodged in my side, and I saw Deena flinch as some pierced her body.

All around us, there appeared weird creatures, completely visible in the moment, as brought to life with a remote control. Bat-like things that flew triangular bodies.

Giant lamprey eels with teeth that rotated in their mouths, their tails opening up as the petals of an orchid. Fox-faced, lumbering creatures on three legs. The air was suffused with them. The lawn was covered in them.

Justice started firing at the things in the air, but they immediately flickered, their outlines becoming amorphous, diaphanous. Then, as the Old One dripped down the rooftop, its flesh dissolving as we watched, clogging the rain gutter, the monsters disappeared completely with a loud, sonic pop.

"Thank God," Deena said, kissing me over and over. "Thank God, you're so smart."

"Shucks, ma'am, it was nothing," I said.

"Hey, guys," Officer Justice (really, now, what a truly silly name!) called to us. "You going to be able to get down from there? Whole place is going up, and I don't think you have a lot of time to waste making out."

As if in confirmation, a large segment of the roof collapsed into the burning hospital, and I was aware of our predicament.

"Damn it, we get rid of psycho rednecks and a whole horde of monsters, and we still have this fire to deal with."

Deena said, "There's a way down, isn't there?"

I shrugged. "I don't know. We'd better find one."

Another section of the roof crumbled down around the chimney, taking a corner of the brick edifice with it. Flames licked up the side of this new breach.

"And quick!" Deena said.

We started searching, while our helpful police officer shouted up, "If you all have to jump, I can try to catch you."

It was a good thirty five to forty feet down to him, so I said, "No thanks. We'll manage."

"Then I'm calling for back-up," he said. "Get an ambulance here just in case." He moved back towards his cruiser.

The villagers had ceased their assault from the woods, and I noticed I couldn't see any of them on the lawn beneath us. At the death of their god, they seemed to have lost all faith, turned tail and rushed back to the comfort of their lives in the forest. I hoped that's what had happened. We didn't need to be dodging stones as well as flames.

As more sections of the roof disintegrated into the inferno below our feet, I was reminded of a game I had played as a child called 'Don't Break The Ice,' in which you hit plastic cubes out from beneath a toy fisherman until he fell through and you lost the game.

I really didn't want to lose *this* game. We had been through so much, survived hellish hardships, and I was sure, in my heart, we'd make it through this last tribulation.

"The trees," I shouted, catching sight of the woods at the edge of the hospital. "We need to get to the trees and climb down."

I ran, holding Deena's hand in my own, feeling its warmth and comforted by the way she squeezed me. As we arrived at the perimeter of the roof, I saw the closest tree loomed a good six feet higher than the roof...

...and five feet away from where we stood. It was quite a gap.

"I can't jump that," Deena said.

I wasn't so certain I could do it, either, but I put on a confident face and said, "Sure you can. Just get into the branches. Then, even if we fall, they'll slow our descent."

Several wooden support beams behind us groaned and succumbed to gravity, plummeting into the blaze. Sparks flew up into the night sky, and the air was filled with the hissing sound of rain evaporating within the fire. It must have been a hell of a conflagration to not be affected by that tumultuous downpour.

"Come on," I said.

Deena looked down at the ground, so far away from us, and she looked back at the huge fir tree, its top wavering back and forth in the wind. Shaking her head, she took a step backwards.

"No," she said. "I can't do it."

"You have to, sweetheart."

The tree shook, swayed even closer to us under the aegis of the storm.

"What if I go first," I suggested.

Her eyes grew worried. "No, Bob. You can't. It's too far away. You'll end up smashed into the ground."

One of the rain gutters came loose to our right, tumbling to the ground with a loud crash. It jolted Deena, and she hugged me close to herself. She was shaking.

"I hate to say anything," Ron Justice said. "But you two don't have long till the whole roof caves in. You going to try anything, you'd better make it now."

"Watch me," I said. "See how easy it is."

She clutched me in her arms. "I love you, Bob."

"I know, sweetie, and I love you, too. More than anything. But, if we don't skedaddle, we're going to be dead, and I can't have that. I just can't."

"I only wanted you to know," she said. "In case anything happens to one of us. In case, we can't say it again."

"Fine," I said, a little abruptly, a little annoyed at this procrastination. "I love you, too. Now, let's get the hell out of here."

Another hunk of roof collapsed into the story below, and little fingers of flames started edging their way towards us. I estimated the remaining roof to suddenly drop off about ten feet from us, ending in a precipice into Hell. There truly was no time left.

Watching the fir tree sway in the wind, I waited for it to swing back towards where we stood at the corner of the roof. It wavered, stood still a moment, then it oscillated towards us. I took a step and leapt into the void.

The wind was loud in my ears. The rain soaked me, and I saw the top of the tree raise out of my view. I was falling, the sensation of weightlessness overwhelming me.

How could I have been so stupid? I asked myself. *How could I believe I'd get us both out of this deathtrap safe and sound? Now, Deena will never follow me off the roof. She'll stay there. And burn. And burn. And burn.*

Then, something clobbered me in the side, and I instinctively reached out, unwittingly catching a branch in my arms. The abrupt stop almost jerked my shoulder out of its socket, but I was hanging on to the tree about three feet below the roof.

I wrapped my legs around the branch, hoping it wouldn't snap off and plunge me to my newly postponed doom. I inch-wormed my way to the trunk, placing my feet on the next branch down, which was a bit larger and sturdier than the one I had caught during my plummet. The tree swayed and bucked under me, threatening to spill me from its upper berth, but I held on tight - so tight I cut the palms of my hands and they bled.

"Come on," I shouted at Deena, who was peering cautiously over the edge of the roof. I had to admit, she looked very, very far away from me at that moment, but I knew I couldn't let my trepidation show. "Come on. Nothing to it!"

She shook her head, terror rolling off her body in waves, almost palpable.

The whole tree shook in the wind, and I had to hug the trunk even tighter

"Sweetie, you have to," I said. "For me. For us. I can't go on without you. You know that."

From below, I heard Ron Justice calling, "There's an ambulance on its way. Ma'am, you'd best be getting yourself off that ledge. Ain't much left of that old hospital."

Silently, I thanked the officer, nearly revising my opinion of him. Nearly.

"Listen to the policeman, Deena. He knows what he's talking about," I said.

"I'm scared. I'm really so goddamned scared."

"Me too, honey. But get your ass over here."

She looked behind her, and I heard a terrible rolling sound, almost like thunder. The rest of the roof was dropping into the flaming cavity, starting at the other end of the roof and progressing towards Deena. She turned towards me and the tree, and she took two steps and jumped.

I held out my hand, ready to catch her. I'm certain Officer Justice held out his arms, too, in case she fell, positioning himself below the tree. The drop was big enough that she might kill him if she landed on him wrong, and I wanted to give the man a big hug.

She reached out her hands, fingers splayed, and she came closer and closer.

The police officer below me shouted something. I couldn't discern what he said, but his voice was suffused with alarm.

I looked into Deena's eyes as she flailed her arms, saw the terror in them, saw the way she knew she hadn't jumped far enough, saw the horror when her fingertips didn't reach the tree branch at my feet.

She fell, and she looked up into my eyes as she dropped towards the earth.

Her engagement ring shone in the flashing, colored lights of the police cruiser. It gleamed, a signal to me, a beacon to draw me down to her. Red, then blue, then red again.

Officer Justice ran towards her, but I could tell he was too far away.

Her leg hit a lower branch, and Deena was spun onto her back, her legs higher than her head. When she hit the ground, just below her shoulder blades, there was a loud crunching sound I could hear all the way up in the tree.

She lay still at least thirty feet beneath me. I could see the rain falling around her, dropping forcefully into the mud at the base of the tree. The wind blew her hair over her face, where it stuck.

"Oh God," I whispered. "No. No, no, no...."

Scrambling down the tree, barely conscious of where I placed my feet, I rushed to her side. Justice was already there, and he motioned to me when I fell from the lower boughs into the mud.

"Don't move her," he said. "I think she's broken her back."

"Is she..." I couldn't say the word, could barely think it.

Placing a hand on her forehead, I could feel the warmth beneath the cool sheen of rainwater. I couldn't feel a pulse in her throat.

No pulse...

Jesus.

Oh, Jesus Christ...

I moaned, sobbed into the officer's shoulder. He patted me on the back, clearly uncomfortable with the manner my grief was pouring out on to his shoulders. He turned out to be a good guy after all.

"What do I do now?" I asked him. "What can I ever do without her? She was everything to me. We...we made it through so goddamn much, and then she dies. She leaves me at the end? How does someone cope with that?"

"I don't know what kind of shit was going on here tonight," he said, gently peeling me away from his shoulder. "But it looked to me like the odds were stacked against you two. You saved her from whatever the hell that thing on the roof was."

"For what? For her to die in a tree?"

He shook his head, unable to come up with any words of comfort.

"I should've let her go first, when the tree was moving towards us. I should've done something different. Caught her hand. Something..."

"You can't blame yourself."

"Then, who the fuck *do* I blame? You, for not getting here quicker? God, for allowing all this mess to happen tonight?"

"Whichever does you the most good, buddy."

I sighed, ran another hand down her hair, adjusting it so it wasn't glued to her lovely face. She looked at peace, as though there had been no pain, no heartbreak. Her eyes were closed, and she almost seemed as if she was sleeping.

Then, she coughed.

Sputtered in the mud.

And she opened her eyes.

I wanted to throw my arms around her, cover her with violent kisses, but Ron Justice stopped me, saying, "Careful. Don't move her. Here comes the ambulance."

I heard the sirens getting louder as I lowered my face to Deena's.

"You all right, sweetheart?" I asked, crying, my tears mixing with the rain. "I thought you were dead."

She closed her eyes again, and my hopes dropped through the sole of my remaining shoe.

"Deena? Deena!"

She said, in a low voice, "I'm...here, Bob."

"Does it hurt?"

"No," she said, and she looked up into my eyes, not moving any other part of her body. "It doesn't hurt at all. Everything's...numb, actually."

"Don't try to move," I said, kissing her cheeks, then her lips, then her cheeks again.

"I...I can't feel anything. Nothing at all."

"Feel this," I said, kissing her long on the mouth.

"I ⬚⬚ feel that. And…and some pain in…my neck."

Behind me, St. Mike's gave a deep groan, and I heard the roof cave in, feeding the fire at its heart. I looked at Ron Justice.

"We're gonna have to move her before the whole place collapses on us."

He nodded. "We shouldn't touch her but . . . you get her legs, and I'll support her head and neck."

I shuffled to a position near her feet and grasped underneath her kneecaps. Deena hissed, squinted her eyes closed.

"Sorry," I said. "This is probably going to hurt, sweetheart."

"On my count," the young officer said. "One, two, three."

We lifted Deena, and she howled, but the sound of another wall collapsing behind us muffled her cries. Taking tiny steps, we moved beyond the tree and the building as the place buckled and caved in upon itself. The final walls tumbled inwards one at a time, until there was nothing left but burning rubble and dust.

The sun peeked out from behind a cloud on the horizon, and the rain began to slacken. The clouds of dust grew translucent as they billowed away from the ruined asylum.

When the sun hit the dust motes, they sparkled in golden arcs. It was finally morning.

An ambulance arrived with drivers and EMTs and who knows what-all. They set about doing what they had to do.

I squeezed Deena's hand. Squeezed it hard.

She didn't return my grip.

She couldn't.

She never would again.

Epilogue

I t's been years since those autumn nights, when my whole life changed, but the incidents remain seared on my memory as if branded there with hot iron. I can't get through a day without something taking me back to St. Mike's on the night of the attack. Halloween decorations give me the kind of shivers grown men aren't supposed to experience. Open fires, especially big ones like bonfires, send me to my car and back home where I can keep safe from the flames. Don't even get me started on jack-o-lanterns - a combination of the dreaded holiday and small fires. I can't go hiking, even after so long, because the woods seem full of things invisible to me, things determined to kill me, to change me - things I can't see that swim through the air all around my nervous body.

And, of course, there's Deena. Every time I see her, the past rushes back to me so fast I can feel the breeze in its wake.

Officer Justice directed the ambulance staff with a supervisory efficiency that surprised and delighted me. Under his careful eye, they got Deena to the nearest hospital, the doctors poked and prodded her, and they set up appointments with specialists and physical therapists. He double checked their references for us. We became his personal project.

He also led an expedition into the woods to the site of the village. I went with him, along with at least ten other cops (which made me feel uncomfortably exposed) and an anthropologist from Penn State. The cave was still there, although the old man who had been left there to die had finally succumbed. His corpse was partially devoured. Forensics would later determine that the teeth marks were mostly human, although a few of the circular rings of wounds baffled the experts. We discovered the nearly abandoned huts of the village, the strange, topiary statues still guarding the far side. Within one plywood shack, we found eight cowering, severely malformed men and women, probably the only surviving individuals from the attack on St. Mike's. Several of them had burns or odd bite marks on them, and they went with the police without protest, sheep being led to a slaughter. I was told later they were admitted to a mental institution, where they'd live out the rest of their days in relative comfort.

Not that I cared. For what they'd done, I could've easily watched them fall in a rain of bullets, executed against a wall. I don't care that they were merely followers, that the cult had been implanted in their minds by a crazed leader. They'd hurt so many others I had loved, I could give a rat's ass about their 'comfort.'

The ashes of St. Mike's were sifted through, and the bodies of my co-workers were discovered, along with the remains of the patients still in our care. There was no sign of the Old One, nor any vestige of the floating monsters. A state investigation was held, but Ron Justice handled everything so that Deena and I came out looking like heroes from a fire set ablaze by bad electrical wiring. I'm still not sure of everything he did, but Justice managed to have the case closed, and I still retained my license.

I didn't go to Pittsburgh. There are far too many mountainous, wooded areas surrounding it. Instead, I took a position at an institution in Columbus, Ohio, a city that seems to spring out of the surrounding flat, innocuous farmland like a toadstool. It seemed safer there. I'd be able to see them coming after me, if 'they' ever tried again.

Deena accompanied me, but she no longer worked by my side. She didn't work as a doctor at all.

During her fall from the roof of the hospital, she fractured her C-7 vertebrae, resulting in a paralysis from the neck down to her feet. She pretty much regained the use of her arms and hands after years of intense therapy, but her movements were awkward, embarrassing to her. She stayed at home, confined to a motorized wheelchair, and she started making calls for various charitable organizations. She quickly became a force in the world of non-profit health care. She enjoyed talking to people, and she had many friends in the neighborhood, but she often felt self-conscious and grew nervous around strangers. Over the phone, they couldn't see her disability. She was just like them, as far as they knew. She liked that.

After our move, I proposed again, and I was shocked when she turned me down, stating that she didn't want to burden me. I protested for a while, but she held firm. We still lived together, but every time I broached the subject, she grew more adamant. Eventually, in 1996, I broke down in front of her, telling her how I felt, that I'd never leave her. Never. She wasn't a burden. She was the love of my life. Sobbing, she wheeled out of the room, the sound of the motor on her wheelchair a whining dissent. Two days later, she accepted, and we threw a huge church wedding with all our visibly relieved relatives and our circle of friends from Columbus. Officer Justice attended as well, serving as my best man. He still visits us a couple times a year, toting along his pretty wife and their three children. We never mention the Old One or what happened on that night when we all met.

So, we survived, and the Old One was blasted to bits. Is it still around, waiting for another Preacher to be born to gain access to our world? Is it determined to achieve a sense of revenge on the puny ants that had somehow stopped it? I don't know. I live my life the best I can, with my lovely wife and my friends. I pray it is gone, hurled someplace so distant it will never get near the Earth again. I often have nightmares, waking screaming and sweating through the sheets. Strangely, Deena is always the one to comfort me. She was the one who was permanently injured, yet I'm the one still having bad dreams. She seems calm and accepting of what happened.

She often tells me, "Bob, you can't do anything about it. We were in the wrong place at the wrong time, and we did all we could. Hell, you probably saved the world. Now, it's out of our hands. We're far away from the woods and everything in it. We're safe."

I often wonder if we really are safe. There are things out there I would have never suspected of existing, things I really didn't want to acknowledge, thriving in other dimensions. Just the fact that there are other dimensions is enough to freak me out sometimes.

And that's my story. Beginning, middle, end.

I hope I kept you entertained. Lord knows, it's a scary story, but I pray I did more than keep you turning pages.

Did you learn anything?

Will you ever go into the woods again?

When the Old One finally finds its way back, will we be ready?

I can't forget that night, how close we came to being obliterated by a cosmic force beyond my comprehension. There are more things in heaven and earth, Horatio.

But, Deena is right. As always. I should have learned this by now.

We need to live our lives in our suburban home, with our dog and our cook-outs. We need to read and experience as much as possible. We need to love as many people as our capacity for love will allow. We can't be side-tracked by the things from other places, the bogey-men of other dimensions. We need our lives and our wives and our beliefs that somehow remain after disaster strikes.

It's usually enough.

Deena's calling for me in the other room. It's dark outside, and I can hear the sound of cars driving down our street, the faint honking of horns. By now, she's already in bed, waiting for me to join her.

Maybe, just maybe, I'll get through this night without being assaulted by the nightmares again.

Maybe.

Somehow, I doubt it.

Acknowledgments

No book is created in a vacuum. The author and publisher would like to thank Joe Mynhardt, Paula Limbaugh, Linzi Osburn, and Lex Jones for their attention to detail.

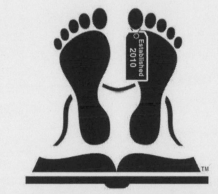

POST MORTEM PRESS
www.postmortem-press.com

About Post Mortem Press

Since its inception in 2010, Post Mortem Press has published over 100 titles in the genres of dark fiction, suspense/mystery, horror, and dark fantasy. The goal is to provide a showcase for talented authors, affording exposure and opportunity to "get noticed" by the mainstream publishing community. Post Mortem Press has quickly become a powerful voice in the small genre press community. The result has been five years of steady growth and successful endeavors that have garnered attention from all across the publishing sphere.

Made in the USA
San Bernardino, CA
17 April 2015